HORSE THIEF

and

Other Stories

by

Anna Balint

CURBSTONE PRESS

Printed on acid-free paper in Canada by Transcontinental
Cover artwork: Caroline Orr
Cover design: Stone Graphics

Grateful acknowledgement is made to the editors of the following
magazines in which the stories listed first appeared: *Briar Cliff
Review*, "The Visit"; *Calyx Journal*, "Gypsies on the Lawn"; and
Clackamas Literary Review, "Wonderbread and Spam".

The publishers wish to thank Jane Blanshard for her fine copy editing.

This book was published with the support of
the Connecticut Commission on the Arts,
the National Endowment for the Arts, and
NATIONAL donations from many individuals. We are very
ENDOWMENT grateful for all of their support.
FOR THE ARTS

Library of Congress Cataloging-in-Publication Data

Balint, Anna, 1949-
   Horse thief and other stories / by Anna Balint.— 1st ed.
      p. cm.
   Includes bibliographical references and index.
   ISBN 1-931896-10-0 (pbk. : alk. paper)
   1. London (England)—Fiction. 2. Northwest, Pacific—Fiction.
   3. Working class—Fiction. 4. Immigrants—Fiction. I. Title.
   PS3602.A5955H67 2004
   813'.6—dc22   200401374

published by
CURBSTONE PRESS   321 Jackson Street   Willimantic CT 06226
      phone: 860-423-5110   e-mail: info@curbstone.org
                     www.curbstone.org

To Mum
for nurturing me with story as well as food,
and for writing your own stories

Acknowledgements

Many people made these stories possible, and I am indebted to all of them. Willie, I couldn't have done any of it without your support and being willing to listen to endless drafts. Special thanks to Teresa Brown for sharing her life, and to Alaina Brown for being so vibrantly alive. To my friend Mariana Romo-Carmona for her guidance and belief in me, and to Michael Klein and Marina Budhos for their insightful readings and feedback. Many thanks to Kathleen Acalá for pointing me in the right direction at a critical moment, and to Caroline Orr, Carolyn Hartness, and Ellen Carmody for their invaluable input and information. Thanks again to Caroline for her beautiful artwork for the cover, and to Curbstone Press for all that they do. To Ben, Kathy, Carlos, and Antonio, thanks for keeping me on my toes. To everyone whose lives intersected with my own and inspired these stories, I salute and thank you.

CONTENTS

"...come celebrate
with me that every day
something has tried to kill me
and has failed."

—Lucille Clifton

Horse Thief
and Other Stories

The Visit

On my way out of the house I took it into my head to spin, my arms up over my head like an iceskater on TV. My pink dress opened round me to a flower. Mama Grace called out from the porch then, Be careful, Annie, in case you fall.

I knew I was closer to flying than falling.

My little brother Frank plodded ahead of me, hanging onto the caseworker's hand like it was a lifeline. Shirley her name was. Red hair bouncing, heels click clicking on the walk. Frank twisted his head to make sure I was coming. He'd asked me after breakfast, would I tell him which one was Mommy when we got there. "Remember the picture." I said. "The one where she's a princess, her hair shiny all down her back?"

Me and Frank took turns sleeping with that picture till it got raggedy corners and a crease down the middle and Mama Grace threw it away. Still, I knew I'd recognize Mommy right off, the way I did in my dreams.

Going into the waiting room through elevator doors was like entering an old dream. Past the guard with his shiny boots and straight up to the Who-Are-You-Here-To-See? Lady sitting behind glass as if she was in a bank. I knew Mommy came next, moaning something about a cigarette, Frank a baby still, crawling in circles on a linoleum floor. Somewhere there was a little room where they buzzed you in.

Shirley sat us on a bench under the window, me in my pink party dress worn especially for Mommy, Frank in his best ribbon shirt. I swung my legs, Frank copied. Lots of watching going on. The guard's eyes from under the brim of his hat, the TV camera's one red eye, my eyes too. All I saw was the same tore up plastic couches. Same cracked linoleum

1

and brown stains on the ceiling. Same tore-up magazines wanting their covers back. Shirley smoothed my hair and the skirt of my dress, said again didn't I look nice. I swung my legs harder and fixed on the light over the elevator. Whenever it crept upward I felt a fluttering in my insides. Inside my head Mommy's feet kept stepping into the room. I dressed them in white skinny strap sandals to show off her red painted toenails. Then the elevator opened its doors and another wrong person got off.

Some complained in loud voices. Some were buzzed in behind the Who-Are-You-Here-To-See? Lady's secret door. Some told to wait. One lady fell asleep in a chair, her water-balloon feet spilling over the tops of her flat Mama Grace shoes. I kneeled up on the bench and looked out the window. Nothing out there but a parking lot and an alley with a garbage truck that roared like a dragon. At the end of the alley a glimpse of McDonald's where Mommy had promised we'd eat lunch. I squished my nose sideways on the glass and breathed a fog to write my name in. When I turned back around the clock on the wall said ten minutes after nine, still no Mommy and Shirley's foot had begun to jiggle. I filled my cheeks with air and popped them.

Then a couple of scruffy-looking boys tough-walked through the elevator doors with a policeman and a blonde lady. One boy was big, the other small. Their jeans were wet around the bottoms like they'd been walking in puddles. The small boy lay down on a plastic couch and fell asleep right away. The other boy flopped down on the other couch, and groaned and flung himself about until the policeman told him Go easy buddy. But the boy jumped up again and yelled at the blonde lady. He was hungry and when the fuck was she going to get him some food. I liked it when he said fuck with the policeman there. The little boy, who was about my size, was snoring by this time. I didn't know little kids snored. Mostly I was hoping for a fight. But nothing like that happened. The blonde lady whispered something behind her hand to the policeman and then put a hand on the big kid's shoulder. Okay Jerome, she said. Let's get something to eat. She shook the smaller boy awake, and they all left on the elevator again.

By that time the clock over the elevator said nine-fifteen. The ruffles on my dress itched and my Sunday shoes were too tight. Shirley tried to tell us a story to pass the time but it got hard to listen when those two boys came back from McDonalds wolfing down their fries. I gave up looking for red-painted toenails in white sandals.

Came a time when Mom left for a party with a six pack tucked up under each arm. She left two bottles of formula propped up in the corner of Frank's crib, and forgot to come back for three days, poor Frank wearing the same diaper the whole time, his butt raw meat. Just about wore his lungs out crying. Lucky for Frank I knew how to refill his bottles with pop. Lucky for me there was Halloween candy lying around even if there was no food in the fridge. Lucky for us a neighbor called the police.

I was Mama Grace's apple pie helper when she told me all that, apples waiting to be cut up in a bowl on the table. We lived in Grandma Addy's house on the reservation by then. I liked that house. The kitchen was big with a wooden table in the middle, all the other rooms small. Out there, Mama wore her gray hair in rollers all day sometimes, kept her feet in slippers. She wasn't always running off to work like before, in the city. Mostly I liked the outdoors with sage grass and tumbleweed, and big skies with chunky animal clouds.

That day Mama showed me how to hold the knife and cut away from myself. Look out for your fingers, she said one minute. Be careful. The next minute she started talking about Mom. Look where careless got your mother. Chop, chop. Another apple cut into four, out with the core and one piece for me. More bad things about Mom while she chopped the other three pieces fast. Chop, chop, chop, chop, chop.

She cut so fast she cut herself. She stuck her bloody finger in her mouth and sucked. I wished she'd cut it off.

Soon as Grandma Addy died we moved back to Seattle. Hated the gray shingle house on a street with not enough trees, hated the wire fence round the house, hated St. Joseph's school with its ugly brown uniforms. The only thing good was Mom calling. The whole year we were away she never called. But I saw a ghost on the railroad tracks one time. A lady with long braids and a long dress the color of river water. She had on a porcupine quill necklace and her hands moved like smoke. Mama Grace told me she was the ghost of a lady looking for her drowned daughter, lots of people had seen her, nothing to be afraid of. I wasn't afraid. I knew it was Mommy looking for me. It got so all my memories of Mom were ghosts.

Just hearing her voice made me cry the first time she called. "Don't cry, sweetie," she said. "Mommy's getting it together for her little girl, going to be driving all the way there to see you, okay, sweetie?" She talked like that, sweetie this and sweetie that, her voice a little rough, like she smoked too many cigarettes.

"Been through rehab for you, sweetie," she went on. "Finished up parenting class and done everything that damn judge told me to do." She called night after night. When she handed me the phone Mama Grace's mouth was a tight little button.

Pretty soon my head started to fill with Mommy everything. Mommy put Doritos and Lemon Hostess pies in my lunch box. Mommy picked me up from school and made the other kids jealous because she was way prettier than their moms. Mommy reading me bedtime stories. Come the night of the St Joseph's potluck, Mama Grace bringing tuna casserole instead of the coconut cake I wanted, kids asked me and Frank how come our mom was so old. I told them: *She's* not our real mom. Our real mom lives in New York and

Hollywood. She travels because she's a model. In my mind Mommy started to look like Cher.

Then one day she really was coming. All the way from Portland. "Guess what, sweetie? Gotta a new friend gonna drive me up there in his Mustang. Be there in a couple of days. And if Grace lets us, we'll take you and Frankie for a spin. Hey sweetie! Maybe Mommy will move back to Seattle just to be near you guys. Find a nice place to live so you can come and spend the night sometimes. How'd you like that?"

Mama Grace always listened in on the other phone. "Don't be making promises you can't keep, Wilma," she said, and told me to hang up. She and Mommy talked on and on, Mama Grace's voice sounding hard and mean. "You need to tell her, Wilma," I heard her say. "Annie has a right to know. She's old enough." And then Mommy said something back to her that made her voice get wobbly. Good, I thought. I'm glad Mommy made her cry. I knew I'd be leaving that house forever soon as Mommy came into town in her red Mustang, with the top down, and her long hair blowing.

The elevator opened its doors again and out rolled a lady in a wheelchair. Mama Grace told me not to stare at people in wheelchairs, but I always did. This lady didn't have legs, just little stumpy thighs. The rest of her I didn't notice much until she'd wheeled her chair nearly on top of me, grinning right into my face, which made Shirley stand up. Then I saw teeth missing on the side of her smile, and her brown face, lumpy like Mrs. Potato Head, her straggly black hair gray at the roots. One of those beat up Indians from downtown. She couldn't stop grinning.

"Annie?" she said. "It's me, sweetie. Mommy." Then to Frank. "Hi there Frankie, big boy."

She put her arms out. I didn't budge. Frank neither. Her voice was right but she wasn't Mommy. Mommy looked like Cher. Then Frank jumped off the bench and grabbed hold of Shirley's arm. Shirley's blue eyes were round as marbles.

"Wilma? Wilma Folson?" was all she managed to say. "That's me!" said the lady in the wheelchair. "And this here's Bob." She spun her wheelchair around and waved toward the little guy in back of her. I hadn't even noticed him till then. He was gray all over. Skin, hair, clothes.

"Howdy!" said Bob.

The lady in the wheelchair had a whole bunch of presents in a canvas bag fastened to the back of her chair. Barbie dolls with different clothes sets, crayons, magnetic letters for the fridge, a G.I. Joe for Frank. She said she'd get us more things when she got more money.

"I'm working on it," she kept saying. "Mommy's working on it."

Bob joined in.

"It's a struggle out there, but we're working on it."

Mama Grace used to complain how for a Tootsie Roll I'd walk off with a stranger. But I liked the toys. I liked the way the wheelchair lady kept saying I was pretty as a picture. "Isn't she, Bob?" I felt cheated too. Mommy had legs. She wore white sandals and red nail polish. Frank wouldn't even touch his toys.

We didn't have to get buzzed into a little room. The wheelchair lady said how about we head over to McDonalds right away, and Shirley said fine. We were allowed to order anything we wanted. I ordered super-size fries, a Big Mac *and* chicken nuggets, and a super-size shake. Then I found out I wasn't hungry. Bob said not to worry, Little Lady, what I couldn't eat, he sure could. Said he was regular vacuum cleaner. I was more interested in the wheelchair lady than food and went and stood by her.

"What happened to your legs?" I wanted to know.

Turning her chair around so she faced me, she took hold of my hands and rubbed her thumbs over the back of them. "Mommy got hit by a truck," she said. I liked the way she made my hands feel. Mama Grace never touched me much.

"See...Mommy used to have some real bad habits, sweetie. I used to be a boozer. As in drunk...How the hell do you explain drunk to a kid, Bob?" Bob had his face full of French-fries, a splash of ketchup on his chin.

"Me and Frank already know about drunks," I said. "Mama Grace shows them to us downtown sometimes. Says we don't ever want to end up like that."

"Good for Mama Grace!" She shot Bob a quick look and let go of my hands, then pulled a cigarette pack out of her shirt pocket and lit up. After a couple of puffs she threw her head back and made a wheezing noise, and her eyes ran and she made all kinds of noise and coughed smoke. At first I thought she was crying. Then Bob started laughing and I figured out that's what she was doing too. I didn't get whatever it was that was funny but joined in anyway. We all three laughed till a zit-faced boy came over in his McDonalds apron and said Excuse me, ma'am, no smoking in this section. So we left. Everyone was done eating by then anyway. Except Bob.

A few blocks away there was a park. On the way there Mom says why don't I sit on her lap and she'll give me a ride. I didn't know whether I was ready to sit on those stumps and made a face. Mom laughed and patted them. "They won't bite you, sweetie." I still wasn't sure, but I rode for about a block. Her stumps felt like warm cushions.

In the park Frank wanted to go on a swing and for Shirley to push him. Then Mom wanted to push him and tried until her wheelchair wheels got stuck in the sand and Bob had to come and pull her out. Right away Frank hopped off the swing and went back to Shirley. I saw a shadow pass over Mom's face. But I'd already worked a swing of my own way high by that time, the skirt of my pink dress flying, my legs stretched and toes pointed. Suddenly Mom was grinning up at me, clapping her hands like I was in a show.

"Gee, you're gonna be in the circus one day, sweetie. Look at her fly, Bob. I used to do that too. Once upon a time."

7

After the swings she made her wheelchair spin around on one wheel real fast.

"Me too, me too!" I shrieked, and climbed back onto those cushion stumps and held tight to the arms of the chair so I wouldn't fall off. Mom spun the wheels with her hands, and the sky and treetops flashed blue and yellow, faster and faster, until the whole world was spinning, with one of Mom's strong arms wrapped round me to keep me safe. We scream-laughed like mad, Mom with her face right next to mine, while behind us our hair flew out in a wild tangle, dancing like kite tails.

When Mom braked, her chair squealed like a racecar and sparks shot out from under its wheels.

"Do it again Mommy!"

Mommy: The word popped out all by itself. No one else could make me feel that dizzy, my whole world turning.

Mommy and Bob insisted on riding back to school with us, and in the end Shirley said, Alright, but there wasn't room for everyone in her little car. I watched Mommy slide onto a taxi seat, slick like she did it all the time. Riding in back with me and Bob, Mommy curled her arm around me and we giggled and winked at each other. Frank rode up front with Shirley. By then it was too late to go back to Mama Grace's and change into our uniforms like we were supposed to.

"Guess you're just gonna have to go to school looking like a princess, sweetie."

Everything Mommy said to me sounded like a song, her face lit up like she'd turned on a magic light inside. Then we got to school and she wanted out of the car. All the kids were on the yard because it was lunch recess already. A bunch of them came running to the fence when they saw Frank get out of the car with Shirley. Every last kid in the school knew about our mom coming to town in her Mustang. I saw how they eyeballed Shirley's carrot-colored hair and milk-white skin. No way was she our mom. Bob hopped out of the car and held the door for me. By then Amanda Hutton had her pug nose poked through the fence.

"Where's your mom?" she asked in her loud bossy voice.

The driver was still getting Mom's chair out of the trunk. Someone else pointed at Bob. "Is that your mom's boyfriend?"

"*Ugh!* He's got cooties!"

Then before I could stop her, here came Mommy with her nutty grin spread all over her face, sliding out of the car and into her wheelchair, a pop-a-wheelie up onto the curb, and *Zoom,* right up to the fence. The whole school laughed.

Mama Grace told me later it never happened like that. Wilma never spent a day in a wheelchair in her life. She never even showed that day. The caseworker waited until ten and then took us back to school. By that time I was so upset I cussed God out on the schoolyard, at recess. As if somehow He was to blame for Mommy not showing up. As if that made any sense.

"All that came of that was you got yourself suspended. Lot of good that did you."

I remembered the cussing.

"I cussed God 'cause I hated Mom being in a wheelchair and kids making fun of me," I said. Mama Grace shook her head.

"No, Annie, that wasn't it."

Mama Grace knew all along the visit was a bad idea. Wilma wasn't reliable. Did I remember Shirley, that redheaded caseworker? Well, Wilma had talked to her, written to her, sent her all the papers from rehab. Shirley said she was willing to go out on a limb and supervise a visit.

"So against my better judgement I went along with it. I shouldn't have. That Shirley was just too young. Fresh out of books. She didn't know your mother. What really happened was Wilma and her boyfriend got in an argument halfway between Portland and Seattle and that was the end of him driving her."

"Who was the lady in the wheelchair then?" I wanted to know.

"Someone you dreamed up."

"Why would I dream up a mother in a wheelchair?"

She didn't have an answer for that.

I was older then. Ten or eleven. Running away every chance I got. I'd already found out things about boys I wasn't sure I wanted to know. I cut classes and smoked in the bathrooms at school. I'd even drunk my first beer by then. It was the running got to Mama Grace in the end. She said I couldn't live there anymore. Frank was fine but her nerves couldn't take me.

I never did see Mom again. Mama Grace said she slid back into her old ways just like everybody knew she would, and in the end she gave up on me and Frank. I never heard anything more about her that I remember. To this day I don't know whether she was the lady in the wheelchair or not. Sometimes, when I'm downtown in Seattle in Pioneer Square, I think I hear her. Walking past the homeless people, the homeless Indians curled up on benches or staring past me out of faraway eyes, I hear that little scrape in her voice and her calling me sweetie. I turn, and it's someone else or nothing at all. Other days I hear her inside my head. Her and me both, scream-laughing and spinning in her chair, the sky above us wide open.

Gypsies on the Lawn

I'd probably be stuck in some London suburb washing nappies if not for my Great Aunt Maria. Instead I'm here. You could say she saved my life. She had this thing about me, partly because I was the girl—all boys in my family except for me—partly because I had her name. "But I'm *Mary*," I insisted. According to Mum I was named for the mother of Jesus and Mary Queen of Scots, not for a crazy old aunt. Great Aunt Maria would bat the air with her hand. "Mary, Maria, de same name. You and me, we are vun, darlink."

Me and my four brothers used to laugh at her. At Grandpa Sándor too. He'd forgotten every word of English he ever knew and his mind was gone. Dad would rescue him from the nursing home for Sunday dinners at our house, where he sat at our dining room table, dribbling on his shirtfront, gibbering away in Hungarian and whatever else he spoke. Romany I found out later. Mum told us to be kind, not to laugh. He was her dad.

With Great Aunt Maria things were more complicated. For one, her mind may have been *strange*—as judged by the average thinking in that still very English corner of London—but it wasn't *gone*. Actually, other immigrants were already moving in, Pakistanis two doors up, West Indians on Willow Road. Enough to put the fear of God into Mrs. Barstow next door. "Gives us a bit more color, more life," Mum used to say over the fence, just to get her riled up. I think Mum used to resent the fact that Mrs. Barstow never saw her as an immigrant. She was quite feisty back then, Mum was. Always in trousers when everyone else wore skirts, moving through the house like a whirlwind with the vacuum cleaner so she could get on and do other things. Always offering opinions. But all that was before she burned her poems.

According to Dad, the problem with Great Aunt Maria was there was no *containing* her. She came and went as she pleased, no one ever knowing her whereabouts, or whether she was even in England or gone back to Hungary again. And then her "get-ups" (Dad's expression), these were embarrassing. Fine on stage or for some Gypsy show in a restaurant in Hungary somewhere, but a bit much in Northeast London.

I'm sure Mrs. Barstow agreed. My aunt's cries of "Zsuzsa! cheeldren! Come kiss me, I'm here!" could be heard long before she finally sailed into view, like a sailing ship in full regalia. This gave Mrs. Barstow plenty of time to make it to her upstairs landing window and peer disapprovingly down onto our side of the fence.

One July afternoon, Mum and I sat in the concrete yard off the kitchen shelling peas. Mum was quiet and shut into herself—it was after the poems business—nothing between us but the pop of the peapods and the rattle of peas into a pot. The air was lazy with heat, wasps buzzing around the empty jam jar filled with water Mum always stood on the kitchen windowsill with the purpose of trapping them. Then here came Great Aunt Maria. First her cries and the click of the gate, and then her big bosom, (one of the things we laughed about) thrust proudly out inside her shiny polka-dot blouse like a ship's bow. My brothers were playing guns in the garden, except I doubt Rollie was. The way I remember it he was still having his crisis, visions and all. It's because of that, and the social worker showing up with his conch shell to help us sort things out, that Mum burned her poems in the first place. So Rollie was inside, stretched out on his bed like a corpse, or sitting on his bed and rocking back and forth while gun and battle noises exploded around him through the upstairs window.

"Oh my God not Aunt Maria now," muttered Mum under

her breath. She didn't want to see anyone or do much of anything then, no one welcome except for Mr. Halifax and his bloody conch shell. If Great Aunt Maria saved me, Mr. Halifax destroyed my mother.

There were always rituals when Great Aunt Maria arrived. First the hugs and kisses. *Cause of death, suffocation from old ladies' big bosoms. Cause of death, asphyxiation from garlic breath.* My eldest brother, Oscar, who was quite the wit, used to come up with lines like that. By the time of that summer visit he was fourteen and sprouting whiskers. He screwed up his eyes and made silly faces when he emerged from the garden or wherever he'd been to get kissed. The only reason he put up with it—that any of us did—was because of what came next, the plump ringed hand reaching into the enormous bosom to pull out five crumpled ten-shilling notes, one each. Great Aunt Maria had done this for as long as we could remember. The value of ten shillings had gone down quite a bit by the time Oscar was fourteen and I was eleven. Still, ten shillings was more than we got anyplace else. The last part of the ritual was palm reading, us lined up in a row with our hands out flat. Who knows whether she could really read palms or not? Her eyes sparkled black and shiny as two coal chips, her big earrings rattling on either side of her head. So maybe she was just having her fun. But she always told me I would travel, that it was in my blood. And here I am. She never told my brothers that, and there they still are.

All this I tell some guy named Sam who I've only known for a few hours. I feel him look at me every so often, quickly, and then away because he's driving. Mostly I look out the car window. Outside is white, and we're skimming across snow and ice somewhere along I-80, somewhere in Wyoming. I still haven't learned to drive. In England I didn't need to. Our red Datsun station wagon follows a V.W. bus. We're a convoy of eight, student radicals from different campuses around the San Francisco Bay Area, delegates to an anti-war convention in Iowa. A few weeks ago Vietnam was carpet-bombed. But you can only talk about what's happening with the war for so long before you start to feel crazy. That's how come Sam and I start talking about ourselves, small things first. The usual getting-to-know-you stuff—where are you from and what's your major? "I don't have one," I say. "I just decided I should take some U.S. and La Raza history courses if I'm going to live on this continent…" Then really talking, our families and histories. I ask Sam first. He's half Jewish, it turns out. This surprises me as he's Black, and I've never met a Black Jew before. But his Mom is from Poland, the only one in her family who survived the camps. His dad didn't survive anything. A Black American soldier in Europe he came home from the war with a Jewish bride and was killed in a foundry accident before Sam was born. "I'm sorry," I say. Then I tell him my family lost people in the camps too, and of course right off he thinks I'm Jewish. I have to tell him, "No, no, my family is Gypsy, on my mother's side."

I look at him, to see how he reacts. I'm used to people asking where I'm from, what am I? It's gotten so I say, Oh, I'm from this planet, how about you? And they get all flustered and say they didn't mean it like that. It's just that I look exotic, as if I was Greek or Turkish or something. I am something, I say. I don't usually tell people Gypsy. I get tired of the questions. Does that mean I grew up in a horse-drawn cart? I hardly ever mention the camps. Sam and I have this in common, I realize now: people making assumptions about who we are based on how we look. We both just did it to each other. I mention this, and Sam throws back his head and laughs.

I like his looks, his dark curly hair and the chestnut sheen of his skin. Most of all I like the way his mouth pulls to one side when he smiles. His hands on the wheel are small, almost as small as mine, although people have joked that I've got big hands for a little person. Pianist's hands, Dad used to say, good for stretching along the keyboard. But it was the violin he tried to get me to play, Grandpa Sándor's violin, a wedding present from Grandpa to Dad, the same instrument Grandpa used to play for my mother when she was a little girl in Hungary. Dad played it for me on Sunday mornings, the only time I ever really felt close to him.

"Do you play a musical instrument?" I ask Sam. He chuckles. "Oboe," he said. "In high school. I was terrible." Then his hands suddenly tighten on the wheel at the same moment he says "Holy shit!" and we sail pass a jack-knifed big rig and a dead deer in the snow. We're quiet for a bit after that, just the hum of the car, its heater, and the sound of the other guy, Dave, snoring in the back where the seat is folded down.

"So what happened?" Sam eventually asks. "What was the big deal about this visit with your aunt? And what's with your mom and the poems?"

My mother is weeping. She stands in front of the kitchen boiler—people used to have those in their kitchens in England when I was a kid—and with one hand she's lifted the top off. It is round, about eight inches across, made of iron turned black from coal dust, a gleaming metal handle fitted into a groove. Mum's other hand feeds torn papers into the hole. An orange glow comes up through the hole, and sometimes a tongue of orange flame licks up toward the scraps of paper as they flutter down. There's writing on them. Mum's back is turned and she doesn't see me in the doorway. Her shoulders heave.

"What are you doing, Mummy?" I ask. I am eleven when this happens. An aspiring ballerina who creates her own ballets in the sitting room, dressed up in Mum's one and only frothy white petticoat. I'm a storyteller and high wire artist. I tell stories to myself under the bedcovers and act them out with Jennifer Small behind the sheds at school. I perform circus tricks for Stephen and Colin on the shiny linoleum of the upstairs landing. I can do anything. Braiding my hair in the mornings, tucking me in at night, Mum has told me I can be anything I want to be.

She turns, her mouth a gash, and when she sees me, reaches out the hand that a moment ago fed the papers. It's empty now. I go to her and wrap my arms around her waist. Still weeping, she tells me those papers were her poems. I don't know how to comfort her. Once she told me her poems were her most precious creations, except for me and my brothers. This after I showed her a poem I'd written at school. My poem was beautiful, she said, and unlocked her secret drawer and took out some sheets of paper with poems on. She read them to me, her words bright as beads. Now all that was left was a few blackened scraps that floated and drifted over the top of the boiler like feathers.

Mr. Halifax the social worker had been at our house the night before. A narrow, red-faced man with flaky skin, he wore a raincoat even in summer. He kept a conch shell in his briefcase, which he fished out for these sessions. "He who holds the conch shell speaks," he'd say, always in a hushed, reverent tone. In our house, given the numbers of males to females, it usually was a "he" doing the talking. I can see us gathered around the dining room table. Mr. Halifax at one end, Dad, sallow-skinned and trying to look bigger than he was at the other end, an unruly lock of hair dropped down over one eye. The rest of us are seated in between, Rollie frozen, staring down at his knees. I pick at the tablecloth. Stephen tries not to giggle, and Mom turns her wedding ring, around and around on her finger.

There must have been some kind of testimonial that night, some kind of outpouring from my brothers and Dad that I can't recall. Why else did it end with Mum talking as if the priest were there to hear her confession? She'd been the wrong kind of mum for boys, not a cabbage mum at all. Forgive her! Forgive her! She thumped the table with the conch shell in a steady despairing rhythm. Forgive her, for not being the kind of mum Mr. Halifax said boys needed, not a comfortable, non-threatening *cabbage* mum. She understood now, that's what Rollie needed to get well.

It was all very confusing. Why would anyone want a mum as tasteless as an overcooked vegetable, and why was this mum good for boys? But maybe my brothers or Dad barely spoke at all, and it was Mr. Halifax holding onto his conch shell himself who talked. Any memory I have of complaints is vague. Something about the wrong kind of food—though nothing to do with cabbage—and other people's mums not wearing trousers all the time. Then Mr. Halifax took his conch shell, his shabby raincoat, and left. Dad saw him out. I wondered as I heard the front door close what kind of a mum a girl needed. Mum was still chastising herself through tears, all us kids quiet. Dad came back into the room looking bewildered. He pushed his hair back from his forehead and offered Mum his handkerchief. "It's not all your fault, Susan," he kept saying—Great Aunt Maria was the only one still called Mum Zsuzsa—and sent me off to the kitchen to make her some tea. "There's a good girl now."

Alone in the kitchen with the teapot and tea leaves, the rest of them in the dining room still, even Rollie, the space cadet, with his hands tucked tightly between his knees, I knew something had shifted. I felt smaller. The next morning Mum burned her poems.

The VW bus pulls into an enormous gas station, so brightly lit it dims the panoramic gleam of the snow. Our red Datsun follows. Dave struggles awake from the back seat.

"Where are we?" he asks.

"An oasis in the snow!" says Sam. "Little America, the biggest gas station in the world!"

Row after row of red and blue pumps gleam under hot white lights and a flutter of red, white, and blue plastic flags. Beyond the pumps is a parking lot and café. We tank up and pile out of the two cars, stretch, and stand with hands in pockets, a hunched huddle for a minute, all talking at once, our breath escaping in great steamy puffs. Then we head for the café. John holds the door for me with a little bow. His knit hat is pulled down low to his pink jug-handle ears.

"How goes it in the red road runner?" he asks, and grins at me through the metal strips across his teeth. Inside, too many for one booth, we are seated in two adjacent ones. I notice nothing wrong at first. Only that somehow Sam ends up across the aisle from me, and I am sandwiched between John and Rebecca. I shouldn't mind this but I do. I glance across at Sam whose hands now remind me of my father's. He moves them as if conducting music while making some point or other to Maggie. Then he picks up the big plastic menu and studies it, unaware that I am studying him.

Gradually, with an uncomfortable prickling sensation, I become aware I am not the only one. Heads are turning to take in Sam's presence. Up front there's a gift shop with postcards and trinkets where two men in cowboy hats and jeans lean on the glass. One chews a toothpick, then lifts up his hat and scratches his head. He says something to his companion. They both stare at Sam.

This is the America I do not know. The one I passed by as I hitchhiked from one place to the next. Now I am afraid. I want to warn Sam. Across the aisle he is laughing. Music starts up on the jukebox and a voice smooth as melted chocolate croons how somebody done him wrong. Talk starts up between our two tables about switching around who rides in what vehicle so everyone gets to know everyone. I only half listen, but hear Sam when he calls out "Not yet, for crying out loud! We're still learning names!" and I know he's waiting for me to look his way. I do, and he winks at me. I wonder if he's really as comfortable in this place as he seems. How can he be with those two men at the counter still looking his way?

A bleached blonde waitress with eyebrows plucked out

and penciled back in comes over to take our orders. She taps her pencil on her pad and avoids eye contact. "What's a BLT?" I ask, and everyone at my table bursts out laughing. Immediately I wish I hadn't asked.

"You've been here how long?" asks John. "I thought they handed those out at the airport when people arrived."

"Not any more, John," says Rebecca leaning across me. "Cutbacks. To pay for the war." More laughter.

The waitress is clearly not amused. She adjusts her apron, and in a tight little voice informs me that it's a bacon, lettuce, and tomato sandwich on toasted sourdough bread. "I'll try one," I say, glad that the men in cowboy hats are leaving. The bells attached to the door jingle cheerily on their way out. The chatter at our table resumes, but I am not a part of it. I watch the waitress as she mops up a spill at someone else's table. Over there she's all smiles. Something about her, her frilly apron maybe, and the fact that she's waiting tables, makes me think of Mum. Suddenly I feel sad. I wonder how Mum is. I picture her wearing one of her frillies to dollop mashed potatoes onto my brothers' plates.

"Penny for your thoughts," says John, snapping his fingers near my face. "Tell me, how did you end up so far from home?"

I'm not in the mood to tell this story right now, not in here. But everyone's heads lean in to catch what I say. I give an abbreviated version. Something about England being too small and me in need of room to breathe. "So I came to New York on a one way ticket with a hundred dollars, a backpack, and a hitchhiking thumb." The waitress arrives with the food. We adjust ourselves to make room for the plates, and Dave complains he ordered slaw not fries. She snatches up his plate again and marches off without a word.

"You hitchhiked?" exclaims Rebecca, incredulous.

"All the way to California. Via the south. Crazy, huh?"

"I'd say. Weren't you terrified?"

"Not really. It was too interesting for that." I wonder what scares Rebecca, and flash on a ride I took from two Black men in Georgia who invited me back to eat and meet their families in some backwater red-dirt town named Griffin. I stayed for two days and was never happier. I wonder have I lost my nerve. I take a bite of my BLT, and declare it okay. I glance at Sam again and catch his eye. He grins at me and gives me the thumbs-up sign.

"I'm stealing zis leetle girl for ze night," Great Aunt Maria announced, and led me out into the garden, where the air was still warm and fragrant with roses. It was dark by then, but the lit rooms in the back of the house cast light in the shape of huge windows onto the lawn. We sat opposite one another in the canvas garden chairs and Great Aunt Maria told me stories. Her wire bracelets tinkled lightly as she held and played with my hands, every once in a while tossing hers to the heavens to give emphasis to some point or other. There in the darkness she made everything real for me. Since then, most of her stories have dissolved the way dreams do. All that is left is odd details. Wide flat fields, firelight on people's faces, the steamy smell of horses.

There are things I do remember: her telling me that Mum once had a big sister, Rozsa, who died in a Nazi camp. Others too. She whispered their names, put a finger to her lips and rocked a little. "Ssh ssh ssh, darlink, because nobody in ze family talks about zat. Ze hurt is too big." She placed one hand over her bosom, drew a deep breath and let it out slowly. "Zen after ze war...in Hungary...the Gypsy life...illegal. No more travelers, you understand? Hard times for Gypsies... maybe vorse zan ze war." She rubbed her cheeks with her hands, and did the same to mine. "But no matter now, darlink, because no more we are Gypsies in our family, you understand? Keep quiet. Forget ze old language. Live in vun place...And votever you do, don't talk Gypsy to Uncle Zoltan ven you go to Budapest. He is very respectable man now, you understand? So!! Zere is only me. No-vun else because now your poor mother, you understand, she too is lost. Only me to show you who really you are."

She heaved herself to her feet and wiped the palms of her hands down the front of her skirt. And there, in that pale rectangle of light on the lawn, she began to sing and to dance, her voice brazen as a brass bell, her big hips swaying and shaking, sending her enormous skirts into a swirl. Everything about her seemed brazen. She clapped her hands and her bracelets rattled. She stomped her feet and the lawn vibrated. I sat transfixed. My little brothers appeared in a window, Dad in another. A light flicked on in Mrs. Barstow's, and in the house on the other side too, whereupon Great Aunt Maria only sang louder, intensifying the rhythm, beating it out with her hands and feet, beckoning with her head for me to join in. Dad opened the French windows and cleared his throat, "Ah-hem, Maria. Let's not forget the neighbors now..." Her voice rose to a trill on a series of tongue-rolling high notes, and I stood to join her. To my excited ears Mrs. Barstow's irritated tapping on glass became the click of castanets. All around me Dad's roses rustled their skirts. What could I do except rustle my own skirt? I arched my back, lifted my arms over my head and let my feet find the earth.

Sam has been so quiet, so intent on listening, I'd almost forgotten he's here. That we're both of us here stretched out in the back of the car. Sam with his hands behind his head, me with a strand of hair I wrap and unwrap around my finger. Up front, Dave is driving. He fills the small, enclosed space with cigarette smoke.

Sam pats me gently on the arm, and for the second time reminds me of my father. This time when Dad gets tongue-tied because he doesn't know what to say. I wonder would they like him, Mum and Dad? Sam pats me again, and twists his head to call to Dave.

"Everything okay up there, Dave?" he asks.

"No problemo."

"Let me know if you want company."

He turns back to me and I feel him looking at me. Outside is stillness, the late afternoon sun a pale waxen ball casting long frozen shadows on the snow. Inside me is all motion, the same excited tremble I felt that night in the garden, and that carried on into the next morning when Dad drove Aunt Maria to the train station. I rode with them and hung over the back seat with my arms wrapped round her neck. I didn't want her to leave. At the station she pinched my cheeks and kissed me goodbye.

"Don't forget what I tell you, my darlink," she said. Then pulled herself free of the car and wrapped her cardigan firmly about her shoulders.

"Cheers then, Maria!" said Dad. And then, "Funny old girl," as we both watched her retreating figure waddle into the ticket office. That was the last I ever saw of her. She seemed to vanish from the face of the earth and no amount of letter writing or phone calling between England and Hungary ever turned up any clues as to her whereabouts.

Years later I changed my name from Mary Burton to her name, to Maria Kovács. But it was that morning, before the train station, that I became Maria. I looked into the bathroom mirror while brushing my hair, and was shown a face I'd never seen before.

For the first time I saw who I really was, in my cheekbones, in my dark eyes and my cloud of dark hair. And there was no turning back. Just as now, in this moment of skimming eastward to some still unknown place with a man named Sam, there is no turning back.

Wonderbread and Spam

One morning in August, Ruthie stood on her tiptoes in front of the stove to stir Top Ramen noodles for her sisters' breakfast when one of the twins let out a scream. "Ruthie, there's somebody dead in the weeds!" They all five rushed to the big window that looked out onto the driveway choked in weeds grown waist high. Sure enough, there was a body. Both twins screamed then, and Ruthie told them to Ssh! in case they woke Mom, what they needed to do was call 911, and Wilma reminded Ruthie the phone was cut off. "Stupid!" So they went out the back door and round the side of the house to investigate, Ruthie carrying Sweet Pea on her hip.

The body was Mom, smelling strongly of beer and faintly of piss, her face flushed a florid pink. No amount of shaking or yelling would wake her, not even when Wilma yelled directly in one ear and one of the twins in the other. Summers in Yakima were fierce, the sun already glinting on the broken glass that lay thick between the weeds so that Mom appeared to be lying on a bed of jewels.

"Dang, Ruthie she gonna melt out here," said Wilma. But Mom proved too heavy to lift without having to drag her some, weighed down as she was with beer. "Like a bathroom sponge filled up with water," explained Ruthie, who at age eight already had a scientific bent. But dragging her would have meant cutting her to bits on the glass— Ruthie's insight again— so instead of taking her back in to the house, they let her be, Wilma the one coming up with the idea of first covering up her face with her yellow straw sun-hat. And then, because she had spotted their friend Hilda's mom leaving for work, Ruthie said forget the noodles, and they scampered across the street to eat breakfast with Hilda.

Hilda, was seventeen and wore eyeliner. She also made excellent pancakes and *quesadillas* and was *very* pregnant. This Mom had noted a few weeks before.

"Damn, that girl got herself knocked up good. Check out the size of her."

According to Mom, the best thing about their Yakima house was the kitchen window, which, besides featuring tire ruts and weeds, allowed a person to sit at the kitchen table and see clear out to the street. "That's useful," Mom had pointed out when they moved in. "Being able to see what's going on without leaving the kitchen. I like that." All that was going on that particular morning was Hilda, standing in front of her own house across the street, hands laced thoughtfully across her splendid stomach.

"Don't you be getting yourself knocked up when you're her age, you hear me, Ruthie?"

At the time Mom was still going through her morning ritual of "getting her head on straight," which sometimes did and sometimes didn't involve hangovers. It always involved drinking the extra-strong coffee she had Ruthie fix for her. Seated at the kitchen window in her terry-cloth robe, hair still in curlers, she was drinking her first cup and smoking her first cigarette when she spotted Hilda. "You hear me, Ruthie?"

It occurred to Ruthie to mention that it was Hilda the wayward teenager who fed them whenever Mom forgot, which sometimes happened these days. She thought better of it. "You had me when you were sixteen," she pointed out instead.

Mom flicked her ash. "That's because I didn't know any better. Never had anyone encouraging me like I encourage you." And she launched into the story Ruthie had heard plenty of times before, but didn't altogether mind hearing again, about the boarding school in Idaho, where the nuns had fingers like pincers, and made you eat soap if they caught you talking Indian.

By then it was late June, the school year barely over. Mom still wound her shoulder-length black hair onto extra large rollers every night, and in the morning still managed (soon as she had her head on straight) to back-brush and tease her jumbo curls into one huge bee-hive helmet. This she sprayed to a hard lacquered sheen with extra-hold VO5 hairspray, as she had done every workday morning of the past eight months of life in Yakima. "Life's a battle, girls," she still liked to say: a line that Ruthie found oddly reassuring. "See what I have to go through for a job at a dump diner?" And then she was out the door, a sleepy Sweet Pea in tow.

That is, until the bright July day Mom decided, with school out and big-girl Ruthie at home all day with nothing to do, there was no longer a need to roust poor baby Sweet Pea from a warm bed and drag her to Mrs. Ortega's at such an ungodly hour. Absolutely no sense at all in wasting money on a babysitter. Although it seemed the money turned right around and spent itself just as quick anyway. With no babysitter to run to, Mom reasoned, it made sense to stop at the Drift On Inn to relax a little on the way home from work. "You don't begrudge me that, now do you, girls?"

Soon after came a morning when Mom, not quite up to fixing her hair, took herself back to bed. If life was a battle, Ruthie figured her mom was losing. She knew Mom was losing when she ditched her morning ritual entirely, lost her job at the diner, and the phone was cut off. "Big deal," was all Mom had to say, "We've managed on welfare before."

Meanwhile Hilda bloomed. By mid-July she reminded Ruthie of a pigeon. Ruthie had memories of pigeons from when she lived in Seattle, a place where pigeons gathered in large numbers on rooftops and telephone wires and dropped droppings on sidewalks. Hilda could be counted on to coo in the same soothing kind of way, especially around Sweet Pea. She waddled like a pigeon too, her round fat front thrust out, toes turned stubbornly in. Luckily for Ruthie and her sisters, given their own mother's absentmindedness where food was concerned, Hilda's waddling led her frequently to the kitchen. Here she chuckled about her own mother's complaints concerning the amount she ate, all the while rummaging in the refrigerator for the makings of a mid-morning or mid-afternoon snack for herself and her little friends. Or while whipping up a tasty lunch of *sopa*, the kind with the little star noodles, that she insisted they sit up to the table and eat "properly."

But for a good deal of the day, like most pigeons, Hilda chose simply to roost. Her favorite spot was her front steps, shaded by an overgrown apple tree, and cooler than inside the house. It was here that Hilda did various other grown-up things that Ruthie and Wilma admired, such as applying eyeliner. This she painted onto her top lid in a thick black line, extending it an impressive extra half-inch of upward swoop past the point where her outer eye ended. Ruthie and Wilma agreed this was "real cool". She also changed her nail polish color a lot, and fixed her hair into various puffy styles. This last gave Hilda ongoing angst, as her layers were taking *forever* to grow out. When she was done with all that, she devoted her attention to brushing and oiling and braiding all of her little friends' hair, admiring how black and strong it was, with not more than a handful of split ends among the five of them. If God were good enough to bless her with a little girl, Hilda would sigh, she'd be sure to let her grow her hair long and keep the ends nicely trimmed. Other than that they discussed names for the baby, mostly girls' names, with a few boy ones just in case.

And so the summer drifted along, until the troubling mid-August morning when Mom's body turned up in the driveway. Even more troubling then, to trot across the street, hungry for a decent breakfast and a few reassuring pigeon coos, to discover Hilda lying disinterestedly on a wrinkled bed-sheet with a pillow stuffed between her knees. In this position, strangely silent and still, a faded blue nightdress stretched tightly over the great mound of her, Hilda seemed to have transformed from pigeon into beached whale. Ruthie had seen a beached whale on TV. It had taken all kinds of people dressed in slickers and armed with ropes and pulleys to move the poor thing. Now that she thought about it, a beached whale was rather what Mom had resembled too. Two beached whales in one morning was a bit much. She stood uncertainly in the doorway of Hilda's bedroom, Sweet Pea on her hip and her sisters jostling and fidgeting beside and behind her.

"Hi, Hilda."

No response except for a low grunt.

"It's me, Hilda. Ruthie."

"Wilma too…"

"All we got for breakfast is Ramen noodles."

"That's nasty for breakfast," Hilda agreed, her voice flat. Still she didn't move.

"'Specially when that's all we ate for supper last night," added Wilma.

Ruthie considered their options. Perhaps if they all five worked together they could move Hilda the way the people in the slickers had moved the whale. But to where? To do what? She had a better idea.

"Come on," she said to Wilma. "Hilda's sick. We gotta make breakfast today."

She had seen Hilda making *quesadillas* plenty of times. The trick was not to burn them, or cut yourself on the knife while slicing the cheese. While the first two were less than perfect, the twins and Sweet Pea didn't seem to mind. And with Wilma's help—"Flip it, stupid! It's about to burn"— Ruthie was soon able to make nearly perfect *quesadillas*. With great pride she carried two of these, only slightly congealed (Ruthie was so hungry she had to eat first) in to

Hilda. But to Ruthie's consternation Hilda showed no interest at all in eating. This was unheard of. Though hardly a problem, Hilda pointed out in a weary voice. Especially as her Mom had opened up the refrigerator the night before and complained about Hilda eating as if she were feeding a whole army instead of just two. A comment that made Ruthie feel even more uneasy. For what if Hilda's mom found out about her and her sisters eating her food almost every day?

"All I want is a Coke," said Hilda. "And to sit outside." With a series of moans she finally heaved herself up and swung her legs over the side of the bed.

"Want me to bring the hair things?" asked Wilma hopefully.

"Not today," said Hilda, waddling out on puffy feet, still dressed in her nightgown. She didn't want to discuss baby names either. Nor did she want to play jacks or cards, or even put on her eyeliner. "She looks funny without it," Wilma whispered to Ruthie. All Hilda wanted was to sit, her fat legs splayed, and stare into air. When Sweet Pea tried to climb onto what was left of her lap she pushed her away. "Not today, *mija*." Pretty soon the twins and Sweet Pea took themselves off to play under the apple tree, which was where they ended up most days anyway. But for the life of her Ruthie couldn't see what she and Wilma were supposed to do.

"What's that in your driveway?" Hilda asked after a bit.

" Mom," said Ruthie. "She's drunk again."

"On her *ass*," added Wilma.

"Oh," said Hilda, and took a swig of her Coke, and fell silent again. For a while Ruthie and Wilma played cards by themselves, until Wilma accused Ruthie of cheating, whereupon Ruthie pointed out *she* was the one cheating, and that was the end of that. With Mom still in the driveway, Wilma a brat and Hilda out of sorts, the remainder of the summer stretched before Ruthie in a most unpromising way. She wrapped her arms round her legs, chin on her knees, and stared off like Hilda to where, under the tree, her little sisters squabbled and played, and fallen fruit lay scattered in the dirt like small pale suns.

The summer before there had been picnics. This as part of Mom's plan to reunite them as a family after their return home from various foster homes. Mom set them up in a little house in Moses Lake, central Washington, a place Ruthie approved of because there were lizards in the back yard, but where one way and another there was a lot to get used to. Not only the twins and Sweet Pea, who Ruthie had barely seen in a year—though Wilma had been stuck on her the whole time like glue—but also the addition of Mom's new teetotaling boyfriend, Vince. Vince wore mirror sunglasses and owned a brown Buick with fins and whitewall tires. Piling with her sisters into the back seat for the first of these picnics, Ruthie found herself face to face with Vince's son, Tony, breathing noisily from behind thick lenses. Mom and Vince thought it important that everybody get acquainted.

The favorite picnic spot was Wanapum, not far from Moses Lake, a place where the Columbia River curved its way through dramatic brown rock canyons. The rides there in the air-conditioned Buick had been fun, even if squashed. The car radio played, and Sweet Pea cooed from the front seat where she sat with Mom and Vince, Mom's new hairdo neatly tucked under a sky-blue chiffon scarf, Vince's thick tattooed arm around her shoulders.

At Wanapum State Park and Campground they all wore swimsuits and played on the beach. They ate tuna and cheese sandwiches and chips, and drank Pepsis. Mom and Vince drank Pepsis too, Vince bragging how he'd never had to get himself on no wagon to where's he could fall off. On those picnics there was nothing much to remind Ruthie that she was any different than any other kid on the beach. Except maybe her Mom and Vince kissed excessively in a way that other grown-ups with children did not. And Mom had an embarrassing habit of kneading Vince's stomach, which rose like dough and spilled over the top of his blue jeans. But sipping on Pepsi, with her bottom in wet sand and toes in the ice-cold Columbia, it had been easy to dream a little. Mom would marry Vince and they'd all be bridesmaids and wear lemon-yellow-down-to-the-ground dresses. Then they'd all move into a bigger house, maybe so big Ruthie would end up with a room to herself because she was the eldest. Of course, Tony would also have a room to himself because he was the only boy. Tony, by that time, would be her brother. Ruthie was never sure how she felt about this last part, not with Tony digging and panting and sending up showers of sand like a dog while Wilma watched in admiration.

Then she didn't need to worry about Tony any more because all of it came to an abrupt end one night when Vince hauled Mom out of a bar. Sorry, sweetheart, Ruthie overheard him say, while depositing a contrite Mom on the doorstep, but it's curtains for you and me. Which from what Ruthie could figure out, was pretty much what happened with Dad. To Mom's credit she soon bounced back. "There's no way better to get over a broken heart than to move, girls," she announced one morning. And piled them all into her old rust-eaten Chevy, which obligingly started up after months of neglect, and with tail pipe dragging and sending up showers of sparks from the road, drove them out past Omak to the reservation to pay a visit to her cousin Grace.

"Guess who?" Mom said, walking through Grace's kitchen door with the five of them in tow. If, after the initial rounds of hugging and admiring one another's children, cousin Grace was put out any over six extra mouths to feed, or finding corners and cushions to make up extra beds in an already too-small house, she didn't let on. They stayed in Grace's little house by the river for what Ruthie hoped would be forever. Grace's two boys aged ten and twelve a lot easier to take than Tony, not to mention the joys of river and tumbleweed, as well as more lizards. But Grace, it turned out, was a good deal too devout for Mom, who after her years of Roman Catholic boarding school said she could handle the Holy Mother only in small doses. "Hell, Gracie, it was the damn nuns drove me to drink in the first place!" So it was, halfway through the school year—Ruthie rather liked the little reservation school on the hill with the cross—Mom packed them all into the Chevy again and drove to Yakima. This, according to Mom, was the perfect place to take root. It had the distinction of being close enough to another reservation to have plenty of Indians around, ("Got right lonesome in Moses Lake"), more opportunities than Omak, and enough distance from any Holier-Than-Thou Catholic relatives and Father Finnegan's home visits to keep from driving Mom permanently back to the bottle. Amen.

They were still sitting across the street on Hilda's steps, the sun at its fiercest, Mom still asleep under her hat (a couple of times Ruthie had run over to make sure she wasn't dead), when Hilda let out a cry and clutched her side. This was followed by a dramatic gush of water from between her legs, cascading down the steps and onto the sidewalk. Why was Hilda going pee-pee on herself? one of the twins wanted to know, as all of them looked on in round-eyed astonishment.

"It's the baby," groaned Hilda, and heaved herself to her feet and staggered back into the house. They all five crowded around Hilda as she dialed her mother's work number and then shrieked and wept hysterically into the phone about not wanting a baby. A short while later a car door slammed outside the house, and Hilda's mom came hurrying up the steps.

"*Ay, Dios mío! ¿Qué está pasando?*"

This when she discovered five extras in her living room, two of them playing midwife to her shrieking daughter who, between writhing and panting on the couch, appeared to be giving birth already. The three little ones cried loudly and only added to the confusion. "Get out of here, *mijas*," she said, crossing herself and shooing them out. "Go home to your mother." A short while later they all five watched from their own front steps as poor Hilda was loaded into an ambulance.

The street became strangely empty after that, as if swept clean of all that gave it life. It was then that Ruthie noticed Mom was gone from the driveway. No sign of her in the house either. She still wasn't back when Ruthie reheated the Ramen noodles and fixed peanut butter crackers for supper. Nor much, much later when she and Wilma fell asleep on the couch in front of *The Late Night Show*. That night Ruthie slept uneasily and dreamed of Cousin Grace's stew, its hunks of tender meat, gravy running over a mound of mashed potatoes the way Hilda's water had run down the steps.

Neither Mom or Hilda came home the next day, so Ruthie made instant oatmeal and reheated some stale Chinese take-out she found in the fridge. She found herself dreaming of stew and mashed potatoes even when she wasn't sleeping. She imagined herself eating plateloads of food, alternating between Cousin Grace's kitchen, and the neat square table of the foster home where white plates were laid out on a blue-and-white checkered tablecloth. That night they had nothing at all for supper. The next morning, still no Mom. When Ruthie discovered the twins in the bathroom sucking the toothpaste out of the tube she decided it was time to go shopping. And because when Mom was sober she never stepped out of the house without looking her best, Ruthie said they should all dress proper.

So it was, some time around eleven, the door to Safeway swung open and in clattered five crimson-mouthed little girls wearing high heels, and with big purses slung over their arms. Ruthie and Wilma led the way, teetering in Mom's three-inch spikes as they surveyed the scene from beneath a pink veil and Mom's yellow sun-hat—this last rescued for the occasion from its time in the driveway. They then resumed their strut, spindly brown legs buckling and bending. The twins followed, and without ever picking up their feet, proved to be the loudest high-heel scuffers ever. But poor little Sweet Pea got marooned just inside the door, Mom's yellow plastic pumps jutting out front and back of her like two wrecked boats.

Of course, Ruthie was the one had to go back and rescue Sweet Pea, a distraction that allowed Wilma and the twins to make a rackety getaway. Ruthie just knew they were heading for the cookie aisle, even though she had insisted no cookies. She'd explained the whole thing. If people saw them taking cookies and candy instead of real food, they'd think they were *bad* kids instead of *hungry* kids.

Sure enough, when she caught up to them, the now barefoot Sweet Pea bouncing on her hip and offending yellow shoes stashed in her purse, she found Wilma and the twins tearing into a pack of Chips Ahoy cookies like wolves with fresh kill. She popped Wilma upside the head and snatched the cookies out of her hands.

"You gonna get us arrested, stupid!"

Whereupon Wilma, cheeks bulging with cookie, kicked at Ruthie and missed, and Ruthie kicked her back harder and didn't miss. This seemed to settle the matter of who was in charge, and Ruthie took off to the bread aisle where they were supposed to have gone in the first place, the rest of them in tow, a compliant Wilma limping now. Here an old lady watched in amazement as the twins snapped open their oversized purses at Ruthie's instruction, into which Ruthie stuffed three loaves of Wonderbread apiece.

"It's for our mother," said Ruthie sweetly, turning to the old lady. And to the others, triumphantly, "Told you it stuffed good!"

Then with a whirlwind clatter of heels they were off again, this time to the canned meat and fish aisle where Wilma's purse was filled with cans of Spam, and then around the corner to the diary section for milk. Stuffing milk cartons turned out to be more of a problem than Ruthie had anticipated.

"*Told* you we shoulda got Kool-Aid!" said Wilma, a remark Ruthie ignored other than to stick out her tongue, quickly resolving the problem by taking the yellow shoes out of her purse and leaving them with the egg cartons. With an extra half-gallon of milk tucked under her arm, and with more clattering and some giggling, they hurried past the check-out stands and out the door, Sweet Pea turning from her perch on big sister's hip to wave "bye-bye" at all the astonished faces.

The front door was open and Mom was home. Bursting into the house, they found her sitting on one end of the couch in a pool of sunlight, smoking a cigarette. She wore a crisp new red and white dress, its skirt spread around her, one bare leg crossed over the other, her top leg swinging light and easy. Her feet were bare too, toenails painted to match her dress, hair freshly washed hanging soft and damp around her shoulders.

"So where have my girls been, dressed up in my things and looking so pretty?" She smiled at them through cigarette smoke, hummed a little tune, and beckoned for Sweet Pea. Ruthie and Wilma looked quickly back and forth between themselves.

"Well?" Mom scooped Sweet Pea into her lap and pushed the hair out of her eyes.

"We been shopping," said Ruthie, and wondered where Mom had been, trying to size up whether this was the right time to ask.

"Shopping! Well, come here and let me see what you bought." She peered into the purses and made a sad face. "Bread and milk. Is that all?"

Ruthie felt indignant. They had gone through a lot to get that food. Besides which, any other mom would ask where the money came from. "We were hungry," she said.

"Hungry! My poor babies! So what were you going to do with bread and milk, Ruthie?"

"Make sandwiches."

This Mom found funny, laughing in a way Ruthie wasn't used to, as light and easy as water running over stones. She combed her fingers through her damp hair. "A sandwich has something in the middle. What are you putting in the middle of yours, Ruthie? Air?"

"No, Spam. Wilma's got it." Wilma pulled out a can of spam and waved it triumphantly for Mom to see. Ruthie waited for Mom to ask about the money, or at least to say something about being sorry for leaving them alone, and with no food. But this new strangely happy Mom just hummed a little more, tilted her head this way then that, smiling first at Ruthie, then at Wilma.

"In that case, bring it all in the kitchen."

After sweeping her empties from countertop to sink, Mom set about making sandwiches, a big pile of them stacked up on a plate. Like it was her idea all along. Like she was any other mom feeding her kids lunch, telling them to wash their hands and sit up to the table. What right did she have? She wasn't the one went through all the hassle of getting her sisters dressed and ready to go, and having to fight Wilma over the cookies. It should be Ruthie tugging the bread slices back into shape from where they were squished. Ruthie cutting the finished sandwiches into little squares. Ruthie dishing them out and reminding her sisters to say thank you.

Mom bustled about, transferring the milk from carton to jug, because nothing was too nice for her girls, she said. "For heaven's sake, Ruthie, take that look off your face and eat."

But Ruthie had lost her appetite. She sat, looking out the window, wishing she'd never had to leave a home where she'd had three meals a day and someone to kiss her goodnight every night. She wondered where her dad was. Took off and married someone else, Mom had said. Ruthie wondered why he hadn't taken them with him. Mom said it was because he didn't give a fuck. Ruthie knew that wasn't true. He just couldn't find them was all. He came back for them, but they'd already moved.

Ruthie saw the police car cruising slowly down the street. It stopped in front of their house, its back end stuck out in front of the driveway. She said nothing, but smiled a secret smile and took a bite of sandwich. There was a curt knock at the front door, which was still open, and Mom went to see who it was.

"Excuse me, ma'am, but there's been a call from the Safeway manager concerning five little girls seen helping themselves to food. We have reason to believe they live here."

"Uh-oh," said Wilma.

"Uh-oh nothing," said Ruthie. The twins sat round-eyed with mouths dropped and food in their mouths. "Close up and chew," said Ruthie. But then her own eyes got round when Mom invited the policeman right into the kitchen, like nothing was wrong. The five of them eating Wonderbread Spam sandwiches and drinking milk. Mom's empties piled up for anyone to see. Ruthie thought quickly, and started shoveling sandwich into her mouth the way she imagined starving people wolfed down their food. Yes, she would tell the policeman, Yes, we're starving. Our mom's a drunk, that's why our dad left her, and she's gone all the time in a bar and there's never any food.

But before she could say one word, Mom proceeded to put on a show. She swirled her red and white skirt this way and that and put her hands to her face: Oh she was shocked, *shocked*. The very idea that she'd sent her daughters shopping and they'd taken it into their heads not to pay for it. "What were you girls thinking of?"

She ran quickly into the back bedroom to get her purse, not any of the derelict ones Ruthie was used to, but brand new, red and shiny to go with the new dress, and fastened with a brass snap. From this she pulled two twenties and flourished them. Ruthie knew right then she'd found a replacement for Vince.

"I am *so* sorry about this. How much do I owe, officer?" Then turning slightly, so the policeman couldn't see her face, she winked at Ruthie. "I'll have a word with you later, young lady." The policeman, who was young and fresh faced, lifted his cap and ran his hand through his hair. Mom thrust the money toward him but he put up his hand to stop her and indicated he wanted a word alone with her. They disappeared into the living room, Mom winking and smiling at all of them before closing the kitchen door behind her.

The twins stared expectantly at Ruthie as if she understood something they didn't. Ruthie put her finger to the side of her head and twirled it. "Mom's gone nuts," she explained.

"I like her nuts," said Wilma.

There were muffled voices for a couple of minutes, and then Mom was heard showing the policeman to the door. She came back humming the same little tune she seemed unable to let go of, picked up the milk jug and refilled the girls' glasses as if nothing had happened. Looking up at her then and wanting to hate her, all Ruthie could think was how pretty she looked without her hair in a helmet. With the sun behind it, Ruthie could see it wasn't black at all, but a deep, deep red, the color of plums. Like the rest of her it didn't seem quite real.

Round the Houses

Summers in London could never be counted on, but the summer of 1970 was worse than usual. It rained at least every other day. Ironically, the place Maria found a job was called Tropical Heat, a shady set-up that operated out of a storefront in Golders Green and sold central heating door to door in immigrant neighborhoods. The boss's name was Sidney Smithers. He had a big belly and a lot of gold jewelry and drove around Golders Green in a maroon Rolls Royce. Most days he showed up in the office when all the girls first arrived and always cracked the same joke about rain being good for business. "Nobody finks about central 'eating if the bleedin' sun's shinin', right, girls?" He'd pinch a few behinds on his way in and wiggle his stubby fingers. "'oo's today's lucky girl gonna give me a quick feel then?" He was disgusting. It was a disgusting job.

This soon became obvious to Maria, but there wasn't much she could do about it. Summer jobs were scarce as sunshine that year with every student in London looking for one. The alternative was to pack it all in, bedsit and all, and spend the summer in Surrey with Mum and Dad. Not likely. Better to stick it out till September when school started up again. Then at least she'd still have her own place to live.

She was one of Mick Hadley's girls. A plaque on the office wall proclaimed him salesman of the year. He had four girls canvassing for him, and drove them out to a predominately Indian neighborhood in his midnight blue Jaguar. There they went door to door in twos while Mick took off to the bookies. Wendy was Maria's partner. She was an old hand at Tropical Heat, having worked there for nearly a year. Nineteen years old, with long legs and short shiny brown hair, she looked like she'd just stepped out of Vidal

Sassoon's and was *nearly* pretty. But the problem was her last name—Thorn—and her rather pointy face. This combination had earned her the nickname "Spikey", which she *hated*. All this Wendy confided to Maria on her first day on the job, the two of them standing under a tree with their clipboards held over their heads while they waited for the rain to ease up. "It's me bleedin' chin," she said. "I look like a witch don't I?" She couldn't wait to get married, she sighed, just to get rid of the Thorn. And then, explosively, "Sod this! Bleedin' rain's making spots all over me blouse!"

Maria liked Wendy right off, but wasn't sure why. For one she called the Indians and Pakistanis "coons." This didn't sit right with Maria, and she felt she should say something on moral grounds, although the very idea of doing so made her feel squirmy. And then, Wendy was so hung up on the way she looked. She wore matching outfits. Day one, red and white. Day two, navy blue and white. Day three, white on white. She was into white. She also wore near white lipstick with nail polish to match. Of course, Maria's own careless "artistic" look—dark hair tousled down her back, colors and textures seeming to land next to one another by accident, (a splash of crimson say, against black velvet)— took as much effort as Wendy's matching outfits. But that never occurred to Maria. No, the thing she liked about Wendy, Maria realized on her third day, was her energy. She walked as if there were a wind behind her, words popping out of her like fizzy water when you took the top off the bottle too fast. After two years of diction and elocution and breath control and learning to walk as if you wore Elizabethan clothing— all standard fare at the Royal Academy of Dramatic Art— Wendy provided Maria with a relief similar to having a tight corset removed.

Alison and Jean were the other two girls on Mick's team. He always dropped them off first because according to him they were a couple of stuck-ups who used up all the air in his car. Maria was weird, he'd say, twisting his neck around to look at her in the back seat. "Fancy yourself the bloody actress do you, darlin'?" And a bit on the dark side. But at least she wasn't stuck up. Maria soon figured out she didn't have the time of day for Mick. "Your job, me lovelies," he liked to say (even Alison and Jean were his lovelies when he was giving his pitch), "is to corner some poor unsuspecting wog or coon and convince them that Tropical 'eat is *exactly* whot they need. Lay it on thick. Coming from a 'ot country to a cold one like this must be very *very* difficult. But their quality of life will greatly improve with warmth in the home. 'an not one bleedin' word 'bout 'ow much electric costs to run. They can throw it out the window after we sold it to 'em for all I care. Just drill it in their 'eads it's cheap to install and give 'em a nice big smile. Sign on the dotted line please, and our salesman will be in touch. Simple."

"Then you go in to make the kill," Maria said the third or fourth time she heard this spiel. She was being sarcastic, but Mick didn't catch that.

"Kill is right, darlin'. Kill the bleedin' lot if I had my way."

Maria had to agree with him though when it came to Alison and Jean. She was cooped up in the back seat with them and saw how they rolled their eyes whenever anybody spoke. Maybe they'd even been *bred* with their long noses, Maria thought: all the better for looking down. One day, they'd barely stepped out of the car when she voiced this idea and instantly regretted it. It made her Mick's mate, the last thing she wanted to be. He laughed all the way to the bookies where he said he was going to put a fiver on a horse for her for giving him such a good laugh. "A fiver for you too, Spikey, 'cause I loves ya." He was really into the horses. He was into Wendy too, when it suited him. He wasn't fat or flabby or anything, and was even good looking in a boring kind of way. Still tanned to the color of a pale carrot from a recent trip to Spain. But Wendy definitely could have done better than Mick. Or so Maria thought. As a special "privilege" he let her ride up front with him, which gave him the chance to stick his hand under her skirt while he drove. Wendy would giggle a little, but mostly slap his hands and call him a dirty bugger. When she got out of the car afterwards she'd be shaking and want a cigarette right off. Sitting behind him in the car, Maria had a daily view of where his toupee joined on. It wasn't even a good match. She wondered how he looked without it and if he took it off in bed. But the main thing about Mick wasn't the toupee or the way he looked. Basically he was just a jerk.

Maria liked her bedsit. Inside its four daffodil-yellow walls she was her own person, and it was here, at age eighteen, that she first claimed independence from Mum and Dad. That had been two years ago. Back then the room had orange curtains, a red overstuffed armchair and a pink bedspread, as well as the yellow walls. The overall effect had reminded Maria of vomit. So she bought two blue-green Indian bedspreads—they were all the rage just then, as was everything Indian—and put one on the bed and one over the chair. She arranged her books and took down the picture of a kitten and tacked up a Picasso print and a poster for Brecht's *Threepenny Opera*. She had her own small wash basin in which she washed dishes as well as her face, and a hotplate. The bathroom she shared with the three other bedsits on her floor, and kept a pile of shillings on the shelf over her basin so that she'd always have money for the meter and a hot bath.

It was in this room that she had begun to emerge as the actress she was going to be, and practiced her lines for Antigone, and for Maria in *Twelfth Night*. That had been a joke: Maria playing Maria. At least it had been to that imbecile, Randy (what a name!), the only American at the academy. He wore cowboy boots made out of crocodile skin and always had money. He swaggered in late to rehearsal like he owned the place. A typical American, Maria thought. This was a view based on years of observing American tourists, which London was full of. They rode the tube train with large cameras slung around their necks and snapped photographs of anything and everything. The men had crew cuts and wore big shorts. The women had bleached and soldered hair-dos and wore pastels. But the thing about all of them was they were loud, and declared everything cute. To Randy, Maria was cute. He sang her unsolicited renditions of Maria from *West Side Story* and told her she looked the part. Was she Greek, Italian, or what?

Because of all these earlier prejudices—which Maria did not see as prejudices at all but only as accurate assessments—she was none too happy to learn from Linda, her next-door neighbor, that the downstairs flat had been "taken over" by Americans for the summer.

"Howdy, I'm Hank, and I beat you to it," said a lanky man in blue jeans and tennis shoes. This when Maria went downstairs to use the pay phone in the hallway one Saturday morning, and he popped out the downstairs door and got to it first. Then right away he gave a little bow, "Ladies first," he said, and handed her the phone. "No, seriously," he explained. "I'm calling Missoula, Montana. Sometimes it takes forever to get through. Just let me know when you're done." He went back into his flat and left the door wide open.

In the entire two years of living in her bedsit, Maria had barely seen the previous tenants of the flat, let alone what was behind the door. She spent the rest of that Saturday morning there, and discovered it had hideous pink flowered wallpaper, a door to a cellar in its sitting room, and that the meter could be picked open with a hairpin, allowing the same shilling to be used over and over again. She also discovered that Hank and his two roommates, Tim and Brian, were students of Friends World College, "a hippy Quaker college" as Hank called it, and they'd just spent six months in Africa. Also, that not all Americans were loud. Tim turned out to be so soft-spoken that Maria had to lean in his direction to catch what he was saying.

She'd been working for about two weeks when Mick dropped her and Wendy as usual at the end of a long row of narrow gray brick houses. Before driving off he rolled down his car window and leaned out.

"Spikey! I told you! Don't be wearing them short skirts on the job. They's for me. All them coons gonna be tryin' to get a look at your drawers!"

Wendy tugged her skirt down round her thighs. "Bloody coons," she giggled to Maria. "Bunch of dirty ol' men."

The moral dilemmas of the job were getting to Maria. She was already perfecting a modified version of the official sales pitch to alert people to the fact that they had sixty days to change their mind after installation. This important piece of information she'd learned from Wendy at the end of her first week when they walked past a house with a twisted heap of Tropical Heat radiators in its front yard. "Stupid coons," Wendy had said then. "Don't even know they can get their bleedin' money back."

Maria waited for Mick to drive off. "They're not coons," she said firmly.

Wendy was still fussing with her skirt. She looked surprised. "Whot are they then?"

"Christ," said Maria, and pulled a pack of Players No. 6 from her pocket. "Wanna fag?" Wendy took one, and they both lit up. "They're people, Wendy. Like you and me. They just come from someplace else, that's all."

"Well, they shoulda' stayed where they come from, shouldn't they?" Wendy was indignant. "An' don't be calling me a coon! I wash don't I? They don't never wash. An' 'ave you ever smelled their 'ouses? Bleedin' stinks of curry! It's all over their 'ouses and it's all over them too."

"Well, just so you know, I'm going in. Starting today."

Wendy gave Maria an "are you crazy?" look and threw her cigarette in the drain. "Mick won't 'ave it. It's against 'is rules."

"Sod Mick."

Wendy walked off to the first house in a huff, and Maria went to the next house. They each stood on doorsteps separated only by a low brick wall that squeezed itself between the two front walks. Usually they leaned over these walls, or sometimes a low box hedge instead, and chatted to one another while they waited for someone to answer the door. Today they leapfrogged their way up the long row in silence, except for the sound of Wendy's low heel shoes, which clicked their way efficiently up to every other front door.

Other than that it was like any other day. Sometimes people peeped out from behind net curtains and waved them away. Other people barely cracked their doors and said "No thank you very much." Occasionally a small child opened the door wide and stood staring up from dark eyes while voices called from inside the house. Even though Maria didn't know the language, she knew these were parents or grandparents asking who was at the door, just like any parent would. And then there were those, usually men, who came to the door and stood hands on hips or folded above their stomachs while they listened to her entire pitch. After about twenty houses Maria got one of these, a young man with his hair in a pink turban. He listened politely and then called to someone inside the house in his own language, and translated the reply that came booming back.

"My father says we need heat but no refrigerator. Ha ha. Come in please." He held the door open and smiled. Wendy stood inches away on the adjacent doorstep. Maria leaned over the box hedge.

"I'm going in," she said.

"Knock yourself out," Wendy sniffed. "I'm waitin' at the gate." Mick's rules were to wait for one another at the gate if one of them got a lead. This to protect each other from all the dirty old men who dreamt of getting inside a white girl's drawers.

The house did smell of curry, Maria didn't mind seeing, as she liked curry better than fish and chips. A lot of English houses stank of fish and chips and stale grease. The front room was full of people, most of them watching television. Two men played cards. The booming voice, an older man with a gray beard and gray turban, came forward and shook Maria's hand and asked her to please sit down. She began her sales pitch, feeling the attention shift from the television to her. Modified or not, she felt less good than ever about what she was doing. She wanted to come right out and tell these people that Tropical Heat was a rip off. But then, she needed the money, and got commission for every lead that resulted in a sale. When she left the house, Wendy was still standing by the gate, smoking another cigarette. She seemed all cheered up again.

"'bout time," she said. "I thought you'd moved in."

"Sorry."

"It's alright. Mick came by. I told 'im you was inside using the loo. 'e's just won some money so 'e's in a good mood. 'e's taking me to the pictures tonight."

They did a few more houses with no luck and then it started to drizzle.

"Sod this," said Wendy. "Let's go to the Wimpy and get a cuppa tea."

They sat in a booth and Maria watched Wendy eat a Wimpy burger and chips. She was always eating but stayed skinny anyway.

"Whot was it like then?" she asked after a while.

"What was what like?"

"The coon 'ouse."

"It was just a house. With a lot people in it."

"Breed like rabbits, don't they?"

"I thought you said your mum had eight kids."

Wendy got huffy again and blew cigarette smoke in Maria's face. "Whot's that got to do wiv it?"

"Nothing. They're just people. That's all."

One day it poured rain and Mick didn't show up. When it rained hard he was supposed to pick up his team and let them sit in the car till it stopped. But there was no sign of him. To make matters worse, there weren't any Wimpy's nearby that day, or any other stores or cafes. Just row after row of the same gray-brick houses. Maria and Wendy huddled under a roadside tree while its leaves dripped all over them. Wendy was furious.

"Bleedin' bastard! 'e's so into 'is bleedin' 'orses he don't even know it's pissing down cats and dogs out 'ere. I'm tellin' you. 'e's gonna cough up for a new jacket if this one gets ruined. Look at me stockin's! I got polka dots goin' up the backs of me legs!"

"I'm getting a lead so I can go inside," said Maria. "Let's go back to that house with the blue door. It's after three. They said come back."

"You gonna leave me standin' out 'ere the rain by meself then? Some friend you are."

"You can come in with me."

"You fink I'm crazy or somethin'?"

"Yes."

The two of them trotted along with their clipboards held over their heads. Maria walked on the outside to protect Wendy's white clothes from splashing cars. When they got to the house Wendy stood by the gate with her clipboard over her head while Maria went up to the front door, her dress clinging to her legs.

"I'm going in," Maria, said a moment or two later.

"Well 'urry up. I'll be under this tree."

Maria had hardly begun her sales speech when the doorbell rang. The woman with a cardigan over her sari, who had answered the door to Maria, got up again.

Maria heard Wendy's voice. "Is me friend 'ere?"

"Yes. Come in."

Wendy stood shivering in the doorway of the front room.

The bottom of her dress was speckled with brown. "Look whot that bleedin' bus did to me dress," she hissed to Maria.

"Please, take a seat," said the man Maria had been talking to. "You are very cold, and in need of a blanket, I think." Maria wanted to laugh when Wendy perched herself on the chair edge as if she were sitting on a nail. The man took a brightly colored afghan from the back of the sofa and handed it to her. She smiled weakly, and draped it across the tips of her knees. A few minutes later the woman reappeared with a tray of tea and biscuits.

"You must warm yourselves," said the man, and nodded at the woman to pour the tea. Maria watched Wendy out of the corner of her eye and saw her pick up her cup gingerly, as if it might blow up. She sipped at the tea but didn't touch the biscuits at first, even though they were Cadbury's Chocolate Fingers and one of her favorites. But by the time Maria finished up her central heating speech she was nibbling on a biscuit. Then a little girl, who had been playing in the corner, came over and hovered by the biscuit plate and stared at Wendy. When Maria next looked over to see how Wendy was doing, the biscuit plate was empty and the little girl had chocolate around her mouth. Wendy dabbed hers with a napkin. The man signed the forms. It was still pouring outside

"Stay in here till it stops raining," encouraged the man. "Reena will make some more tea."

Suddenly, the little girl climbed onto Wendy's knee. To Maria's amazement she let the little girl take hold of her hands and examine her long painted fingernails.

"You like me fingernails then, do ya?" she asked the little girl.

"Pinkie likes you," said the man.

"She's 'bout the same age as me baby sister," said Wendy.

They stayed in the house for an hour. Maria enjoyed herself immensely. Which part of India were they from? she wanted to know. What was it like there? How long had they lived in England? Did they like it here? It must be hard, wasn't it, coming to a country so different from their own, and sometimes so unfriendly? The little girl lost interest in Wendy after a while, and Wendy just sat, forcing a smile every so often as she sipped at her tea. But Maria could tell she was listening to every word that was being said. Then a car drove past, honking madly, as if someone had their hand held down on the horn.

"That's Mick!" said Wendy, and jumped up. Then on her way out the door. "Ta ta, Pinkie."

Maria thanked everybody for the hospitality. "Our salesman will be in touch," she said. And then thought better of it. "Don't buy it," she said to the man. "Tropical Heat is a ripoff. Get gas instead."

Mick was fuming. "Where in bleedin' 'ell 'ave you two been? I got better things to do than drive a round all day lookin' for a coupla tarts."

"Yeah, like sittin' in there in the warm and dry bettin' on bleedin' 'orses while I'm out 'ere getting drowned. Look at me dress. It's ruined," said Wendy, turning on the car heat full blast. Alison and Jean were already in the back seat, bolt upright, with their knees pressed tightly together. Their hair was plastered to their heads and water dripped down their faces and necks.

"I'll 'ave you two know I lost a good bet 'cos of you two bleedin' idiots. Where the fuck where you all this time anyway?"

"In that house," Maria said. "Nice people. They gave us tea and biscuits."

Mick slammed on the brakes. "Whot!? Whot!? I use up 'alf a tank of petrol and drive around 'alf of bloody London lookin' for you and you're in there 'ob-knobbing with some bloody coons? You're supposed to sell to 'em, duckie, not socialize with 'em. Spikey, I 'ope your not picking up any funny ways from our artist friend. She's prob'ly 'alf coon herself by the looks of 'er, but *you're* not goin' in 'ouses no more. You 'ear me?"

Wendy folded her arms across her chest and stared out of the car window. "You go in 'em. An' I will too if I feels like it. You don't own me."

The downstairs flat always overflowed with visitors. On Sunday mornings when the landlord came for the rent the extra people hid in the cellar. All except for Maria. She was just visiting from upstairs. "Hello, Mr. Richman," she'd beam (his name was a running joke) and hand him her rent money. There were six people living in the flat now, including two Africans Mr. Richman didn't know about, one from Burundi and one from Kenya. They were Friends World College students too.

"I thought it was an American college," Maria said.

"*World*, baby, *world*," said Hank. "Which in today's screwed up world does mean American."

"With a couple of token black faces on scholarships to keep up appearances," said Osano, the Kenyan. And everybody laughed.

Maria spent more and more of her spare time downstairs. She'd never had so much opportunity to talk politics and hear different ideas exchanged. The Vietnam War was a constant topic. Try to talk about that at the Royal Academy and half the time you got shouted down, or laughed down. New words entered her vocabulary: colonialism, neo-colonialism, imperialism. Or perhaps they weren't new words at all, but had just taken on new meaning.

One Saturday she spent most of the evening talking to an American G.I. named Scotty who was back from Vietnam and now stationed in East Anglia. He was on leave for the weekend. He talked urgently, hunkered down on his haunches beside Maria's chair, constantly running his fingers through his tufted blonde hair. Listening to his stories, Maria realized there was nothing so simple as Donovan's anti-war song about the universal soldier who really was to blame, which was currently high on the charts. By the end of the evening she'd learned more new words: fraternization and cannon fodder.

The next morning, she came down after the over spill of people had done their usual disappearing act into the cellar, and Mr. Richman was just leaving. She'd barely walked into the room when the cellar door flew open and hit the wall with a loud smack and Scotty burst into the room. He flattened himself against the flowered wallpaper, shaking all over. Sweat and tears streamed down his face and his blue eyes rotated madly in his head.

"What happened?" whispered Maria to Tim.

"Shell-shock," Tim whispered back. "I guess the cellar set it off."

Midsummer the weather cleared up a bit. Wendy still went into the houses with Maria anyway. She said she did it just to bug Mick, but Maria noticed she didn't use the word coon as much as she used to. They took longer breaks these days too, at Wendy's suggestion. No point in running themselves ragged working when all Mick was doing was the horses, was there? Or maybe he was doing Gloria. "'e has another girlfriend, you know," Wendy had confided one afternoon, sounding rather ashamed. Maria said she wasn't surprised but managed to keep her mouth shut from saying anything more. A few times they went back to Maria's bedsit, and heated up baked beans on the hotplate. It was only five minutes on the bus from the area they were working. One time they ran into Osano coming out as they went in.

"Cheers, Maria," he called out.

"A friend. He lives downstairs," Maria explained, in answer to the look on Wendy's face.

Another time Wendy looked at Maria's books. Plays mostly. She pulled the collected works of Shakespeare off the shelf and flipped it open and read a few lines out loud from *As You Like It*. She said she didn't know what it was talking about but it sounded nice, even in cockney.

"Read it for me proper. You mus' be crazy giving up being a famous actress to work in a place like Tropical Heat."

"Who's famous?" laughed Maria.

Mostly they still took breaks at the Wimpy whenever there was one nearby. Nothing filled up a body as good as a Wimpy burger and chips. They were sitting across from one another in a booth one afternoon, Wendy at work on her second plate of chips, when she asked Maria would she like to come over to her house tomorrow night for a nosh up.

"We don't 'ave much money you know. Me mum 'as to take in other people's wash since me dad got sick. An' we live in Kings Cross."

"So? I don't live in Buckingham Palace do I?"

"Kings Cross is where all the tarts 'ang out."

"I know. I'd like to come."

Wendy's family lived in a flat above a barbershop. Heavy food smells hung on the air. The front room was crowded with people: her mum and dad, all her brothers and sisters and an uncle. Her baby sister was asleep in a playpen in the corner of the room. Wendy's dad sat yellowed and frail-looking in a wing armchair pulled up close to the TV. His face was hollow but his stomach was swollen up like he was pregnant. Liver problems. Too much booze, Wendy whispered. The uncle played cards with a couple of the younger children.

" Sit down luv," said Wendy's mum. She had big red hands that she dried on her pinafore. "I'll bring you a nice cuppa tea. We'll eat in a jiff. Soon as I've made more chips. 'ope you don't mind eatin' in the kitchen."

Supper was in shifts because there were too many people to fit around the kitchen table. It was a fry up, Wendy's favorite: bacon, eggs, chips, fried onions, fried tomatoes, fried bread, and lots of ketchup. Drying racks hung with clean clothes were tucked in every corner of the kitchen. One of Wendy's little brothers smeared ketchup on a clean shirt and got a slap on the back of his knees. After supper Maria went with Wendy into her room, which she shared with three other sisters. There were two sets of bunk beds, one on each side of the room. Wendy slept on a top bunk and had a picture of Mick pinned on the wall above her pillow. They sat on the bed together and smoked cigarettes.

"You've got a nice family," Maria said. "Real friendly. Too bad about your dad."

Wendy was quiet and blew smoke rings. Maria guessed she was thinking about her dad. Earlier she'd told Maria that he was going to die soon.

"I know what you fink," she said at last.

"About what?" asked Maria, surprised.

"About me 'ome. You're finkin' it's not that much different."

"Different from what?"

"From them 'ouses. The coon 'ouses."

"Well…in some ways it's not that much different is it?"

"No. Not really." Wendy blew smoke up to the ceiling. "But at least it don't smell of curry in 'ere."

That weekend Maria took the train to Guildford to see her parents. She was dressed in a black velvet minidress and platform-soled shoes. The platforms were not very high— Maria really didn't like an overly clunky look—but high enough to infuriate Dad. Of course, she didn't think of it that way. She was just making a visual statement about being in charge of her own life. After all, the point of this visit was to tell her parents that she was *not* going back to drama school in September.

The train window was fogged with soot and smeared with pigeon shit. The world beyond reminded Maria of watching an old worn film, with flecks of dirt that projected onto the screen. Rows of chimneys and rows of wash flashed by until suddenly the narrow walled-in back gardens of London gave way to a patchwork of fields. Dad was at the station to meet her. He winced, Maria thought, when he set eyes on her, but only said something about he could see she was wearing her skirts as short as the rest of them. They didn't talk much in the car. Classical music played on the car radio as usual. Dad hummed along and on and off conducted with one hand as he drove.

"How's the job then, Mary?" he eventually asked. He still insisted on calling her that even though she'd officially changed her name on her eighteenth birthday.

"I like it."

"You could be spending the summer out here with us."

"I don't like it out here, Dad."

That wasn't strictly true. Maria did like Guildford, especially the hilly cobbled main street that the Morris was groaning up at that very moment. She liked the old bookstores at the top of the hill, and the river running below. What she didn't like was being in her parents' house. That's how she thought of it now: Her Parents' House. Something quite different from *her* home. "Deserters!" She'd screamed when two summers ago they moved out of London. "I'm not going!" And she didn't. She won an acting scholarship and stayed behind to go to the Royal Academy instead. "La de da," said her brother Colin at the time. At first she had enjoyed weekend visits to Guildford. But after a while everything that had bothered her before in the old house now seemed to be worse than ever. There never seemed to be enough space, or air. It was odd, because the London house, red-brick and narrow, had been hemmed in on one side by Mrs. Barstow's and on the other side by the Carruthers, whereas this new house was detached and had grass all the way around. But inside those walls the routines and roles of different family members seemed to have hardened into something unyielding. It was a smaller, tighter, family now, with her gone and Oscar, her eldest brother, married. The three brothers that remained Maria thought of as the Three Kings.

Mum, as usual was in the kitchen. She had flour on her hands and apron front.

"You're just in time to help me, darling," she said when Maria walked in. She kissed Maria and got flour on her black dress. "Don't you look smashing?" Whatever else Mum found wrong with Maria, she always admired the way she dressed. Maria had a natural talent for the dramatic, according to Mum. Although increasingly there was also a problem with this, Mum explained now: Maria needed to understand that to be so dramatic was to be powerful, which was very intimidating to men. "Uh-oh," thought Maria, "she's been reading her psychology books again." This proved to be a difficulty whenever Maria came home, Mum continued, and explained why she often experienced hostility from one or other of her brothers. "They feel threatened by you, darling."

All this while rolling out and trimming the pastry for a rhubarb pie.

But Maria liked to believe that under all her current domestic tranquility, Mum wanted out. Locked away inside her was the same Mum who had taken Maria on ban-the-bomb marches when she was eight and nine years old. Under blouses and brooches and floury aprons, the old Mum waited to re-emerge in stretch pants with a copy of *The Second Sex* tucked under her arm. Or if not that, at least to cheer Maria on. "Do all the things I never got to do, darling." Except she never got around to saying it.

"What about your scholarship?" she asked now, the very question Maria dreaded.

"What about it?" They had moved into the morning room by this time so Mum could catch up on a little ironing before lunch. It was horrible, Maria tried to explain, the way theatre people called everyone else "darling" and then stomped all over each other to get a part. Maybe two years ago she had wanted to be a Shakespearean actress. But she'd changed. Just look at the past two years, Mum. How many bombs had been dropped on Vietnam? Bombs were being dropped this very minute. All over the world black and brown people were oppressed, (another new word). In America, since Martin Luther King had been murdered...

"Martin who?" asked Stephen, wandering in at that moment. He swung a paisley shirt back and forth in front of him.

"I just can't be in plays any more," said Maria passionately. "It all feels so meaningless."

"Is she turning on the dramatics again?" said Stephen. And then, just as dramatically, his hands clasped together in mock prayer. "Please, Mum, please. Just iron this one shirt so I can get out of here before she really gets going."

"Why don't you iron your own bloody shirts? Mum and I are talking. Mum, are you going to let him treat you like a servant?"

"Who asked your opinion, Maggie Smith?"

"He asked me very nicely, darling."

Good! Good for King Stephen! Boy oh boy this house was claustrophobic! The whole of England was claustrophobic!

"Nobody dragged you here this weekend, darling. What's the point in coming if you get upset with everybody?"

No reason. She just thought Mum and Dad might like to know that *she*, Maria, had reached a point in her life where she needed to *do* something. Travel. See the world. Stir her blood. But that was something that Mum, stuck behind her ironing board, would probably never understand. "I'm going to America, Mum."

Mum's nose crinkled as if she smelled something bad. "What on earth do you want to go to America for?" She spat on the bottom of the iron to see if was hot enough for Stephen's shirt. "They don't even know how to make a decent cup of tea. Ask Dad. He's been there. Lukewarm water and a teabag on the saucer, that's all you'll get."

Near the end of summer, Wendy had a big row with Mick. Bigger than usual. She came to work wearing a new powder-blue two-piece suit. When she stood against the light you could see straight through the skirt. Mick noticed on the way to the car and threw a fit. Called her a bleedin' cheap tart and a bleedin' prick teaser who wanted all the bleedin' coons after her. Wendy yelled right back at him. They were in the car by this time, Alison and Jean too, doing their usual number with their eyes.

"You're jus' jealous!" yelled Wendy. "Prob'ly worried I'm gonna run off wiv a younger man! An' they're not coons anyway! They're people. Jus' like you. But nicer."

That got him riled. Especially when Maria started laughing.

"Sod off! Go on. Get outta 'ere. Sod off! Gloria's a better fuck than you anyway. Sod off and take your arty farty friend with you!" He leaned over and opened the car door and pushed Wendy out. "You too, fuck-face," he yelled to Maria.

"Hey, Mick the Prick, I thought you'd like to know your toupee needs adjusting," said Maria, and flipped it off his head and into his lap. She hopped out of the car and slammed the door as hard as she could. But not before she heard Jean laugh. Mick sped off and knocked somebody's dustbin flying. Wendy stood on the corner, crying, with mascara all over her face. Maria handed her a Kleenex and put an arm around her.

"Come on. Let's find the Wimpy."

They shared a plate of chips and sucked on pickled onions. After a bit Maria asked, "Why do you stay with Mick?"

"Don't know. Love 'im I guess. 'e's awful sweet sometimes."

"Sometimes."

"Most of the time."

"I don't see it."

"You don't like 'im."

"I don't like him because I don't see it."

They were quiet for a bit. Maria offered Wendy a cigarette. She took it, and they puffed into each other's faces. Then Wendy started to talk. Real softly.

"I tried to kill meself once you know. Look." She pulled up her sleeves and showed her wrists. There were pale scars. Maria realized she'd never seen her wearing short sleeves.

"What happened?"

"I was pregnant and didn't know it. It weren't Mick. It was before I knew 'im. Anyway, nuthin' was showin'. I was worried though. One day I was over me boyfriend's 'ouse and I 'ad these bad pains. I went to the toilet and there was all this blood and the baby came out in the loo. It was real little. But I could see it. Sort of. I was real pregnant I guess. I never tol' me mum. I just cleaned meself up and waited for Georgie to come 'ome. But 'e didn't come. I was scared. I got so lonely and scared I couldn't stand it. I knew Georgie was getting' ready to dump me anyway, so I went in 'is bathroom and got one of 'is razors and cut meself. Then I realized I didn't wanna die. But it was too late. Blood was gushin' out me arms. There was no phone at 'is place. So I wrapped bath towels round me wrists and went outside. I called to people on the street. I told 'em I didn't wanna die. I asked someone, please help me, I'm dyin' But no-one stopped. The blood soaked all the way through the towels, but I managed to get to the phone booth and call the emergency number. Then I passed out. I was in hospital for two months. They shut me up with the loonies."

Maria reached across the table and squeezed Wendy's hand. She wanted to say something beautiful about life and Wendy being important. But the words weren't there.

"How old were you?" she asked instead.

"Fifteen."

Usually when Wendy had a row with Mick he made up with her the next day. He'd show up at work with some chocolates or flowers. That was one of the things Wendy thought was nice about him. Maria thought that even if he'd given her a diamond ring instead of a crummy box of Macintosh's Assorted Cremes, it would never make up for the way he treated her.

This time Mick wasn't even around to make up. Maria arrived at work the following morning to find Wendy weeping in the office. She was dressed up in her white and red two-piece with the sailor collar. Mick liked her in that outfit. There were already big wet mascara blotches on the collar by the time Maria got there.

"What's up?" she asked. "Mick?"

Wendy nodded, sobbing.

"Mick went to Spain," said the receptionist from behind the desk. She was enjoying herself. She'd always had the hots for Mick, and was jealous of Wendy.

"Wiv Gloria," sobbed Wendy.

"Gloria! How do you know he's with her?"

"'e was the last time."

"Mick's had this holiday planned for a while," said the receptionist smugly, filing her nails.

"'e never tol' me," wailed Wendy.

"Well, Mr. Smithers wants you girls to go out with Bob this week."

"Mr. Smithers can want," Maria said. "Come on, Wendy. Let's get out of here."

They left, with Wendy still crying and the receptionist waving her nail file at them: they'd lose their jobs if they didn't come back, she threatened. There was a piece of brick lying in the curb outside. Maria picked it up and made like she was going to throw it through the window.

"Where we goin'?" sniffed Wendy.

"To get something to eat."

Maria took her to an Indian restaurant. "It's time you tasted curry," she said. "I'm treating you."

Wendy was amazing. After so much fuss about curry she tucked in like she was eating fish and chips. She cheered up as soon as she'd eaten too, just like Maria knew she would.

"I'm dumping 'im this time. When he comes back from Spain 'e better not fink 'e'll find me waitin', 'cause he won't."

"Good. I'll drink to that."

"Come on. We gotta pick up a paper. I need me a new job."

That evening around ten thirty Wendy showed up at Maria's place. Her face was pink and glowing and she had no make-up on. She wore a pair of bellbottoms and a tight sweater. Maria was in her dressing gown with her hair wrapped up in a towel. She'd just put a shilling in the meter for a hot bath.

"Don't we make a lovely pair?" said Wendy. "'ope you don't mind me coming so late. I been calling the phone downstairs but it's been busy all night."

"That's Osano," said Maria. "On the phone to Africa." She put the kettle to boil on the hotplate. "What's up?"

Wendy stood center room clutching her handbag. "You're gonna think I'm ever so silly. But I couldn't wait till mornin'. Promise you won't laugh?" She reached into her bag and drew out two lavender-colored sheets of paper, and handed them to Maria.

"They're poems," she said. "I wrote 'em meself."

Her handwriting was neat and even and sloped backwards. Maria had seen it plenty of times, on the clipboards they filled out. She never thought anything of it before. Now it looked vulnerable, arranged so neatly on the page, as if wanting to be approved of. She felt a sudden panic. Maria was picky about poetry. She knew they'd be about Mick. What if she didn't like them? She read them. They were sad, but not sentimental. She read them a second time, and realized they were quite good.

"'So what happened is seen / through frosted glass, not clearly /and with such a weight of sadness...' That's beautiful Wendy. I didn't know you wrote poetry."

"Me neither. But English always was me best fing in school. I'm glad you like 'em. You can keep those. I wrote 'em over for you."

Neither of them went back to Tropical Heat. Wendy got a job in Woolworth's and Maria didn't look for another job. She'd already booked a flight to New York and was getting ready to leave. Her parents were in a flap. "This is madness, Mary. You don't just chuck in a perfectly good scholarship and take off for a foreign city on a one way ticket." Wendy came over after work one day to take Maria out for curry dinner to say goodby. She ran into Maria's dad as he was leaving.

"That your dad, then? 'e don't look too 'appy. Nor do you." Maria was standing in the middle of her room crying, surrounded by half-packed boxes of books. "Come on, then."

"I'm alright," said Maria. "I'll just be a minute." While she waited, Wendy picked up Maria's Shakespeare out of a box and started looking through it again. She read the balcony scene from *Romeo and Juliet* out loud, doing both voices, and soon had Maria in stitches. Maria said keep the book, she was through with William.

Over dinner Wendy told Maria she didn't know how long she'd be able to live without Mick if he came and asked her to go back, but she'd try. She was still writing poems she said. She pulled another poem out of her purse and gave it to Maria as a goodbye present. It was called "Friendship" and wasn't as good as the others had been. Maria liked it anyway. Wendy also gave her seven pair of knickers, each with a day of the week embroidered on them.

"A nice girl can never be too prepared." She'd miss Maria, she said. Maria said she'd miss her too. They both said they'd write. They both cried.

Maria didn't get to see her after that, because she stayed

at her parents' house the week before she left. But later, in the US, Maria got three letters and a poem from her. This when Maria had a job as a temporary au pair in Connecticut, and a real address for a while. The first two letters said she still wasn't seeing Mick but thought about him a lot. Woolworth's had turned out to be a real drag and she missed going to the coon houses with Maria. The poem was called "Standing On My Now." The third letter said she was in love with this terrific bloke named Pete who was assistant manager at Woolworth. The only problem was he was married. Then Maria didn't hear from her any more, which didn't surprise her because she no longer had an address and was moving around a lot. Eventually Maria gave up trying to stay in touch with everyone but her mum and dad and Osano. She'd gotten a lot fonder of him than she ever planned. He was back in Kenya by then. But sitting on a beach on the West Coast of Vancouver Island on the lookout for whales, she suddenly flashed on Wendy for no obvious reason. She wondered what Wendy was doing at that very moment. "Probably in bed with Pete," she thought. "I really must send her a postcard." But she never did.

A year later Maria went back to England for a visit and to sort out her visa. She'd decided by then to stay in America even if it meant marrying someone to do it. One day she went to Kings Cross to look up Wendy. But her family had moved. She went to Woolworth's, but she didn't work there any more. Nor did anyone named Pete. She went by the Tropical Heat office, and it was all boarded up.

Small Item in the News

I'm standing in the dining room looking out at the garden through the French windows. The garden is beautiful. So green and lush in the rain, everything gleaming and holding light, the pink and yellow of the roses almost fluorescent.

Rollie always enjoyed the garden. He liked to sit on the bench alongside the lawn, even sat there when it was raining once. I remember that, his coming in with his hair plastered flat to his head, dripping all over the kitchen floor and making a mess. I was quite cross with him, but of course he cleaned it up.

I should start clearing the breakfast dishes from the tables instead of standing here pressed up against the windowpane like a small child. We have so many guests at the moment and today they all want cooked breakfasts. The air still smells of bacon. But I can't get on yet. I need to be here, need to be looking at this. Rollie should be here is what I'm thinking. Should be here where somebody cares about him. We should never have let him go. Maggie says we did the best we could and there was no way to stop him. Maybe she's right. But it doesn't feel right.

It amazes me the way rain releases colors hidden at other times. The patio stones are full of color just now. When they're dry they look plain gray. But it is pleasant on sunny days to open these windows so guests can walk out onto the patio and sit outside if they wish. There are times we could do with one more table out there. Except this year has been so wet, even for England, that no one wants to go out. It's hard to believe it's July already. It seems only yesterday that Rollie showed up on the doorstep in time for Christmas. I'm glad he came to us. He seemed so happy helping us decorate the tree, and playing Christmas carols on the piano for the guests. How wonderful it was to hear him play again, a wonderful Christmas, Julian home all the way from New Zealand, and he and Rollie getting on so well. And then there was Maggie's daughter and the baby...I wish we'd taken more photographs.

Maggie's going to come in here any minute to see what's happened to me. We're supposed to go over the supply list together this morning. But I can't think about that right now, and I can't think about clearing tables. Oh, look at that sparrow! He's taking a bath in a puddle and having so much fun. I'm glad to see someone enjoying the rain. Now he's flying up to the bird-table, the one you built for us. Do you remember, Rollie? One Saturday you just took it into your head to build that bird-table. Quite the handyman you turned out to be that day, so busy with the hammer.

When was it that you first came to us? I have a hard time remembering. Was it five, or six, years ago now? I know it was summertime. Such a clean-cut young man you were back then. I opened the door and there you were on the doorstep looking as if you'd just stepped out of the barbershop, and wearing a tie. So different from Julian with his bushy hair and old sweaters. Business wasn't good back then. I remember that. Maggie and I were just getting started, and most of the rooms were empty even though it was summer. What did two fifty-five-year old widows know about running a guesthouse? We'd been housewives and mothers for most of our lives. Of course, we knew about cooking and cleaning, but there were other things. We had to learn how to ask for money for our work. You can't imagine the novelty of that in the beginning, of being paid for what we'd always done. Then there was the advertising, and building a reputation. Word of mouth helps. And there are always people who come back.

You always came back, didn't you, Rollie? The first time you just stumbled across us by accident, that's what you told us. You were walking up the road toward the old city center when our sign advertising vegetarian meals caught your eye.

That and our wonderful location. Only a five-minute walk to the Royal Crescent and Queen Square, the Botanic Gardens right around the corner. And so quiet here in Bath after London, you said. Yes, this really is a very pleasant spot, and we've always attracted a fair number of people because we offer vegetarian meals. That's definitely one of our selling points. Of course, we have meat dishes too. Both Maggie and I eat meat. But you stopped because you don't.

In the beginning you reminded me of a choirboy. Such a clean scrubbed look, your gray eyes fresh and clear as rain. All that changed. People do change. You were always here then, that first summer, working in the garden with old Thomas. You got quite brown from being outside so much. Thomas should be here later today, and he'll probably ask about you, he usually does. "Have you heard from Master Roland?" he'll say. Mind you, it's raining so hard today maybe he won't bother coming at all. What can he do out there in this wet? Oh, how I wish you could see the garden right now, Rollie, at this very moment, everything shining.

I should have done more for you. Done something more or differently. Maggie always gets irritated with me and says we did far too much already. But I disagree with her. The problem was we couldn't let you be around the guests any more. Still, we might have tucked you away in a corner of the kitchen for a night or two. You never minded a sleeping bag on the floor, did you? But it would never have worked. Maggie is right about that. You would have ended up being underfoot in the morning. We're very busy in the mornings, with breakfast, and you were never a morning person, were you? But perhaps Maggie and I could have doubled up and I could have let you use my room for a while. You needed help, that's the point. You came to us because you needed help. I know what Maggie would say, and maybe she's right. That the two of us couldn't provide the kind of help you needed. It's all we can do to run this business and keep ourselves afloat, whereas you needed professional counseling and somewhere proper to live. A halfway house or a group home, some kind of support system and some structure.

None of that was obvious at first. You just came and went, that was all, we didn't know where. One day I asked you. Where are you when you're not with us, Rollie? You gave me a knowing wink. Connections, was all you said. You had connections. We thought maybe you had a girlfriend. That didn't seem so farfetched in the beginning. The point is we didn't think it our place to ask you too many questions when you first came, Rollie. We did wonder about you, of course. Who was your girlfriend, if you had one, and who was your family? Did you have a family? And why was it that you couldn't work a regular job? You did tell us you had health problems, but never told us what they were, and questions always seemed to make you so uncomfortable we didn't want to pry. We did worry about you though. Over time you lost your choirboy glow and your face became quite lean, almost sunken. You began to look frail. I remember you at the piano. You reminded me of a willow tree, the long curve of your spine and the way you drooped over the keyboard.

The first time you played the piano was such a lovely surprise. You'd just arrived and we were showing you around. Would we mind if you tried out the piano? you asked, and we said we'd be delighted, there weren't many guests around at that time of day. But we didn't know what to expect. Then you played Chopin, exquisitely. We peeked in at you, and you were smiling with your eyes closed, your head tipped back, your fingers long and delicate over the keys. In the beginning you played often, and some of the guests enjoyed hearing you play. They would come out of their rooms to listen, and sometimes they made requests. You could play anything, it seemed.

Once in passing, you told us that your mother taught you to play, but that she had been dead for many years now. That was all you really ever told us about your family, other than to mention that your father was an army man, and you didn't like him. We never knew who you really were. You came and went and all we ever had was little snippets of information. I remember one time we were raking leaves on the lawn, just the two of us, talking about schools and education. Do you remember? You told me that you had gone to Eton and Cambridge, and that both were a waste of time. You only had a year to go at Cambridge when you came to us, you said, but you couldn't do it anymore. Too much pressure. You liked it here with us because it was peaceful. By then I wasn't sure whether or not to believe you. But what else was I to believe?

Then suddenly you stopped playing the piano. One week you were here and playing, and then back again a few weeks later, shut into yourself and refusing to have anything more to do with the piano. Until last year at Christmastime. We took that as a good sign, that you were getting back to your old self. What made you stop playing so suddenly, Rollie? What happened? What happened in your life before you came to us?

Maggie and I used to speculate. Early on we wondered if you had a drinking problem. But it wasn't that. Yet you deteriorated, the way alcoholics do. Two weeks ago, sitting in our kitchen, you looked so disheveled. Your hair had grown long and needed combing, your clear eyes turned to mud. You smelled musty, not a choirboy at all any more, your hair streaked gray and even your face turned gray. You told Maggie you'd been sleeping out of doors. When I came in you hung your head as if you were ashamed. I wanted to hold you then. I think you needed to be held. But I just stood there asking silly questions about how you were, where had you been. He's been sleeping outside, said Maggie to me. We can't have that, Rollie, can we now? She wasn't scolding you, but you thought she was, mumbling something about St. Vincent's Mission and things not working out. Then Maggie gave you something to eat, some macaroni cheese and cold-slaw, and your hand shook as you lifted the fork to your mouth. We'll find somewhere for you to go, for you to stay, I said. Somewhere temporary until we could help you sort things out. There was nothing to sort out, you said. Nowhere left to stay. We insisted of course there was and I went out to the hall telephone.

I tried, Rollie. I did try. I was ringing up everything I could find in the telephone book that day, the last time you were here. I told myself, there must be something. Then Maggie told me you'd already left and not to bother. Why did she let you leave? I don't understand that. She got quite annoyed with me when I asked her. She said you wanted to go and there was no way she could stop you. I suppose she was right. But it didn't feel right.

I called St. Vincent's first and asked would they take you back. They said no, you had become too much trouble. They had to consider the needs of the other residents. You had become belligerent. Belligerent? I couldn't believe my ears. That wasn't the Rollie we knew. But the woman on the other end of the line was quite clear. She seemed pleasant enough, I didn't feel rushed or put off. They had done what they could, she said. Had even tried several times to contact your mother and father in Surrey, but unfortunately there was no answer. Perhaps they were away on their summer holidays.

His mother? I asked. But he has no mother. She died a long time ago. No, no insisted the woman. Roland's mother was very much alive. In Surrey. She talked to her once before, about a year ago. A very nice woman, his mother, both his parents, very nice people. So difficult, to care for the mentally ill. Such a strain on families. She didn't think institutionalizing people was the answer, but what was? There are so many Rolands in the world, she said. They just fall through the cracks.

I was shocked. How did this woman know all this? We'd known you for years and never knew. How did she know how to find your mother? You learn to ask the right questions, she said. You do what you can. You find out things. You kept your mother's name and address in your address book, Rollie, under E for emergencies. I never knew you had an address book. Why should I? I never checked your pockets. You have a whole family, Rollie, all of them alive, both parents, brothers and their families, even a sister and nephew and niece living in America someplace. And the only time your father spent in the military was in the air force, in World War Two. Your father is a music teacher, Rollie. What happened? What happened in your life? Why didn't you tell us the truth about your family? If only you'd told us everything, right from the beginning.

There I was, going through the telephone book, intent on ringing every shelter and agency listed, even though the woman at St. Vincent's had tried to reassure me. He'll take off for a while, she said. He'll go back to Surrey and then he'll be back. But his family's not there right now, I protested. Besides, he's changed, you told me yourself he's not himself. I still had the phone in my hand when Maggie came and told me you'd already left...

Look. The rain has stopped. The sun is trying to push its way out from behind the clouds. Raindrops on the rhododendron leaves are glistening like jewels. I really should clear the breakfast things, but I'll just step out on the patio for a moment. The air is so clean after the rain. Maggie sees me from the kitchen window and I know she's calling me. I hear her tapping on the glass, but pretend I don't. She knows I'm upset. She's upset too. It's just that she handles things differently from me. She's going to polish everything in sight for a week.

Maggie was the one who saw it first. She pointed it out to me. A tiny article on page three of the morning paper. They found your body in the river, Rollie. You left here and went directly to the river, didn't you? I was still making those useless telephone calls while you were already heading toward the river. All these days and nights passed and you've been lying there, your body swollen with river water. I should have held you in my arms, two weeks ago. I should have held you like a son, Rollie.

The Blue Pontiac

Neela barked one short bark. Outside the window a woman was on the lot. Her dark wavy hair gleamed in the sunlight, her skin tanned against the white straps of her sundress. She seemed interested in the red Subaru, and pushed her sunglasses up on top of her head as if without them she could get a better look. Above her, the brightly colored plastic flags that decorated the lot hung limp. Beyond the fence a bus roared past, belching smoke.

Faramaz mopped his face with his handkerchief, pushed open the screen door of the ten-by-six hut that served as his office, and went outside. His dog, Neela, a German Shepherd with lean sloping haunches, had already resettled under the solitary tree to which her leash was attached. The gravel ground-cover scrunched under Faramez's sandals and caused the woman to swing around. For a moment, seeing her dark eyes and strong nose, he thinks she is Persian. He speaks in English anyway.

"Hello there. You like the Subaru?"

Up close he noticed tiny crease marks around her eyes and a faint scar across the bridge of her nose. The hair around her temples was streaked with gray. But it was her body language, the way she shifted her weight, that told Faramaz she was not from his country.

"It's nice, but not what I'm looking for."

"What *are* you looking for?" He pulled his handkerchief from his pocket and wiped his face again. He never liked the heat. Not even in Iran. He should have settled some place other than Berkeley, California.

"I'm not sure. Something bigger. Maybe even a camper or a van."

"Planning a trip?"

"Yes. I'm driving to Seattle in a few weeks. I want my kids to be able to stretch out and get away from each other. Maybe that way we'll get there without anybody being murdered."

Seattle, thought Faramez. That's where he should have gone. Seattle was cool, with plenty of rain. "How many children?" he asked.

"Two. Boy and a girl."

He followed the woman to the Toyota pick-up with a camper shell. She was small, and looked almost girlish herself from the back.

"Little ones?"

"No, thirteen and ten. The ten-year-old thinks she's twenty. When they argue, it's dangerous." She opened the back of the shell and peered inside. "My goodness there's a lot of dog hair in here."

"Yes. My dog, Neela, has been sleeping in there. But I will clean it for you so good if you buy."

The woman laughed. "I'm not buying yet. Just looking." She walked over to a VW van. "This is nice. Something like this would be perfect. But too expensive."

Faramaz was at her side. "No, no. This is very cheap. Very cheap. This is a special."

The woman laughed again. Her smile was wide, generous, her teeth strong and white. She is strong, thought Faramaz. She reminded him of his lost fiancée, Nasrin.

"$2000 is about my limit..."

Faramaz was already inside the van and opening the sliding side door for her. He extended a hand. "Come inside and look. So much space. Your kids will love this. You give me $2000 and I finance the rest. You like it? Let's go to the office and talk business. How's your credit?"

"I have no credit. I'm a widow." Another laugh, she laughed a lot. "According to the bank that makes me an automatic risk."

Neela began barking furiously and straining against her

leash. At the far end of the lot a couple were looking at the Audi. The man wore a suit. Neela always barked at suits. No business sense, that dog. Men in suits had credit. Faramaz reached into his pocket for a pencil, paper and business card.

"Give me your name and daytime phone number," he said to the woman. "Here's my card. Take your time. Look around. Maybe in a week I'll have a cheap camper for you. Excuse me." He hailed the couple. "Hello there. You like the Audi?"

A week later, when Faramaz was in the middle of negotiating a sale, the woman returned. Her name was Maria. Faramaz had made a mental note of it when entering it into the logbook of potential customers. He wondered if she was recently widowed. She didn't appear to be in mourning. This time it was a foggy day and she wore blue jeans and a T-shirt. Her shoulder-length hair was pulled up into a ponytail and large colorful earrings danced on either side of her face. Today she reminded him even more of Nasrin. With her was a boy in oversized sagging pants, darker than she was, but with startling light eyes. He looked around from under the rim of his Oakland Raiders' baseball cap as if on watch for something. The son, Faramaz guessed.

"Nothing new?" Maria called out. She sounded dis-appointed.

"Not yet. Sorry." Faramaz turned his attention back to his customers. It had been a bad day for him. He had a headache and wanted nothing better than for eight o'clock to arrive so that he could lock up and leave the lot to Neela. He pictured himself lying on his bed in the cool and dark of his room, the bamboo shade all the way down. Yet he also dreaded going home. His little apartment around the corner on Dwight Way was not as peaceful as it had once been, not because outside the traffic volume had grown any worse, but because inside was his nephew, Hassan, who was still at war. Instead of speaking he yelled. Only this morning, standing in front of the open refrigerator door, he had screamed that the milk carton was empty. The veins on his neck stood out like purple ropes, his head thrust forward at an alarming angle. Coffee slopped over the top of his cup, and his hand, when it poured the drip of milk that was left into his coffee, shook terribly. All this Faramaz studied from his seat at the kitchen table where he drank his own morning coffee black. An ounce more tension, he had thought then, and Hassan's body would ignite itself before his very eyes and explode.

"It's only milk, Hassan," he said gently. "We can buy more."

It mystified him how quickly Hassan had been able to adjust his taste from black tea to coffee, how readily he now tucked in to French fries and hamburgers, and how seemingly overnight he had become addicted to cop shows on TV. Yet in other ways he was unable to make the smallest adaptations. This morning Faramaz had taken the cup from Hassan's shaking hand and placed it on the table and wrapped his arms around his nephew's slender body, amazed at the wild flutter of his heart.

What did Bahman Servat know or care about Hassan?

It was unfortunate then, very unfortunate, that this afternoon Bahman, the plump and pomaded owner of Used Autos on San Pablo, should happen to make his weekly stop when it had been unusually busy and impossible for Faramaz to be all places at once. Worse still that Bahman should witness Hassan in the act of trying to sell a car which, true enough, resembled an act of assault. Faramaz cringed, remembering this. It hadn't mattered that Faramaz pleaded his nephew's case. Please, Bahman, please. Hassan has been in the country only six months. He doesn't understand American customs yet. He shouts because he still has the sounds of shells exploding in his ears. He's only here in the afternoons, when things are at their busiest. Bahman had fired Hassan anyway. In English too, scolding him in front of customers as if he were an errant schoolboy. Faramaz could only imagine the outrage he would have to endure that evening, and rubbed between his eyes, wishing desperately that this couple would make up their minds whether they wanted to buy the Buick or not. He glanced around to see if Maria was still about. It occurred to him that he had been unnecessarily short with her a minute ago. But she was nowhere in sight.

"Why don't I let you talk between yourselves?" he suggested to the couple, and smiled, graciously he hoped. "I'll be in my office."

What Bahman didn't appreciate was that Hassan was making progress. That very morning, for example, for the fifth day in a row, even after the milk incident, he had managed to leave the apartment without punching any walls. True, his right foot, encased inside the special shoe Faramaz had saved for, had punctuated the wooden floors with its usual unnecessarily loud clunks as he slammed his way around, gathering up his schoolbooks. But no fists. And today the routine pause by the front door, the hearty shout of "Goodbye, Uncle," was followed only by the soft click of the door closing.

Faramaz picked up the phone to call Bahman, who in his estimation had long ago ceased to be a countryman. He was a man consumed by a capitalist mentality. He had no compassion. Not even for the veteran of a terrible war, for someone who was but a confused boy when his foot was blown off. The grenade no doubt hurled by an Iraqi boy as young and as inflated with the glory of God as Hassan had once been.

It was unheard of for Hassan not to be home to shout a greeting to his uncle when he walked in the door. Besides which, at this time of day the TV was usually on, volume full blast, announcing Hassan's presence before Faramaz even had the key in the lock. Instead the apartment was quiet. At first Faramaz tried to tell himself that it was a blessed quiet, took two Tylenol, and lay down on his bed with a wet towel pressed to his pounding forehead. It wasn't long before he realized that it was a cursed quiet, for where was Hassan if not at home? He slipped his feet back into his sandals and went across the hall to Violet's door.

"Whoever you are and whatever you selling I don't want it," said Violet the first time he knocked. But the second time, his face close to the door, calling out to the old lady inside that it was just her neighbor, Faramaz, she came and undid the bolts.

"Come on in, sugar."

Inside her apartment Violet had red plush furniture and plenty of advice. This latter she liked to lavish on Faramaz after first feeding him and then settling him into one of her armchairs. This evening however, after refusing her invitation to sit on down and have some fresh biscuits and gravy—and yes, her apartment did smell deliciously of warm biscuit— Faramaz remained standing and insisted, somewhat apologetically, that he just wanted to know had she heard Hassan come home this afternoon.

"Well, no, sugar," she said, "Now that you mention it I never did hear him."

Violet had taken issue with Faramaz about Hassan's shoe from the first. Said there had to be something better looking and better sounding than that dinosaur hoof. Least he could do was put felt on the bottom so the boy didn't make so much racket coming and going.

"You ask me, Faramaz, 'bout time that young man got out more. Can't be stuck up under you all the time. He's in America now. Instead of turning yourself gray-headed over him you need to get on and live your own life 'cause God only gave you this one. Heck, that boy's probably out there having a good time with some girl while you still don't have you one."

"Thank you, Violet. I'll keep that in mind."

After which Faramaz walked all the way up Dwight Way to Telegraph Avenue, and onto the UC Berkeley campus, looking for Hassan. He wandered around Sproul Plaza, drawn to clusters of dark-haired young men in white shirts, catching snatches of conversations in various languages and remembering his own student days. But it wasn't until it was nearly dark that he told himself this was foolishness. Hassan was still studying for his high school diploma, why would he be here? He had no idea where he might go. It made more sense to go home and wait, more than likely Hassan was already home. But when he got back the apartment was as quiet as when he left it. Dark now too, and with no phone messages blinking on the machine. Faramaz massaged his still throbbing head for a few minutes, and then got into the shower. But no sooner had he turned on the water than he realized he wouldn't hear the phone if it rang. He washed hurriedly and wrapped himself in his bathrobe. He told himself he really should eat, even though he had little appetite, and sat at the kitchen table, picking at the leftover chicken and saffron rice he had warmed for himself, and wondered when it would be appropriate to call the police. As far as he knew there was no other recourse when it came to missing persons, even though he had little confidence in or liking for the police. But perhaps it was still too soon, or perhaps he should seek out Violet's advice on the matter. He had started out across the hallway again when he decided against the idea. Partly because it was late and he knew Violet went to bed early, and partly because he already knew the speech Violet would make on the topic of the police and all the reasons not to mess with them. Returning to his kitchen table he sat there with the day's newspaper, pretending to read it, and watching the clock.

It was nearly midnight when a stiff breeze began rattling the blind in the living room. Faramaz crossed in the dark to close the window, and turned to flip the light switch only to discover Hassan lying corpse-like on the couch. At first, with a gasp, he thought he was dead. But then Hassan's eyes blinked open, and he stared at the ceiling as if that was what he had been doing for a long time, only to be interrupted by this sudden burst of light.

"I didn't hear you come in, Hassan," said Faramaz. "I've been worried."

A long pause followed before Hassan answered. "I've been here all the time, Uncle," he eventually said. His voice was uncharacteristically flat.

Faramaz felt suddenly silly, and angry, both at himself and the boy. Was it possible that Hassan had lain there all along, so quiet and still and hidden from view by the back of the couch that Faramaz had not noticed him? And then Faramaz reminded himself that the couch was also Hassan's bed. Where else would the boy lie down if he was upset and wanted to think, or just be quiet for a change?

"You should have let me know you were here, Hassan," he said reproachfully.

No answer. Just the dark eyes continuing to fix on the ceiling, the long delicate hands crossed loosely across his chest.

"I called Bahman this afternoon," Faramaz added. "To plead for your job back."

Hassan remained silent. "No one answered the phone. So I left him a message."

Faramaz stood for a minute more, not knowing what else to say, then took the neatly folded blanket from the back of the sofa, shook it open and covered Hassan. He turned out the light and tiptoed from the room.

"Thank you, Uncle," came Hassan's voice through the darkness.

Bahman relented. After all, it was cheaper to keep Hassan than to hire another American at a proper wage. That young fellow, Johnny, with his flashy shirts and the way he cracked his knuckles, girls always hanging around the lot, hadn't been to Bahman's liking at all. Too bad Ali had taken himself off to graduate school after all these years.

"Teach your nephew to sell cars and he can stay, Faramaz. Otherwise hire someone else," said Bahman the next time he visited the lot, adjusting his gold cuff links with an air of importance. But two weeks of intensive training seemed to have borne little fruit in Hassan's salesmanship, and it was still his estimation that all Americans were born cheats. More than once Faramaz had had to intervene and cool him down, apologizing to customers in English and re-explaining to Hassan in Farsi that they are in America now. In America anyone who takes their time or comes back for a second look is not a cheat or a nuisance but only serious about buying. Patience was the key, and charm.

No one aggravated Hassan more than Maria. In two weeks she had been back four times and test-driven six vehicles. Faramaz was not surprised then, when one afternoon his phone call to a customer was interrupted by Hassan's voice, shrill and unrelenting, and he looked outside to see Maria again.

"No more test drives. You buy first. Then you drive. You buy, it's your car. Then you take where you want."

Maria stood hands on hips in front of the gleaming blue 1979 Pontiac LeMans station wagon that had come in two days before. Her daughter was with her again. By this time Faramaz knew both her children by name, with a definite preference for the girl and her dimples and exuberant hair over her sullen brother. Something about the brother, his tense jaw and unsmiling eyes, was an uncomfortable reminder of Hassan. Faramaz told his customer he'd call him back, grabbed the key to the Pontiac and came out of the office smiling broadly.

"Hello, Maria. Hello, Sofi. So Maria, you want to drive the Pontiac. Big American car. Lots of room for your kids. Yes, Maria. This is the car for you. Only 80,000 miles. Great deal. Let's go." And then to Hassan, who was yelling in Farsi for Faramaz to beware of that woman. "Hassan. I didn't talk Bahman into giving your job back for you to lose it again.

Remember. Be good to the customers. It is Neela's job to bark, not yours."

Back on the lot, Maria thought she wanted to buy the Pontiac. It gleamed a silvery blue in sunlight, chrome hubcaps polished to a high shine. It appeared to have been well taken care of. Maria walked around it, opened and closed doors, and fiddled with the radio. And then to her daughter's obvious embarrassment, and Hassan's amazement, she lowered the back seat, climbed in and lay down.

"Mom...!" exclaimed Sofi.

"We're going to have to sleep in this thing, sweetheart. Just checking."

"American women are crazy!" yelled Hassan, clunking his way into the office in disgust. "Where is her husband?"

"Faramaz, honey, the question is not whether or not the boy *should* go home, it's *why* he wants to go home. If it's 'cause he's homesick like you say, then there ain't nothing you can do to change it, so you may as well let him go. Lord knows you come to the wrong person if you want me to start speechifying about how great this country is."

Faramaz sighed, and dusted cornbread crumbs from his knees into a napkin. How could he explain to Violet his doubts, the aftermath of eight years of war in his country? The old lady heaved herself to her feet and readjusted her housecoat over her large chest.

"Maybe he just needs to go on home and see his mama and then come back again. Here, wrap up some of my cornbread and take it on over to him. My show's fixing to come on."

"Thank you Violet, but Hassan does not enjoy corn-bread."

"Well, that about says it all. My cornbread is one of the few things worth staying in this country for."

Back in his own apartment, Faramaz found Hassan sitting intently in front of a *Kojak* rerun, and was tempted to point out that there were no American infidel cop shows in Iran. But he kept his mouth shut. He knew what Hassan was going through. He went into his room and took the picture of his parents from the dresser top and stared at it. They stared back, his father from beneath fierce brows and over the top of a bristling mustache, his mother wanly, her left eye already milky from the beginnings of the cataract that had since left her blind in that eye. Her head was loosely covered. The picture was taken before the new Islamic regime enforced the wearing of the *chador*. Over the years light had drained the color from the photograph. The olive grove in the background, once vividly green, now looked as if it had been painted in watercolor. Even his memories of Iran were drained of color these days. Yet there was never a day he did not dream of returning.

The next day Faramaz drove the Pontiac and Maria to *Consumers* on Telegraph Avenue to have a diagnostic done on the car. He liked taking customers there because the wait was usually an hour or longer, which gave him time to go to BongoBurger and eat a Persian burger. Sometimes the customers went with him, sometimes they browsed the vendors' stalls that lined that part of Telegraph, and sometimes they waited at *Consumers* and hovered anxiously around 'their' car. He hoped Maria would come with him. She did.

"You hungry, Maria?" Faramaz asked when they were seated at one of Bongo Burger's yellow formica tables. He asked as if he meant to buy for her, then wondered if that was his intention.

"No thanks. I'm just having coffee."

Their table was next to the window. Outside was a parking meter, on either side of which someone had thought to plant sunflowers. Under the canopy of these a man slept, stretched out on a grimy bedroll. Beside him a shopping cart was parked, laden with empty bottles and cans. After all these years he still had not got used to seeing such sights in America.

"Very Berkeley," remarked Maria, and Faramaz agreed without knowing whether she meant the sunflowers or the obviously homeless man, or both. It suddenly occurred to him that he might ask Maria's advice about Hassan. After all, she had a son who seemed in his own way to be as unhappy and angry as Hassan. It must be difficult for her, raising two children alone. Perhaps she had some insights. He opened his mouth to say something but then realized he hadn't ordered and went over to the counter, where he chatted briefly with Muhammad. Glancing back at the table he was startled by the angle of Maria's head and the lean of her body as she still gazed out the window. For a moment he thought she was Nasrin. It was uncanny, really, this likeness.

"So Maria," he said when he returned to the table, leaning forward on his elbows. But before he could go on, Maria spoke.

"What part of Iran are you from?" she suddenly asked.

The question caught Faramaz off-guard. "You know I am from Iran?"

"Of course. Your accent. Your name. Your looks." She gestured at the Persian menu written up above the counter and laughed. "BongoBurger!"

Faramaz smiled. It was not often that anyone showed an interest in where he was from, much less recognized his accent. "You are a detective. I lived in Tehran before I came here. But I'm not from there. I'm from north of the capital. My family is from Rudbar, a small town near Rashat. A very beautiful part of the country, near the Caspian Sea. Olive trees grow there." Muhammed came over with Faramaz's burger and Maria's coffee. Aware of Maria watching him, Faramaz bit into his Persian burger and immediately wiped his mustache with his napkin.

"So, how does an American lady know about Iran?"

Maria laughed. "I was a student radical in San Francisco.

I marched with the Iranian Students Association years ago. Up and down Market Street. The Iranians wore paper bags over their heads so they wouldn't be recognized. We used to chant, *Marg bar Shah! Marg bar Shah!*"

Faramaz choked on his mouthful of burger and took a quick swallow of water. "*Marg bar Shah!* Death to the Shah! You know that too? It's been a long time since I've heard it."

"I had some Iranian friends," Maria went on. "In college. They went back right after the Shah was overthrown." She looked intently at Faramaz while tracing the rim of her coffee mug with her finger. "Later I heard some of them were killed by Khomeni."

Faramaz said nothing, and chewed his food slowly. Who is this woman? he wondered. He wanted to ask her more about herself, but didn't dare. Instead he stared through the window at the homeless man who was awake now and rolling his bedroll. Then he wiped his mustache again and leaned toward her.

"I haven't been home for seventeen years, Maria." His voice was soft. "I was one of those Iranian students with a paper bag on his head. Perhaps we marched side by side, you and I. And yes, it is true what you were told. About those who went back."

Suddenly he felt as if he could tell Maria everything, all the things he usually kept locked into himself, the things even Violet had not been able to pry loose from him. He reached into his pocket for his wallet and took out a ragged photograph.

"This is my fiancée, Nasrin. I took this picture of her myself one hour before she boarded the plane that took her home. She thought she was going back to the most democratic country on earth. That's the way we all felt then."

He watched Maria's face as she looked at the photograph of Nasrin standing beside her suitcase with her arm raised and fist clenched. He wondered if Maria saw anything of herself in the picture, but if she did she didn't say so and only commented that Nasrin looked triumphant. She handed the picture back to Faramaz.

"Where is she now?" she wanted to know.

"Nasrin was one of those who disappeared," said Faramaz quietly. "It was intended that I go home with her, on the same flight. We were going to get married. But then, at the last minute, I had responsibilities here to finish up. So I stayed behind."

"And lived."

"Yes." He ran a hand through his hair, then brought it to rest on the tabletop. It occurred to him, staring down at his trembling fingers and delicately boned forearm, each of its black silky hairs curving in a crescent against olive skin, that it could be Hassan's hand and arm he was looking at. He did not want to lose this boy.

"My nephew, Hassan, the one who shouts, was only twelve years old when he was marched off to the front. His father was my eldest brother…who died in the war…as well as one more brother and three cousins. Before that my uncle was killed by Shah's troops." He ran his hand through his hair again. "Through all of this my mother and father and Hassan's mother and sister have somehow survived. By some miracle I bring Hassan here with me."

Maria said nothing, and they sat there quietly, both gazing through the glass. The homeless man was gone now. Muhammed came and took away Faramaz's plate and refilled Maria's coffee. He said something in Farsi in a low voice, and Faramaz shook his head and waved him away. He wiped his eyes with the back of his hand, aware that Maria was watching him.

"And now?" she said gently. "What is your life now?"

"Now?" Faramaz smiled suddenly and tipped his chair back against the wall. "Now it is 1990 and history is history. Now I am in BongoBurger with you. Now I am a used-car salesman in America. Now I try and teach my nephew how to sell cars." He let his chair down with a crash and threw back his head and laughed so loudly people at other tables stared.

They walked back to *Consumers* in silence.

The phone was already ringing when Faramaz unlocked the office door. It was Maria, and she sounded annoyed. The car was no good, she said. It died three times on the way home last night and had no power.

"Bring it in, Maria," said Faramaz. "My mechanic will fix it for you. You have my word on it." Suddenly he felt happy. The day before he had given her the keys to the car and shaken her hand. It was nice doing business with her, he said, very nice. Afterwards he wished he had said more. He should have asked what happened to her husband, told her how glad he was to have met her, someone who knew about Iran. This morning gave him another chance.

Outside was foggy. A slight wind tugged at the plastic flags and made them dance. Faramaz sat under the tree with Neela and sang softly in Farsi. He enjoyed the cool air on his face. Maria arrived in the Pontiac, which died as if on cue when she drove onto the lot. He watched her get out of the car. She wore pink pants rolled halfway up her calves. He liked her small ankles and the way the arches of her feet lifted inside her sandals as she walked over to him.

"Enjoying the fog, Faramaz?" She sounded strained, and looking up at her it occurred to Faramaz that perhaps something more than the car was wrong. He felt uneasy but smiled anyway.

"You're starting to know me, Maria."

He called to his mechanic, who was generally only ever seen by customers as legs extending from beneath various cars. A young Vietnamese man came wriggling out from under a Volvo. Faramaz slapped him on the back.

"This is Huy," he said. "The best mechanic. He fixes anything." Huy nodded, smiling shyly, and popped the hood of the Pontiac.

"What did I waste forty dollars at *Consumers* for if he's so good?"

Faramaz noticed Maria was shivering. He put a tentative hand on her arm.

"Come inside, Maria. You are cold. Have some tea while you wait."

"I should have worn a sweater."

Brown-padded kitchen chairs lined one wall of the office. Maria sat on the one furthest from the open door. Faramaz made Lipton's tea in a styrofoam cup and offered a cookie. She shook her head. "I can't wait long," she said. "I have to pack. I'll take the bus home and come back later."

"I thought you weren't leaving until the school year was over."

"Change of plan." She put the tea down on the desktop. "I really should get going."

Faramaz handed the tea back to her. He didn't want her to leave just yet. "Give Huy a few minutes. Sometimes he works miracles that fast. If not, you drive your old car home and come back later." He turned on the little black-and-white TV that sat on top of the filing cabinet. "You watch soap operas?"

Maria shook her head again and sipped the tea. But he left the TV on anyway. On the screen a blonde woman was crying. It seemed to Faramaz there were always blonde women crying on these soap operas. Maybe it was the same woman.

"So Maria, why the sudden change of date?" Faramaz wondered how long she would be gone, if he should call her when she got back, offer to cook her dinner perhaps, some Persian food. Certainly, this didn't seem to be the right time to ask if he might see her again.

"It's my son," she said. "I need to get him out of here. Fast. Oakland schools are a war zone."

"So bad? What happens when you return? Maybe try Berkeley."

"It's this whole area, Faramaz." Suddenly her voice was desperate. "Josh is only thirteen years old and up to his neck in it. Gangs. They recruit kids at the schools. Last night I caught him with a gun...I'm not planning on coming back."

Faramaz saw Hassan through the screen door with his schoolbooks under his arm, staring in disbelief at the blue Pontiac where Huy was half hidden under its raised hood. Why was he here so early? Hassan must have sensed the question because he clomped into the office waving his arms and shouting excitedly, something about a class cancellation. Then, catching sight of Maria, he turned and made a little bow.

"Good morning," he said. "My uncle says I must be good to customers. How are you? You don't like your American car? Too bad you buy it."

Faramaz shook his head, and handed him some tea. He was about to ask him, in Farsi, would he please give him a few moments alone with Maria when a voice from the TV leapt urgently into the small space. This was a program interruption, said the voice. Iran had suffered a massive earthquake. Tens of thousands were feared dead. The quake had hit northern Iran, near the Caspian Sea. There was footage, views from the air of flattened villages and the chop chop chop of the helicopter as it flew overhead. The populations of whole villages and towns were feared dead.

Hassan sat down opposite the desk. He sipped his tea. Suddenly he seemed to crumple. His head dropped to his knees and his tea dropped to the floor. Just as quickly, Faramaz was at his side. He lifted his nephew's head, cradled it against his chest, stroked his face and his hair. He circled his arms around the boy and rocked him. He thought of his parents' faces in the photograph on his dresser, and noticed that Hassan's shirt was blue today, the same shade of blue the sky would be by three p.m. when the fog burned off. He watched as the spilled tea spread into rivulets and trickled toward the door.

"I'm so sorry, Faramaz, Hassan, so sorry…"

Faramaz did not hear Maria leave the room. Only the gravel scrunching softly under her light walk outside. Then her voice again. "I'll be back for the car later, Huy. I have to go now." He heard Huy say okay, and explain in his still choppy English that he was cleaning the carburetor, that the car would be very good by this afternoon. Then Faramaz heard only the chaos inside his head.

Burying the Cat

I know who she is soon as I look at her. Huddled on my porch she's as wet as if she'd just pulled herself from the river. With her dark wet eyes and long slick hair she looks like a river otter and my sister Wilma both. Besides, who else would come looking for Mom and Lou?

"*Annie?*" I say, and hear the disbelief in my voice.

She nods, miserable, her teeth chattering. "I'm looking for my grandma and my brother," she says again. I tell her come in and take off her wet coat and shoes. Right away she spots Tiger lying in state in his cardboard coffin just inside the door.

"Is that cat dead?" she wants to know.

My little one, Tina, steps out from behind my back.

"That's *my* cat," she pipes up. "And you're making him wet! When the rain stops we're going to bury him."

Annie states the obvious. "He's going to get wet in the ground anyway."

I don't particularly like where this is heading and send Tina for a towel. I haven't liked where this whole day is heading. Lousy timing, old buddy, I told Tiger this morning when we woke to his screams and him belly crawling around the house. My anatomy exam is Monday morning, and I'd planned to spend the whole weekend studying. So much for that. What could I do except call the vet? Thankfully she was open, except, not so thankfully, there wasn't anything she could do for Tiger. And who's prepared for euthanasia first thing Saturday morning? I thought we'd leave Tiger right there to be cremated. But oh no, Tina insists, he has to have a proper burial. It's bad enough we *murdered* him. Least he should have a cross on a grave with his name on it. We'd been about to go out and scout about for what my eldest,

Brad, cheerfully calls "Public Burial Grounds" when the skies opened.

Now this: A ghost shown up on my doorstep.

Tina comes back with a bath towel, by which time Brad and Rhonda have torn themselves away from the TV to gawk from the doorway. "It's your cousin Annie," I tell them. "Come for a visit." Part of me wants to pull her close and hold her face in my hands. Give her a good looking over. I don't dare. She's too much like Wilma used to be. So I carry on with the introductions. "I'm your Aunt Ruthie," I explain, "and those three over there with the staring problem are your cousins." Then I'm all nurse, practical, help her out of her shoes and jacket, throw the towel over her head and start rubbing. She's nothing but bones under it.

"Where's grandma and Lou?" she asks again, from under the towel.

"Your grandma's in the hospital and maybe won't be back." I keep rubbing. What else do you tell a kid you haven't seen since she was knee high about an old drunk lady with no liver left to speak of? I don't know what to say about Lou.

"Find your cousin something dry to wear," I tell Rhonda, and make a face at Brad and Tina that means get lost. I figure Annie doesn't need an audience right now.

"Where's Lou?"

My hands stop rubbing and I take a breath.

"Lou's dead."

I give no details. Can't. Just thinking about Lou is still a quick sudden cut, all the way to the bone. I feel Annie stiffen under the towel, but she doesn't ask anything more. I'm not sure what I expect. I'm just thankful when Rhonda comes back with the clothes and I can send the two of them off to the girls' room for Annie to get changed.

"Hang her wet things on the edge of the bathtub, Rhonda," I call after them.

Truth is, this business with Tiger has me stirred up again. I work in the VA hospital, but since Lou I can't handle death.

Which is nuts, seeing as these days I'm running back and forth from Veterans to Harborview Hospital to see Mom, who could croak any day now. Don't ask me how I feel about that one. Her turned yellow and pickled in her own juice, the sticky sweet smell of death rising from her like perfume from a flower. We never got along in the first place. Lucky for me, where I am, on Spinal, patients don't die too often. They just stay forever. In wheelchairs and strung up with pulleys. All that will change if I pass my board exam this spring. There's no R.N. positions open on my floor, so who knows where I'll wind up.

I always was good at feeding kids. In no time I have Annie seated between her girl cousins on the couch, a plate of spaghetti on her knee. "Thank you, Auntie," she says, sweet as can be. What's next? I wonder, and seat myself on the arm of the couch to watch. She's pushed the too-long sleeves of Rhonda's sweatshirt up to her elbows, one skinny arm curved round her plate, the wrist of the other making little jerky movements as she winds spaghetti round and round her fork, sucking the noodles in when she can't get it right. I've seen Lou eat spaghetti the exact same way. Her black eyes glitter. She barely takes them off the TV. The last time I saw her she was a grimy three-year-old in a torn T-shirt, leaning against the leg of a cop. I should have taken her that night, when I had the chance. Lou too.

Wheel of Fortune comes on, first prize a minivan. Annie gets excited, and starts rooting for the black lady with big hair, cheering with her fork thrust in the air. I wonder at that. How quickly she's moved herself in, laughing along with Rhonda and Tina. Half an hour ago she was an orphan under a bath towel.

Soon as she's done eating I figure it's time to find out exactly where she blew in from. Last I heard she was bouncing from foster home to foster home because no one could put up with her. I turn off the TV and send Rhonda and Tina to clean up their room. Brad's in the kitchen with the phone stuck to his ear. Annie sinks down in the couch cushions.

"Okay, Annie. So where'd you spring from?"

"Dunno." Already she's picking at her sleeve.

"You don't know?"

She shrugs. "Some boy's house. I was kicking it at some boy's house."

"And?"

"He left to make a beer run...I mean a *root* beer run." She darts me a look to see how I'm taking it. "So I went with him." Another shrug. I can't believe what I'm hearing. Except, yes I can. I just don't want to. I fold my arms across my chest.

"How'd you end up here?"

"Dunno." More shrugs and sleeve-picking. "He drove up the hill...with the building that looks like a castle on top...and I recognized it." She laughs, and looks me in the eye, and suddenly she's on a roll. "So I told him my Grandma's house was round here someplace, and please pretty please could he help me find it. I remembered it was next to a park, and blue, a kind of faded blue, with the front porch just about hanging off. Well, he was real *real* nice and drove round and round till there it was! So I got out of the car and stood in the rain in the park across the street." As if she's reading my mind she adds, "I was scared to come in at first. The last time I was here Grandma didn't want me."

I haven't a clue what to say to all that.

"What last time?"

"You know...the last time. When I was s'posed to live with Grandma. A long time ago."

"No, I don't know."

" My caseworker bought me, a long time ago, and me and Lou played all day. Then Grandma changed her mind and said she was getting too old to take more kids, and told the caseworker to take me away again."

This is the first I heard about any of this, though it sounds like something Mom would do. "Well, your grandma doesn't live here anymore. And last I heard, you were in a foster home someplace."

"I was. But I left."

It's not altogether true that I never got on with Mom. The day Tina was born she showed up at the hospital with balloons, a tub of ice cream, and an outfit for Tina. She'd never done anything remotely like that for the other two. With Brad she was in the middle of one of her binges and never even noticed there was a baby in the house till he was a week old.

"What gives, Mom?" I asked, when she sat down on the bed. I hadn't seen her for a couple of weeks, maybe longer. She looked as if she'd come straight from the beauty parlor. Roots touched up, make-up fresh, nails done. Her hair so black and parted down the middle she reminded me of Morticia from *The Adams Family*. I knew something was seriously up when she leaned over and kissed me. Then she pushed my hair back from my forehead the way she used to when I was little. That is, whenever she happened to turn round and notice me, which wasn't often. "Such, a pretty face. Why cover it up with all this hair?" I have to admit I liked it.

"I'm turning over a new leaf, Ruthie." I groaned. How many times had I heard that line before? She put up her hand. "It's different this time. I've found Jesus."

It was all I could do to keep from busting up laughing. Would have if I hadn't been so sore from birthing Tina, who was peacefully asleep when Mom came in, toasting herself in one of those warming bassinets with a stocking cap on her head. I'd named her Tina after Tina Turner because I wanted her to have a take charge attitude. I used to sing *What's Love Got To Do With It?* when I was changing her diaper. Love never seemed to have too much to do with how any of my kids came to be, least of all Tina with her here-one-day, gone-the-next daddy.

By this time Mom's snatched her up to crow over, whisked the cap off, telling her she's the most gorgeous baby she ever set eyes on, just look at all that hair.

"Wake up, little one! Look at the balloons Grandma's brought you."

"I thought Jesus was the one that messed you up, Mom? Having him rammed down your throat at the rez boarding school all those years."

"Hey, that was me mixing up apples and oranges, Ruthie. Jesus wasn't the one doing the ramming. It was the nuns, and the damn B.I.A. The Pope too. Damn, it was the whole damn Catholic Church. But Jesus was innocent. They just used his name."

"What about Mary?"

"What about her? I don't hold no grudge against Mary. The way I figure, they used her too." By this time she'd handed Tina over to me, whipped out a couple of plastic bowls and spoons from her purse and began dishing up rocky road ice cream. "We need to celebrate, Ruthie. I know I haven't been the best mom over the years, but this is a new beginning, with a new little granddaughter to mark the occasion." She leaned over and breathed on Tina. "Check your grandma's breath, sweetheart. Minty fresh, and not a hint of booze."

"So who enlightened you on all this, Mom?"

"My neighbor, Minnie. You remember Minnie, the little lady with the white gloves? Well, she invited me to her church and I went, and it was beautiful. Music to send shivers up your spine. Indians and black people understand each another. We suffered the same burdens. It's all in the music."

"So now you're Baptist?"

"Amen."

It took my guard down. I enjoyed Mom like that. She spent more time with me the first few weeks of Tina's life than any time I could remember. We talked more. She shared feelings I never even knew she had. About losing her own mom and dad in a car wreck, about my dad, about leaving the rez, about city Indians, and how she hadn't meant to turn into one. She wasn't so sure it had done any of us any good. Maybe she'd go home, she said. Except now her grandkids needed her, and Lord knows my sister Wilma needed her help to get sober. She moved Wilma and her kids into her house. Then, of course, there was her church. Her anchor, she called it.

They say timing is everything. Mom was at a church retreat when Wilma went missing. Mom called me in a panic soon as she got back. The police were at the house: a neighbor had called them. Could I believe Wilma had gone off on one of her binges and left her kids on their own for days? I didn't think it the right time to remind her that's exactly what she used to do with us. I just bundled Brad and Rhonda into their jackets, strapped Tina into her Snuggli with a bath towel folded over her head, and walked the eight blocks to Mom's in pouring rain. I found Mom sitting at the kitchen table with her arms wrapped round Lou, talking to a cop and a social worker. Annie leaned against the cop while he fed her candy, and the baby, Frankie, perched bright-eyed on the social worker's knee. My kids dripped rainwater all over the floor.

"We got it figured out, Ruthie," Mom said, and fake-mopped her brow with the back of her hand. "Thank you, Jesus. I've been on the phone to my cousin Grace and she's willing to take Annie and the baby, because heaven knows you've got your hands full. Lou can stay here with me. Right sweetie, you want to stay with Grandma?" Lou peeked at me over the rim of Mom's arms and nodded. The social worker beamed.

"We like to keep them with family," she said.

All I felt at the time was relief. Relieved too that somehow I'd managed to keep Tina dry. I asked the cop would he give us a ride home. A few weeks later Minnie died, and before I knew it Mom's relationship to Mount Moriah Baptist Church was history.

The next morning is bright and cold. Everything dusted with sparkling frost. "Perfect funeral weather," says Brad. "No chance of early rot."

After breakfast we head for the arboretum, the five of us, plus Tiger in the box. The shovel is in the trunk, the drum under the front seat. I see Annie's face in the rearview mirror as I drive. She has a red knit hat of Rhonda's pulled over her sleek dark hair, and her face is as bright and shiny as a new copper penny.

"This is a dumb idea, Brad," Rhonda keeps saying. "You can't just show up in the park with a shovel and start digging. Tell him, Mom. You're not going along with it are you?"

"What's the big deal?" says Brad. "It's not even a regular park. It's not like we're going there to throw a bunch of trash around. It's all organic." His voice has started to break. Sometimes he sounds like a man and sometimes a boy. He is exactly half my age.

On the way into the arboretum we pass a University of Washington sign and I have serious misgivings. None of this would be necessary, I think, if our damn landlord hadn't woken up one morning and realized that our house, perched up high on Beacon Hill and sagging off its foundations, was a potential gold mine. Now it's sold to a pioneering yuppie couple. A month ago they stood at their own peril on our rotting back deck to exclaim about the view of the Olympic Mountains, which on that particular morning were stretched out white and clean as someone's laundry along the horizon. Oh, the gems to be found in poor inner-city neighborhoods if people are only willing to look! Oh, the proximity to downtown! Just imagine what a little well-invested money will do!

Now me and the kids are out a home. I thought we should bury Tiger in the backyard anyway, along with all the other animals Mom buried over the years. But Tina wouldn't hear it. "The new lady will dig him up, Mommy." I chuckle now, as I park my old Chevy between two shiny sports utility vehicles, thinking about that woman—who just *loves* to garden—and the look on her face when she discovers she's digging up a pet cemetery. Mom liked to rescue animals, stray cats and dogs mostly, but she wasn't any better caring for them than she was for us.

We set off along a trail, Brad in the lead with the shovel, Tina with Tiger in a box, almost as big as she is. But she won't let anyone else carry it. I carry the drum. Tina insisted I bring it to make a proper prayer for Tiger, though I don't know how. Mom's the one knows, when it suits her. About as traditional as I ever got was a couple of pow-wows Mom took us to when me and my sisters were little. That's before alcohol was banned at pow-wows, or maybe Mom just sneaked it in. I don't remember much. I do remember Mom throwing up on the blanket we were sitting on. That, and the sun beating down, and how bad I wanted some shade.

Sun streams down through the open spaces between trees. These, I note with more misgivings, have important-looking nametags on them. All around us tree trunks, branches, and fallen, semimulched leaves glitter with frost. The ground underfoot is hard and crunchy. Annie spins about with happiness, runs ahead and then back to me, linking her arm through mine: "Hi, Auntie. Just checking in."

We've hardly gone any distance at all when even cold as it is, someone jogs past in shorts, exposed legs a brilliant pink. Then comes a lady wrapped up in a muffler with two snuffling dogs on a leash. Obviously this is not a good idea. Brad still thinks differently, and points triumphantly to a flat smooth spot between two trees.

"See!" he says. "Perfect!" and leaps off the trail to attack the frozen ground with the shovel. He digs for a minute or two, and then a man comes by with a cellphone and a Great Dane.

"Come on, Brad," I tell him. "Rhonda's right. This isn't going to work."

The man has stopped to stare at Brad, but it isn't until he tells whoever he's talking to he's gotta go that Brad stops digging. Maybe Brad thinks he's about to call the university police.

"Let's get out of here," he suddenly says. Then on the way back to the car: "Too many roots anyway."

Lou's funeral was the hottest day of the year. We didn't have money for a funeral tent. I stood at the graveside and sweat trickled down the inside of my dress. I'm not one for dresses, but I wore one for Lou. Like it made any difference. Like any of us made any difference. There was more family gathered than I remembered having, more than Lou ever knew he had. Mom called them and they came, somehow scraping together the planefare, trainfare or gas money, an uncle and his wife, my twin sisters from Vancouver and Omak, one with husband and kids, the other without, my baby sister, Sweet Pea, all the way from New York. Even Mom's cousin Grace showed up with Lou's little brother, Frank who she'd adopted by then. Go home, I wanted to scream. Every last one of you! You're too damn late! There was even a teacher from Lou's school, his classmates, and a few other kids who claimed to be friends. Only Wilma and Annie were missing. No one knew where Wilma was, and I think we'd all forgotten Annie even existed. After we had Lou in the ground Mom came over and draped her arms around me and cried for forgiveness on my shoulder. I shook her off.

"Forgiveness for what, Mom?" I backed away from her. "For letting a fourteen-year-old boy out the door at eleven o'clock on a Tuesday night?" I kept backing up, her coming after me with her arms outstretched. "For forgetting to even ask where he was going?" My voice rose, the whole funeral crowd turning to stare. "For forgetting to ask who he was going with? Who was it, Mom, out there in that car with the custom gold rims?" I was glad of the shocked faces around me. I screamed the last part. "Or is it something else you want my forgiveness for after all these years?" I turned and walked, over short springy grass, over other graves, over flat headstones. Not looking back, unable to bear the sight or to hear any more of Mom, or anyone else, not even my own kids.

Back at the house I'm firm: no more running around looking for burial spots.

"Not today, guys. I've got an exam tomorrow morning to study for. Tiger will to have to wait."

"He's gonna start to smell, Mom."

Rhonda's probably right again. Some kids seem to come unhinged when they turn thirteen. Rhonda's the complete opposite.

"We'll put him out on the back porch. It's cold enough out there."

"Can't do that, Mom. Raccoons."

I start to feel itchy across my stomach and back, and know I'm breaking out in hives again. It happens these days, whenever I get too stressed. If I don't settle down to study soon I'll turn into one big red blotch.

"I know, Auntie," says Annie brightly. "You can put Tiger in the freezer. I seen it on TV. Cryonics."

"That's when you freeze something live to bring it back later, silly," says Brad. "Tiger's already dead."

"Either way, I don't want a cat in my freezer, thank you."

But Annie's given me an idea. I send her and Brad to Red Apple Grocery for a block of ice and a styrofoam picnic cooler. It passes through my mind, as I retreat into the bathroom to pat calamine on my itching welts with a cotton ball, that I still haven't said anything to Annie about how long she can stay, and she hasn't asked me. She hasn't asked me about Wilma either. You'd think she might want to know where her own mother is. Though, if she does ask, there's nothing I can tell her. Strange too, not another word about Lou. No questions about how or when he died. My conscience prods. Annie should have been with me all along, I tell myself. Her and Lou. What judge in their right mind would let a kid stay with Mom?

No sooner do I have this thought than the phone rings. I swear Mom has some kind of sixth sense that tips her off to whenever I'm thinking less than charitable thoughts about her. "It's Grandma, Mom," calls Rhonda. I explain to Mom that no, I can't make it in to see her today, I have an exam in the morning and I need to study. She starts to cry, and reminds me I didn't make it yesterday either. Have I forgotten about her? "No, Mom, I could never forget you." Never a truer word spoken. "I'll be by tomorrow afternoon."

Brad and Annie arrive back from the store and we re-settle Tiger on ice, and put him in the corner of the bathroom, which most of the time is the coolest room in the house. "You're on your own now, kids," I say. "There's left over spaghetti and stuff to make a salad in the fridge." I pick up my books and retreat to my room. Just as I'm closing the door, I hear Annie's voice: "Cousin Brad, please get your feet off my bed." So the couch is *hers* now, I think.

I study till late, torn between getting this anatomy stuff nailed and some sleep. My hives have subsided. It's after midnight when I head for the kitchen to fix myself a snack. The living room is bathed in a pale glow from the street lamp outside. Annie is asleep on the couch, her arms wrapped around Tina's gray rabbit. I stop to look at her. It's hard to believe she once tried to burn down Cousin Grace's house, which is what I heard. She looks younger than twelve, a scrap of a girl, with bones like twigs. A gust of wind could blow her clear away. I lean over to stroke her hair away from her face the way Mom did me, the way I still do my girls. Her hair is damp and warm at the temples. I think of Lou, the skinniest little boy I ever saw, with a round happy face and dimples to die for. Most of the time he looked like a piece of dark wood furniture in need of dusting. The first thing I always did when he came to my place was throw him in the tub. By the time I finished with him he'd shine all over. Sometimes it was days, or even a week or two at a time, till Mom called up and told me to send him back. Like a fool, I always did.

One Christmas, I gave him a phone book, pocket-sized, with a red cover. I wrote his name in front with Mom's name and number, my name underneath. Keep it with you, I told him. That way you will never come up missing.

As it turned out the phone call came to me.

"Ruthie Fallon?"

"Yes."

"There's been a shooting."

I'd been cleaning out a brown syrupy mess from the bottom of the refrigerator. One of the kids must have stuck an open can of Pepsi on the top shelf, and it had tipped over. I was just home from my shift and still in my nursing scrubs. I opened the fridge to get milk for my coffee and saw the mess.

"We need you to come to the morgue to make an identification."

Outside was beautiful. One of those days when Seattle redeems itself from so much rain, sunshine beaming its way through the branches of the tree outside the kitchen window, the linoleum carpeted with leaf pattern.

"Did you call his grandma?" I asked. "Jeanie Fallon? She's his legal guardian."

"Mrs. Fallon could not be reached."

On the way to the morgue everything shimmered, nothing quite real. As I crossed the Twelfth Avenue bridge, Puget Sound glittered with a thousand points of light. I drove like a maniac, as if somehow I could save Lou if I got there faster.

Cheap cat food caused Tiger's problem. That's what the vet said. It plugged up his urinary tract, a quite common occurrence in male cats. She was nice, stroking poor Tiger's flank, telling him to go easy, old boy, she wasn't going to hurt him. There was an operation, very expensive, but in Tiger's case she didn't recommend it. Tiger was too far gone. It can happen that way, she said. A seemingly healthy cat frisking about one day and sick like Tiger the next, although usually there were warning signs. Had any of us seen Tiger trying to pee in funny places?

Waiting for her to come out of the back room with Tiger's body was almost more than I could bear. She appeared with him wrapped in the towel we'd brought him in, and laid him, still warm, across Tina's lap. Brad and Rhonda crowded round and they all three stroked him. I stood in back. I couldn't stop crying. The vet gave me a squeeze on the arm and handed me a piece of paper. If we were planning on another cat, she said, here's the cat food she recommended. It cost more, but in the long run it was worth it. I wiped my eyes with the back of my hands and told her how sorry I was. All I could think of was Lou.

I know I'll let Annie stay. Whatever the judge says I need to do, I'll do it.

Morning comes, the sun barely up as I struggle awake. Already I'm reciting the names of bones. Like a homing pigeon, I head toward the kitchen and my morning coffee. On the way I stumble across the couch. It's empty. I run from room to room calling Annie's name. I flick on all the lights, as if I'll find her hiding behind a door or under the table. The kids shake themselves awake and run round the house calling her name. Brad runs outside in pajamas and bare feet. I call him in. She's gone, I say. No sense him freezing himself to death out there.

I don't want to think about what Annie's wearing, or not wearing. Her jacket's right here. I hug it to me, as if it's her I'm hugging. I shoo Brad into the shower to warm up. I tell the girls to go on and get dressed. Tina can't stop asking questions. I don't have any answers. I can't let go of Annie's jacket. A little later, Brad comes out of the bathroom with a towel around his waist. So much steam might not be good for Tiger, he points out. It's then we discover Annie has taken Tiger with her.

Suddenly Tina's face brightens, and she runs to check on the shovel, which she remembers leaning up against the wall, just inside the front door. "It's not here, Mom!" Her voice is triumphant, as if somehow its being gone represents some logic on Annie's part. Annie stepped out at six a.m. to bury a dead cat. I don't have the heart to mention we left the shovel in the trunk of the car.

Dust

Salvador brought his wife home from the hospital at one o'clock. Lunch time. "Are you hungry for some lunch, Consuelo?" he asked, already knowing what she would say. How could he ask her a question like that at a time like this? Besides, didn't he know that for the past week that place had been trying to poison her? The food there wasn't fit for a dog, not that she had anything against dogs, but her stomach was ruined.

She said all those things, then sighed and dangled her arms while he helped her out of her coat. They were still in the hallway. She didn't look so good. No reason she should, thought Salvador, those doctors didn't know what they're doing. For one week they run tests, then send her home with puffy hands and feet and tell her to stay in bed for another week. Well, they didn't know his wife. She was not the type could sit around, and especially not now. He had heard her.

"Doctor," she said. "At home my own son is right now dying. How can I do nothing? I have to do something."

Which was Salvador's own feeling exactly. Only that morning, the first one up as usual, he had swept the kitchen floor, watered the plants, and made the coffee—but then found himself unable to sit down and drink it. He took out the trash, which was still nearly empty from when he'd done the same thing the night before, and brought in the newspaper. Of course this he couldn't sit down and read. Who knows, maybe he'd come across one of those little articles about someone found dead in an alley somewhere in back of Market Street, with a needle in their arm, and no one knows who they are. For years, whenever he came across a newspaper article like that he always thought of José. Thank God José would die here, in a bed, with his family all around him instead of alone on the street. Because there was no dignity in a death like that, no dignity at all, just as there was no shame in liver cancer. Cancer was a terrible disease, but there was no shame in it. Still, he didn't need to read anything to remind him of how it might have been. God knows, for the past twenty years at least, ever since he was a teenager, José's life had been one long drawn-out close call.

What he could do with was a drink.

This Salvador had thought to himself this morning, standing uncertainly under the arch that separated living room from kitchen, still dressed in robe and slippers. But no way, not a chance. He had promised Consuelo. He left the liquor cabinet alone, and the paper too, still rolled up with the rubber band around it, and for the want of something better to do, straightened out the slipcover on the couch. Then went around with a Windex bottle and a rag, squirting and wiping everything in sight.

Now, hanging Consuelo's coat on the coat stand, and picking up someone else's from the floor, he felt anxious about getting back to the kitchen, to fix himself a sandwich. Not that he had much of an appetite, but not eating didn't help anyone except the fat man, which Salvador prided himself he was not. A sandwich, carefully made, perhaps salami with jalapeños, would give him something to do with his hands. He would make one for Consuelo too, though without the jalapeños, and wrap it in plastic wrap so that if she felt hungry later it would be ready for her.

Naturally she needed to look in on José right away.

She hadn't seen him at all since the doctors sent him home. It was too late, they said, there was nothing they could do. Nothing she could do either when she was still stuck in the hospital herself. And while Salvador had tried to warn her how José looked—he could barely bring himself to go into that room—there was no way really to prepare her. He was right behind her now.

"Hello, *mijo*. I'm home." He marveled at that. The way

Consuelo could suddenly brighten her voice. But right away there were complications. Miguel was in the room helping his brother with the bedpan, and the moment Consuelo popped her head around the door he yelled at her.

"Get out, Mom! For Chrissakes, José doesn't want you around right now!"

Which on the one hand Salvador understood, because if he were José he wouldn't want his mother (may the saints preserve her), or any woman, looking at him at a moment like that. It would be humiliating enough to have to use that thing in the first place. On the other hand, he was not José, and who knows, maybe when you get to be as sick as he is you don't mind any more.

Either way, there was no need for Miguel to yell. Loud enough, too, to cause Salvador's teenage granddaughter, Roberta, to come out of her room, which these days was an event in itself. Of course she still had the telephone stuck to the side of her head, and was still talking into it, but paused long enough to ask, "What's going on Grandpa?" while forgetting to say anything at all to her grandma.

"Nothing, *mija*," said Salvador, and indicated Consuelo with his head, so that Roberta added, "Oh, hi Grandma," before going back into her room and closing the door.

Already Consuelo was in tears, and who could blame her? And they hadn't been home even two minutes yet, still stuck in the hallway, Salvador now holding Consuelo's elbow with a firm but gentle grasp, his idea being to steer her into the living room and settle her into the easy chair with her feet up on the hassock. On the way he murmured a little prayer to the statue of the Blessed Virgin, her face chipped from the time she was toppled out of her niche above the hall stand by an earthquake, but benevolent still. "Please, Holy Mother, keep Angelina downstairs. For the time being at least."

A month ago, the night José showed up, unshaven and haggard, and told them he was ill, Angelina had complained to her mother. "Mom, are you going to let that drug addict stay here? Under this roof? With my daughter?"

This in the doorway to the bathroom where Consuelo smeared cold cream on her face before going to bed, leaning close to the mirror, because without her glasses she could scarcely see a thing.

"Your daughter?" inquired Consuelo.

"Yes, my daughter, your granddaughter. Don't play games with me, Mom."

"You mean Roberta? The one we give a bedroom up here with us because there is no space down there with you in that little mother-in-law apartment, and everybody knows teenagers need space?"

"Yes, Mom. And you know I appreciate everything you and Dad have done for her and for me. But *José!* You know how he is. Are you forgetting the time he stayed here while you and Dad were away and left his dirty needles right here in this bathroom?"

"I'm not forgetting anything." Consuelo by this time had finished with the cold cream and was examining her hair. "*Ay, Dios mío…*look at all this gray." She picked up her glasses—too big for her small face—put them on and turned to face Angelina. "It is you who forget, Angelina. That drug addict is my *son.*" And she swept past her first-born child, the divorcee who thought she was so much better than anyone else, and into her bedroom and closed the door.

Now Angelina, appeared at the top of the stairs with a large uncooked pork roast on a plate. In truth, she had been feeling guilty about her brother, who it turned out was so sick that barely had he laid himself down in his old bed in his old room than he had to be carted off to the hospital in an ambulance. But they didn't keep him there, and sent him home again, to die, the Hospice people now coming and going, and her mother ill too. The least she could do was cook. Seeing her mother in the easy chair took her aback just a little. "Hi, Mom. How are you? I didn't know you were home yet." She put the plate down on the edge of the dining table which was mostly buried under rolled-up newspapers and unopened mail, and kissed her mother on the cheek. "How are you?" she asked again.

"Not so good," said Consuelo, eyeing the pork. "What are you planning to do with that pig?"

"Roast it. Up here, if that's okay? My oven's so small. Don't worry, Mom, you won't have to do a thing...except eat a little when I'm done."

Consuelo leaned back in her chair and closed her eyes. "My stomach is ruined, *mija*. But help yourself. This is your house too."

She started to doze a little, listening to Angelina console her father, who it seemed had cut himself while cutting his sandwich, and curse at the gas oven, which took its own sweet time to light. But finally she heard the shudder of the back bedroom door that she had been waiting for—the door was warped and sounded different from all the rest—and Miguel came into the living room. Right away she stood up. "I don't need to breathe the same air as a son who speaks to his mother that way," she said, and swept out, as best she could on swollen stocking feet, ignoring Miguel's caution that José was now asleep. Sweeping out was something she had perfected over the years, as a way of dealing with irritating offspring with as few words as possible. Of course she was glad Miguel loved his brother the way he did, but he needed to remember that she was the mother.

She sat on the chair beside José's rented hospital bed and looked at her eldest son. The one who had always caused her so much heartache, whom she had beaten with a wooden spoon and shut in his bedroom in an attempt to keep him safe, who ran with the wrong crowd and did terrible things to his own body. "*Ay, mi travieso!*" There before her very eyes was the evidence. Thick purple track marks crawling up the inside of his arm like snakes. She turned the arm over.

Yet his head on the pillow was still beautiful. Oh, her handsome son, even with his skin turned yellow and thin to the bone he was handsome, his hair still so black. She stroked his cheek and his hair, wept a little and pleaded with the Holy Mother to be merciful. *Ay ay ay...*How could it be that he had so little time left? "*¿Por qué, mijo? ¿Por qué?*" She put a hand on his forehead and felt that it was cool. But his breathing was awful, such a rattle in his throat.

Looking around the room she could see the problem. It was shameful. Why should a dying man breathe dust? In Mexico when someone was dying you cleaned everything. Even here, in this country, they cleaned the hospitals. Why, only yesterday they had woken her out of a perfectly good sleep to change her sheets. And then the noise of that floor polisher! But at least the hospital floor was clean.

This room had become everybody's junk pile. The dresser piled high with a mountain of old magazines and bits and pieces of junk. The peak of the mountain that ridiculous sombrero of her husband's, the one he won in Las Vegas, now covered in dust like snow on the top. And then there were Angelina's boxes! So many of them! She knew that apartment downstairs was very small, so why had she brought everything with her from that big house here? Stacked four feet high and higher, her boxes were a wall, even covering part of the window and making the room so small and so dark. Consuelo ran a finger along the top of the wall. Just as she thought. Dust.

Tentatively, she lifted a box from the top of the pile. To her surprise it wasn't so heavy. She dropped it to the floor with a soft thud and dusted it with the hem of her skirt. So nicely sealed. What was in it, she wondered? and pushed it under the bed with her foot. Although she remembered perfectly well that the doctor had told her not to lift anything, she reached for another box, which turned out to be even lighter, weighing so little that when she dropped it, it almost bounced. A quick dust and she pushed it under the bed alongside the first one. The third box, however, was heavy. Unable to lift it at all, she succeeded in pulling it off the pile. It landed on the bare floor with a loud thump that caused José to shudder in his sleep.

"Sorry, *mijo*," she whispered, and sat down again because suddenly she felt dizzy. She fanned herself lightly with one hand. But see! Already there was more light in the room. What did those Hospice people think when they came to see José and found him surrounded by dusty boxes and junk as if he were in a storage unit? She remembered many years ago when this very room had been José and Miguel's bedroom, with the model train set their father liked so much set up in the middle of the floor. Back then it had been bright in here, with those yellow curtains with the trains on them. Back then everything had to be trains, trains, trains, because their father worked for the railroad.

Now, one or two more boxes, she thought and that would do it. Then at least she would be able to open the window and let some fresh air in. Except right now she wasn't sure if she could move another box, or do anything except lie down like the doctor said she should. It was all she could do to shove the third box under the bed with the other two. She fanned herself again.

"I'll be back later, *mijo*," she whispered to José. "Let me rest for just a little while."

But from late afternoon and into the evening people came and went. Miguel's wife and kids, Mrs. Díaz from across the street, and José's old girlfriend, Maria, who Consuelo and Salvador had once hoped he would marry—even if she was a widow with two children—and so nice to see her again after all this time, though so sad under the circumstances, and couldn't she stay a little longer? Also Angelina's best friend,

Rose, who had gone to Mission High with Angelina and José, and once had a crush on him. Who could blame her, he used to be so handsome. Also two ordinary-looking people from when José worked for the telephone company, and three not so ordinary-looking people (not in this neighborhood at least, though maybe on Polk Street) who Miguel whispered were from José's theatre days. These three Consuelo and Salvador looked at askance. Particularly the black man named Rueben who had bleached blonde hair and a diamond stud in his nose. It was people like that gave San Francisco a bad name.

"So what do you do, Rueben?" inquired Salvador, not sure whether or not he wanted this man in his house, although how could he deny him under the circumstances, seeing as he was a friend of José's.

"I'm an actor," said Rueben.

"You too? Our José tried his hand at that."

Everyone took turns popping into the back bedroom to see José, some with flowers or a card, and Rueben with a party blower. Miguel cautioned each of them not to stay too long and wear José out, while Salvador told people proudly how it was Miguel who did everything for José, getting up for him in the night, that bedpan business, washing him down, even giving him his morphine shots. To which Miguel—with a harried look on his face and running his fingers through his hair—explained both to his father and to Mrs. Díaz how if anyone had told him a year ago he'd being doing all this for his brother he never would have believed it. A year ago he wanted to kill José, and as it was he wasn't sure how long he could keep this up. Then suddenly he remembered again the Hospice people saying José only had a day or two left, three at the most, and broke down and cried, disappearing with his wife into his parents' bedroom to be comforted.

Mostly people ate. Angelina's pork roast a big hit, except with Rueben who didn't put anything impure into his body, especially not pig meat. Angelina, who was very good at this sort of thing, circulated, and made sure everyone had food on their plates, and whipped up another salad in no time at all when the first one was eaten. She also found some of her mother's beans in the freezer, and thawed these out for Rueben in the microwave, even though he told her not to go to all that trouble. These were so delicious, especially wrapped inside a warm flour tortilla, that several other people had to try them and Rueben absolutely had to have the recipe. Which is how come Consuelo, who Angelina had insisted to "Just stay put, Mom," and keep her feet elevated like the doctor ordered, eventually found herself sitting at the kitchen table with Rueben. The secret to her beans, she explained was when and how, and how much salsa to add to them, because that's what gave them their flavor.

"Do you like to cook, Rueben?" she inquired.

"Oh yes. Love to. As long as the ingredients are pure."

Salvador by then was nursing a shot of whisky in a glass, after all, it was late enough in the day, and was doing the rounds with the bottle. So far the only people who had taken him up on his offer of a drink were the rather pale, quiet little man from the telephone company, and Mrs. Díaz.

"Drink, Rueben?" he asked, though wondering whether it was the smart thing to do to offer any oddball friend of José's alcohol. Next thing he'd be raiding the liquor cabinet like José himself used to do.

"Oh no, no, no. Thank you," said Rueben, putting up his hand. "I *never* put anything impure in my body."

"Just this once, Ma, please," José had pleaded with Consuelo ten years ago when he wanted her to come and see the play he was in. "I'll get you and Dad front row seats."

What on earth made him want to be an actor? Why not the railroad, like his father? His sister sold hosiery in a department store, what's wrong with that? His brother was a plumber, making good money too.

"You forget Ma, I worked for the phone company for years. That's how I paid for my acting lessons."

But in the end they went, front-row seats like José said, Salvador dressed in his suit, Consuelo in her navy dress with the pearl buttons. Although it seemed everyone else there wore jeans, the man next to Consuelo with a stud in his nose. And such a small place, some of the seats patched up with duct tape. And then the play! True, José had a lot of lines and he said them well, as well as so many cuss words could be said. But why did he have to scowl so much and wear such tight jeans with those rips in those places? Okay, okay, okay. It was the way it was supposed to be, and, yes, maybe life could be like that, but why would anyone want to write about it, much less pay money to go see it? If he had to be an actor, why not be more like Rock Hudson? With some nice clothes and a nice shave José was every bit as handsome. Instead he was hanging around all those sorts of people who get mixed up in theater these days, homosexuals and people with rings in their noses. Which wasn't a good idea at all given his problem. Everybody knew rock stars and people in the theatre were drug-users and alcoholics.

"Ma, Rock Hudson was a homosexual."

"Well, that just goes to show you."

The following afternoon Salvador sat and listened to Miguel snore from where he was stretched out on the couch, and the faint sound of Roberta talking on the telephone in her room. He was too worn out from the day before to do much of anything, as was everybody, although he had stayed up way past midnight in an attempt to get Consuelo to bed. She had refused to leave the kitchen until every last dish was washed and put away. Thank God she was now asleep and the house was quiet.

Salvador closed his eyes, and thought he might doze off himself. Consuelo had arranged for the priest to come by later on, and Angelina was downstairs making a huge batch of pasta salad because more visitors were expected. Several times Roberta had been obliged to come out of her room, her telephone conversations interrupted by the call-waiting beep as yet another person called to inquire about her Uncle José.

Perhaps Salvador did drop off, wandering briefly into a dream where José was still a little fellow dressed up in a sailor suit with pomade in his hair. Salvador carried him on his shoulders to keep him safe from some danger on the ground, José bouncing and giggling, Consuelo running after them with a comb, trying to comb José's pomaded hair. But then he started to hear something outside the dream. Nothing much, some clinking, the dull thud of something falling on the floor, drawers opening and closing. Then the warped shudder of José's door, but this time loud, as if someone had kicked it. He flicked his eyes open and saw Consuelo stagger into the hallway, weighed down by two bulging grocery bags. He was on his feet immediately.

"Consuelo! I thought you were asleep. What are you doing?"

Consuelo harrumphed. "Taking all this junk to the garage where it belongs."

On the top of one bag Salvador saw his prize sombrero he'd won in Las Vegas. On top of the other, one of his model trains built from a kit. But he knew his wife. When she got that tone in her voice and that gleam in her eye it was better not to argue with her. He took the bags. If she wanted them to go in the garage, then into the garage they would go. The thing was for her to rest.

But oh no no! No way in her right mind could Consuelo rest just now. Tears began streaming down her face. Didn't Salvador understand? All these years she had seen her son like a wounded animal caught in a trap, and could do nothing. Now that he was dying she could do something. At least she could clean that room for him! They stood directly outside Roberta's door, so that when Consuelo's voice began to rise in her distress, the door popped open and Roberta peeked out—naturally with the telephone in hand. She looked from her grandma to Salvador, and for the second time in two days asked her grandpa what was going on?

"Nothing, *mija*. Close the door."

Salvador put down the bags and placed his hands on his wife's shoulders. Consuelo clasped her hands as if in prayer, and spoke in a fierce urgent whisper.

"Salvador. As José's mother, the one who gave birth to him, I must clean that room for him. I must make sure he lies between clean sheets and opens his eyes to the Holy Mother." It was then that Salvador noticed that the Virgin was no longer in her niche in the hallway, an absence that caused him to cross himself.

Consuelo sighed. "But still he needs flowers. There should be more flowers. The air should be full of the smell of roses." Which meant she needed to go down into the garage to find the clippers and gardening gloves so that she could pick some roses from the garden for José. Because even though their garden had become an abandoned place since she herself was not well enough to care for it, the roses nonetheless were beautiful. After the roses she would rest.

So they went down into the garage together.

A single fluorescent light bulb dangled from its ceiling, lighting up the oil stains directly underneath while leaving much of the walls and the corners in shadow. Cobweb-covered cans of paint and other odds and ends could dimly be seen stacked up on and under shelves, including that lamp Salvador never got around to fixing, and yes, here were the small gardening tools down at the end in the white bucket. But ay ay ay, here were more of Angelina's boxes.

They both spotted José's things at the same moment. Not even in boxes like his sister's. Just in a pile. Like his life. They stared at the pile, as if maybe it would grow bigger, or rearrange itself and look like something more than it was. A small stack of books, a twelve-inch TV, a pair of Frye boots, a few clothes, and on top of it all José's old leather flight jacket.

Consuelo let out a little cry and put her hands to her face. "You remember that jacket, Salvador?"

Salvador nodded, and put down the grocery bags close to José's pile. How could he forget it? For years José had worn that jacket as if it were a second skin, and now it looked like something a snake had cast off. Consuelo picked it up, and held it against her as tenderly as if it were a baby. She rubbed her face against it, opened it, and sniffed at what was left of the lining.

"It still smells a little of him," she whispered. And smiled as if she had just discovered treasure. The same smile that had caused Salvador to fall hopelessly in love with her on the edge of a lettuce field, thirty nine years ago.

"Remember, Salvador? That cologne he used to wear?"

She held the jacket out for Salvador, and together they remembered. Not the cologne, but the night fourteen year-old José sauntered in wearing a leather jacket with its collar turned up. He'd saved his money from delivering newspapers, he said, and bought himself a new jacket. Consuelo had looked up from where she was setting forks and napkins around the table, Salvador from his work boots, which he was unlacing.

"What kind of jacket is that, *mijo*?" Consuelo wanted to know. Its leather shone, supple and new. And it smelled new, though from the expression on her face it might as well have stunk of rotten fish. José looked cocky with his hands in the pockets, his hair slicked back and a red bandana round his neck. But he smiled sweetly.

"You've never seen a bomber jacket, Ma?"

Consuelo paused for a beat and took another look.

"No. And I don't like that name. *Bomber*. So much aggression." Then returned her attention to the forks. But as soon as José left the room she picked up a fork and waved it at Salvador, who had said nothing. "You're the father," she said. "You need to do something because I'm telling you, that jacket means trouble."

Before they knew it, José took to wearing nothing but an undershirt under the jacket, the red bandana now tied round his head. "It's the *cholo* look," he explained. He'd given up his newspaper route by then, and everything was *cholo, chico, chicano*. Words that to right-minded parents born in Mexico should never be trusted. And where was he going dressed up like that? With who? Who were his friends? Why not bring them to the house?

"Stay off the streets, son."

Always they told him that. Though Salvador recalled now, in the garage with the jacket in his arms, how his words had always sounded as light as ping-pong balls, and merely bounced off José's leather-clad back as he walked out the door.

He wrapped his arms around his son's old jacket and around his sick and stubborn wife, and smelled the musty smell of the leather still laced with a hint of cologne, and the sweet powdery perfume of Consuelo's cheek. He thought of all that he had lost, and was about to lose, and might lose soon, and wept.

Consuelo sat at the kitchen table and stirred honey into the tea Salvador had just made for her. With the roses in the room she felt much better. Especially when José had opened his eyes, looked around the room, and said, "Someone's been busy," and smiled at her. Then, all of a sudden, everyone was awake, upstairs, out of their rooms and crowded around, pointing fingers and telling her to stay away from José, not to be clattering around him and making all that noise. Had she no consideration?

Consuelo continued stirring. "What noise? He slept. You slept. There was no noise. Only a little cleaning to make the room a nice place for him to be in."

There was actually only the three of them, Angelina, Miguel, and Roberta, but they felt like more, Angelina pushing her face close to her mother's, spitting out words as if her mouth was full of broken glass. "He's *dying*, Mom. Don't you understand *anything*? He doesn't care about dirt." Miguel, wringing his hands, holding his head, groaning (maybe he's the one should have been an actor...) "Gee, Mom, what were you thinking of? How could you put that statue up? He doesn't even consider himself a Catholic." Then Angelina again: "Why do you always have to be so difficult, Mom? Why do you always have to be the center of attention?"

A big wind who wants to blow her mother away is what she is, thought Consuelo, the wind now whispering to her own daughter, "You see, Roberta? You see how Grandma is?" That silly little Roberta nodding her head up and down as if it was on a spring, because, oh yes, she understood how Grandma was.

Consuelo stopped stirring and tapped her spoon on the side of the cup.

"Angelina," she said, her voice very calm. "Yesterday, the same day I come home from the hospital, your father tried to make my kitchen clean for me. Then you come upstairs to cook, to make my kitchen a mess. That's okay. That kitchen down there is so small it's not a kitchen at all. But why don't you clean up after yourself?"

"Come on, Mom. You know very well I would have cleaned up this morning."

"Why should I leave that big mess for cockroaches to find?"

"You don't get cockroaches overnight, Mom."

"We don't have cockroaches because I keep this house clean..."

"Oh here we go. My mother the martyr..."

"...and I didn't hear anyone complain this morning when they found clean cups for their coffee. Oh no! But it's the same thing. It's me who cleaned the cups. Just like it was me who cleaned the room."

"You did it for yourself, Mom. You weren't even thinking about José..."

"And you were?" Consuelo was on her feet now, jabbing the air with her teaspoon, her eyes ablaze. "You! The one who wanted me to put him on the street!"

Miguel rubbed the sides of his head and groaned again. "Drop it, Mom, just drop it."

Consuelo swung around.

"Ha! He talks to me like I'm a dog with a stick. Well, now I don't feel like dropping anything." She shook the teaspoon at Miguel and growled as if she were a dog. "You think you are better than José? You think it's okay for me to clean for you but not for him?"

Salvador waved his hands in the air and tried to get their attention.

"Leave your mother alone," he said. "She knows what's best. And she should be resting..."

The only one who noticed him was Consuelo.

"Why don't you speak up?" she said in a loud voice. "They don't listen to you either." Her voice began to climb. "Because this is *los Estados Unidos! En los Estados Unidos* children don't have to listen to their parents!"

Then from the back bedroom came José's voice, surprisingly strong and clear.

"Fuck *los Estados Unidos!*"

For an instant there was a stunned silence. Then a cheery voice from the hallway: "Hello there!" Father O'Connor's boyish face appeared around the side of the refrigerator, his cheeks flushed pink, his blue eyes sparkling. He waved one large hand at them and beamed. "Hello there!" he said again, and stepped entirely into the room. "Anybody mind if I come in? I rang the bell, but no one heard me...And, ah well, the door was open."

Between themselves, when they were on better terms than currently, Angelina and Consuelo both referred to Father O'Conner as Father What-A-Waste, because he was so young and good looking.

"Oh no, Father, no," they both said at once. "Come in and take a seat." And of course Salvador offered a seat too, although no one heard him. But no matter, because Father O'Conner said he didn't mind if he did, and lowered his lanky body into the nearest chair, smoothed his cassock over his knees, and beamed around at all of them.

Later on, José allowed him into the room, although, he confided to Miguel, this he was doing mostly for Mom's sake. But whatever happened in there between them seemed to satisfy Father O'Connor—a couple of toots on Reuben's party blower were overheard, followed by a few loud guffaws of laughter— because he came out smiling as broadly as when he went in. He was ready for that cup of coffee now, he said, rubbing his hands together eagerly, and reassured the rest of the waiting family that José would now be accepted into the Kingdom of Heaven.

Whereupon Salvador thought it time he looked in on his son directly, which he hadn't yet done all day. He left his family with the good Father and knocked on the back bedroom door.

"Hello, son."

"Hi, Dad."

Salvador came in and stood uneasily at the foot of the bed. *Dios mío*, he wasn't sure if he could do this, not with José looking like that.

"It must get pretty tiring...all these visitors. I don't want to wear you out, son."

José looked up at his father brightly for an instant, his eyes huge and glittering.

"Don't worry, Dad. I'm still your basic party animal." He laughed. "Hey, I've got hassle-free drugs and a great social life. What's more to need?" He sucked in air between his teeth, and glanced away, swallowing hard a couple of times. "That was a joke, Dad."

Salvador sat down cautiously in the chair beside the bed.

"I know, son. You always were a joker. But that's good. It's a good thing to laugh."

"Yeah...except now the laugh's on me."

Salvador felt tears well up behind his eyes again. He patted some part of José under the blankets and looked around the room. Consuelo had done a good job. The roses on the dresser top were beautiful, the Virgin from the hallway peeping coyly out from underneath a bloom. Propped up next to her, leaning against a vase, was a picture of José as a teenager, sporting a big pompadour and wearing his leather jacket.

"Hey, I look pretty good, don't I? Sis found that old picture, and I asked the Father to put it up there for me. He's an okay guy...as priests go. I told him he could keep my party blower."

Salvador's shoulders began to shudder.

"I'm okay, Dad. Really...Hey, Dad, look at me." Salvador turned his head, wiped his eyes, and nodded. José ran his tongue over his lips. "I had this dream, Dad." He swallowed. "Remember Squinklé? My old buddy...the one who used to call up all the time, and you and Mom complained how come you never got to meet him...till finally I brought him to the house and you told me to never bring him back again?" His voice was becoming scratchy, as if he'd been shouting a lot and was now running out of voice. Still he managed a chuckle.

Salvador nodded. "I remember Squinklé."

"Well, in my dream I was waiting on this corner...and I was really bored. Man, it was like I'd been waiting a long, long time and was ready to go...someplace. Then up pulls this red Camaro, real shiny and clean, with nice whitewall tires, and out leans Squinklé. Hey Bro, he says. *¿Qué hubo? ¿Qué pasa?* I tell him nothing, nothing's happening. He tells me I got it wrong, I been getting it wrong for years...it's all just beginning to happen. Hop in, he says. He's taking me for the ride of a lifetime...And there in the car with Squinklé are

Sonny and Loco…and Gabriel, and a pretty girl named Estela I once had my eye on…but who died of an overdose before I had a chance to put the make on her." José paused and sucked in air through his teeth, his eyes glittering. "All my old friends, Dad." He sucked again. "From way back…all the ones who passed on. They're waiting for me."

He stopped, and closed his eyes, and swallowed a couple more times. Then he opened his eyes, reached up and touched his father's cheek. A little touch, his fingers dry as dead leaves.

Wesley

I don't sleep nights no more. Not since. I've moved since too. Now I live some place where there's no children. I don't need children to remind me. I still don't sleep nights though.

1345 Eleventh Avenue was my place, my home. It had been my home since way back. Thirty-six years I lived there. Moved in when Charles was in eighth grade. Lived there twenty-two years before my husband died. I thought I'd die there.

It had these two windows I liked to sit by. One in front and one in back. I had my big green chair pulled up to the one in front. I could view the street good from there. All the comings and goings. Some days I'd sit up front most all of the day. I liked to watch the children. So many children on that street it sounded like a schoolyard sometimes. I watched the little ones wobbling along on their bikes with training wheels, and the big ones doing pop-a-wheelies or playing ball in the street. Then some car comes speeding through the middle of their game and just about knocks somebody over. More than once it was police cars did that. They always came driving like they owned the street and everybody on it. In summer time I watched children all ages running after the ice cream truck.

The window in back was different. That was my bedroom window. It was set in the back corner of the house. I could see everything from there, my yard and the yard next door too. Some days my hip acts up. Days like that I'd just sit in my rocking chair and look out on the yard. Didn't even bother dressing. Just sit in my robe and look out at my plum tree. Watch the birds coming and going from it. Watch squirrels playing tag up and down it. I liked spring best. Then there'd be blossoms all over my tree, like white lace.

I watched the yard next door too. There's an orange tree in that yard. Some years there'd be a whole lot of oranges and they'd hang so heavy they'd pull the branches way down. One year the kids that lived there then had an orange fight. They messed up the yard something shocking. I remember thinking it was a shame to waste all them oranges. Another year the girl brings me a bag full of oranges. They weren't very sweet, but I liked her bringing them just the same. Sofi her name was. I never forget children's names.

That house suited me just fine. I used to promise myself I'd die in that house. I remember the day Wesley moved in next door real good because it was the same day Charles tried to talk me into moving. He wanted me to live in an old folks' home. He came by with a big bouquet of flowers like it was Mother's Day. I fixed him his coffee and we sat down in the front room. I sat in my green chair.

"I'm worried about you Mama," he says. "You know Jeanie and I would love to have you stay with us but we don't have the space."

"I'm fine where I am, Charles," I tell him. "You and Jeanie don't need to worry about me. I just need help getting my groceries in and getting to my doctors appointments, that's all."

Charles stirring sugar in his coffee. I'm wondering how long he's planning on stirring the same spoonful of sugar. Wondering what he's got planned. Finally he tells me.

"Well, Mama, Jeanie and I went ahead and did what we thought was best. We made arrangements for you to move into the Sunshine Retirement Home. It's a beautiful place, Mama. You'll like it there. Quiet. Nice gardens..."

"I'm not moving no place, Charles. And if that's what you came here to talk about, you can leave." I've never spoken to my son that way since he was grown, but his words hurt me. I looked out the window so he wouldn't see the tears in my eyes.

I was sitting there like that, biting my lip, when this U-Haul truck pulls up to the house next door. The place had been empty for more than a month. Then here comes this truck and parks, so I'm looking. Looking real hard, biting my lip, trying not to hear Charles talking about being realistic. I watch a tall skinny man come piling out of the truck. Right behind him is this woman who would be pretty if she didn't look so tired. She has her head wrapped up in a scarf and she's holding a baby that's sleeping. The man stands scratching his head looking at the house. It ain't much to look at.

Then I hear Charles. "I'm leaving now, Mama. We'll talk more some other time."

I say, "I ain't moving, Charles." And all the time I'm watching the new family. I see the woman turn her head back toward the truck and holler over her shoulder into the open window.

"Wesley! Wesley, wake up. We're here." She hollers so loud the baby wakes up and starts to fuss. Out of the corner of my eye I see Charles walking to his car. I know he's waving to me, but I don't pay him no mind. I'm waiting to see who Wesley is.

The truck door swings open and this little blond-haired boy about six years old comes sliding off the seat. He stands all sleepy-eyed next to the truck like he don't know what's happening to him. He keeps rubbing his eyes and pretty soon he wakes up and starts to look around. He sees me looking at him from the window. So I wave to him. And he smiles at me. A big old jack o' lantern smile. The biggest smile I ever saw. That was Wesley.

Halloween was a few days later. Charles comes over with all these little bags of candy for me to hand out. He don't say anything about the Sunshine Retirement Home. I don't either. I just scowl so hard he gives me the candy and leaves. The doorbell starts ringing early. I sit in my green chair to be close to the front door. The kids all know I'll be home and have something for them. I like Halloween. It's about the only time I see the kids up close.

I see Wesley and his mother walking over from next door. My house is their first stop. Wesley's dressed like a devil in one of those red plastic outfits that come out of a box. He's carrying a red plastic devil's fork. His smile isn't devilish though. Just wide and cute. With his top two teeth missing.

"Hello, Wesley," I say, and put two packages of candy in his hand.

"How you know my name?" he asks.

"I heard your mama calling you outside."

"Oh! What's your name?"

"Don't be asking people their names, Wesley. Just say thank you for the candy."

"Thank you."

"You're welcome, Wesley. My name is Mrs. Jacobs. Come back and see me some time. And welcome to the neighborhood." Wesley's mother smiled a hurried tired smile and turned to leave.

Mostly Wesley just waved to me from the street or his back yard, but he did come to visit me once in between that Halloween and the next. My doorbell rang one day and when I opened the door there was Wesley standing on the porch.

"Hi," he says, beaming. I see his top teeth is growing in. "How come you always sit in the window?"

"Because I like to watch what happens outside."

"How come you don't come out?"

"Too hard for me to get up and down steps, pumpkin. But you can come in. Would you like to come in?" He pokes his head in the door and looks around.

"Nope. I can't. My Mom says I can't go in no place she don't know about. Do you live all by yourself?"

Just then Wesley's mother appears in her front yard with the baby on her hip. She looks up and down the street.

"Wesley! Wesley Jr! Where are you?" She spots him on my doorstep and gets mad. "Wesley, get over here this minute! I told you, leave that lady alone!"

Sometime before the new baby came Wesley's mother threw the skinny man out. I saw her on the street with Wesley right before that. She was real pregnant. That was the day Wesley had a black eye. He'd just taken the training wheels off his bike and he wasn't real steady yet. He's pedaling fit to bust. I'll never forget his face. His smile's so wide it look like it's about to cut his face in half, and this big purple bruise around his eye. His mother's out there cheering him on, trying not to act so weary like she always is. I enjoyed seeing them having a good time together.

A few days later it had just turned dark and I heard this banging and carrying on coming from next door. I looked, and there was the skinny man pounding on the door with his fists. He was crying like a baby and calling her name over and over.

"Barbara! Barbara!" That's how I learned Wesley's mother's name was Barbara. But she never did open the door and I never did see the skinny man after that.

Then the house was real quiet for a few days and the car was gone. One afternoon I see the old Chevy pull up to the house and Barbara gets out with Wesley, the little one, and a new baby. She's looking more tired than ever. I start to see Wesley in the back yard on school days, and I know he's not getting to school like he should be. And the yard got to be so raggedy it weren't nothing but weeds. Barbara gave up trying to tend it a long time ago. Some days when the back door was open, I heard her carrying on like she's mad at the whole world, and the kids all fussing and crying up a storm.

The day that changed everything was one of the days I didn't get dressed. My hip had me laid up for nearly a week. That day was my first out of bed. It was a pretty day. I'm sitting in my rocking chair and I got the window open to let some of the sunshine in. I'm watching the squirrels and I'm waiting to hear the front door open because I know Jeanie is stopping by. Charles and Jeanie both been coming by everyday since I been sick. And they been talking on and on about Sunshine Retirement Home too. I watch a squirrel chase another one right over the fence into Wesley's yard. That's when the back door catches my eye. I see it swing open. It opens maybe a third of the way and I'm thinking Wesley's little brother will come running out like he does in the mornings sometimes. But he never comes, and the door just stays that way.

Then I hear something. A whimpering noise like I've never heard before. Then I see something. On the ground. A hand. A little pink hand. It's reaching round the side of the door. Then I see a blond head. Then I see Wesley come crawling around the door on his belly. He's moving real slow. Dragging himself onto the concrete. I'm wondering what he's up to. Is this some new game or what? He stops for a minute and makes the whimpering noise. Then he pulls himself out further. He's wearing pajamas and his feet is bare. But his legs is wrong. They're trailing. His legs just trail behind him. He reminds me of a bird with a broken wing.

He pulls himself across the strip of concrete by the door and into the grass. Then he turns himself, real slow, until he's facing my window. He lays on his belly in long grass and reaches up an arm toward my window. He lifts his face up out of the grass and looks right at me. His face is scrunched up and red. He's crying. He tries to call out to me. But no sound comes. Not even the whimpering noise. He flops down in the grass and lays still.

I'm shaking. I've never been so scared in my whole life. Don't know what to do. Seems like he's hardly flopped down when the back door opens wide and there stands Barbara. She's got a bag of groceries in her arms. Wesley's little brother is holding onto her leg. I hear the new baby crying some place back in the house.

"Wesley?" she calls. She calls like she's not sure he's out

there. She doesn't see him at first. The weeds and grass are so long they've covered him some. Then she sees him and drops the groceries and runs to him.

"Wesley! Wesley! What are you doing out here?" She picks him up and carries him back in the house. I keep telling myself over and over that he's OK now. His mama's come home and is taking care of him. Then I hear my door and Jeanie comes in. She's brought me some chicken soup. She goes on about how it's good to see me out of bed, but how she'd be more at peace in her own mind if she knew I was being taken care of properly. I don't touch the soup. I'm thinking about Wesley.

For two days I watched his house real close. At night I lay in bed listening. I never saw anyone go in or come out of the house. I never heard anything either. The Chevy stayed parked right out front. I told myself it weren't none of my business anyhow. That's what Charles always told me, "Mama, you got to keep your nose out of people's business. It ain't the same here as how you grew up."

The third morning I see a man in a suit knocking on the door. No one answers. I don't know who the man is but I know they're all home. I'm thinking, maybe it's a man from the school. Maybe he's checking on Wesley. I'm thinking, Wesley needs to be checked on. I know he does. Even if it is none of my business. But I'm scared. I'm thinking about Wesley's smile. I'm thinking about him riding his bike without the training wheels, his smile so wide, and with that black eye. How did he get that black eye? I know what I saw in the yard. A bird with a broken wing. So finally I call the police. I don't know what else to do.

A police car shows up and parks in front of Wesley's house. Two policemen get out and knock on the door. No-one answers. They start pounding on the door. They start yelling,

"Open up. It's the police." Someone lets them in. Barbara I guess. I hear all kinds of crying and shrieking come out of the house. Then two more police cars show up and I see another one down the block.

The ambulance comes. The gurney comes out of the house and the sheet's all the way up. But it's flat, almost like no one's under there. I know it's Wesley. I can't hardly breathe now and there's a pain in my chest. Barbara comes running and crying after the gurney. A policeman catches hold of her. It takes two of them to hold her back. A policewoman brings Wesley's little brother and the baby out of the house. The little boy's crying and the baby's looking around. She puts them in a police car and it drives off. The two policemen got handcuffs on Barbara now. They put her in another police car and it drives off. Another policeman comes knocking on my door to ask me questions.

Since then I stopped sleeping nights. I told Charles to sell my house. Told him I'm ready for the Sunshine Retirement home. Won't talk about why. Of course he knows. My name was in the papers and I had to be a witness at the trial. But I won't talk about it. Not with him or anyone. I'm just here, looking out on big green lawns. Charles was right. It's beautiful here. But it ain't home. And it ain't no use. I can't forget nothing.

I think about Barbara sometimes. Me boxed up in my little house looking out windows. Her boxed up in her little house with three children and tired all the time. Now she's boxed up in jail. Mostly I think about Wesley. He'll be with me till I die.

Horse Thief

My boyfriend, Sly, wants me to meet his mom. This he springs on me when we're riding the Beacon Hill bus back to my Aunt Ruthie's. Sly's mom lives on the Hill too.

"I don't know," I tell him. "Moms make me nervous." All the moms I've ever had flash through my mind. My real mom. Mama Grace, who was supposed to adopt me and didn't. This one foster mom who made us call her "Mother." At least six others. Their faces are a blur. Sly rubs his face against my cheek the way a cat rubs against your legs.

"My mom's different. She's tough, but she's cool."

This is news. A week ago she was a *bruja* for throwing him out the house and changing the locks on account of his gang-banging. As far as I'm concerned, she's no different than the rest of them. Except for one thing. She birthed Sly.

The bus groans on its way up the hill. Outside is a pretty day, the Puget Sound sparkling in sunlight. Maybe we should have gone to the waterfront instead of downtown to that tattoo parlor. But you know I appreciate the fact Sly had my name tattooed over his heart. It cost him sixty dollars. I never ask where he gets his money. I just like that he has it. I like how he leans on me now, still trying to persuade me about his mother. His lips and mustache fuzz are so soft against my face I have to turn around and kiss him.

The rest of the way we ride with Sly's hand under my shirt—his shirt really. Mine don't fit anymore and I left most of my clothes in the back of someone's car by mistake anyway. He cups my stomach, feeling for heartbeats. Sly's the one who wants this baby. Before the tattoo parlor he *made* me see a doctor. Marched me right into Harborview Hospital like he owned the place, found the right clinic, and walked up to the lady at the desk. Told her I was fifteen years old, six months pregnant, and had never seen a doctor. Now I was having funny pains. Was that normal? All of it was true except for the last bit about the pains. He made that up to make sure they'd see me right away. Mind you, by the time you finish filling out all their forms the baby's just about born and running around. What am I? this one form wants to know. I cross out American Indian and write *Indigenous*. I like to use words like that because no one expects me to know them. Then soon as I'm done with the forms, up pops some social worker with a smile, asking all about where I'm staying, and wanting to call my Aunt Ruthie right there from the hospital.

"She's at work," I explain. "She's a nurse and she works hecka long shifts." I thought that sounded good enough to get the smile off my back. Aunt Ruthie doesn't even know about this baby yet, and I don't need her finding out from some eager-beaver social worker. I hate people into my business. Next thing this lady's asking is my aunt my legal guardian? You know I told her yes. Finally I get to see the doctor. He's this preppy guy thinks he knows everything. Telling me I'm too thin, and making speeches about what I should and shouldn't eat. He was nice though. He gave me these vitamins big enough to choke on that I have to take every day. All of that makes Sly real happy, throwing up gang signs right there on the sidewalk outside the hospital. Just because we've got an estimated due date. Anyone would think he was the father.

Me and Sly hooked up at a New Year's Eve party. That's three months ago now. I like the way Sly tells it. How the place was wall-to-wall bodies, the bass cranked so high the house had a heartbeat. Sly was mostly chilling, sipping on an ice-cold *Corona*. His homeboys had hooked up with a couple of girls the moment they walked in the door, but Sly hadn't spotted anyone he liked yet. Early on he danced with a couple of *putas* in shiny little dresses, the kind that barely covered their asses and held up with spaghetti straps. Not his style, he says. He doesn't like a girl who throws it all away. But it seemed every girl there was wearing one, even the big girls with thunder thighs, their breasts rolling around like a couple of puddings. He was bored with all that. Nothing to do but watch everyone get pumped up trying to be with the person they wanted to be with. Then suddenly, there I am. On the other side of the room, propping up a wall and nursing a beer. I'm in jeans and a jacket, my collar turned up like I'm cold or something. Yeah, right! I was wearing the jacket on account of my pants zipper not zipping on account of my fat stomach on account of being pregnant. I would have been all the way bummed out if not for the beer.

But the part I like is what comes next. How most of all Sly spotted me because I had the face of an angel! That and my hair, cascading over my shoulders like some kind of waterfall. He watches me from his side of the room, trying to figure me out, whether I'm with anyone, whether I'm sad or happy. Well, I wasn't exactly laughing was I? Sly puts up his hand. He doesn't like interruptions when he's telling this. The wall-to-wall bodies are some kind of ocean, moving in waves with the music, covering and uncovering me. I slip from his sight, and then the bodies part or sway to one side, and there I am again. Until suddenly I'm not there, and he gets this sick panicky feeling and twists his head and scans the room. Presto! I'm back, on the same patch of wall, with a new beer. A *Corona*. Like he's drinking. Like that's a sign.

But Sly, being sly, bides his time. By now he's figured out I'm not going anyplace except to the bathroom if I head through the bedroom, or for more beer if I head for the kitchen. He swears one time he follows me on a beer run and stands right behind me while I reach into the cooler, close enough for him to smell the peach shampoo in my hair. I'm so out of it he says I never even notice. Finally, right before midnight, he decides it's time to make his move. The way I'm knocking back beers he wants to get to me before I'm totally messed up because he doesn't like a girl who's drunk.

Besides he *knows* it's time, with midnight moving in and the New Year waiting to be let in the door. He knew we needed something major to mark the beginning of our relationship. He means to have me in his arms and dancing right on the stroke of twelve. But then I spoil everything by heading for the bathroom again. There's already a bunch of fools yelling the countdown, so he figures "fuck it," we may as well be in the bathroom as anyplace—which I think is twisted. He follows me there, through the bedroom, which is packed as everywhere else, the coats on the bed buried under bodies grinding on more bodies. There I am, my back to him, framed in the bathroom doorway, the light blazing behind me, my blue-black hair shimmering down my back all the way to my butt.

And this is where I have to take over telling this thing, because wouldn't you know it someone had puked all over the toilet seat? I just back right out of there, automatic reverse, straight into some jokester's arms.

"I'm not gonna let you go till you promise to be mine," says this trying-to-be- sexy voice in my ear.

"Fuck you! You're crazy!" I tell whoever it is.

"Crazy 'bout you," says the voice. "I've been watching you all night." By this time it is midnight, the whole place nuts. People cheering and blowing those party blower things, the bodies on the bed bouncing up a storm.

"I want to kiss you."

"Fuck you! I don't even know who you are!"

"I want to kiss you anyway."

To this day Sly swears the little purple groove on his shin came from me twisting around and kicking, trying to make him let go of me. "Shit yeah," I say. "You deserved it!" He could tell I wanted to get a look at him though, which is true. Wanted to see the pervert that was holding me. So he turned me around, gently as is possible while holding someone in a vise grip, and brought his face close.

"Take a good look," he said. He likes to brag about how

girls have a thing about his eyes. How pretty they look with his dark skin. And they were pretty. Light colored, like moonstones.

"You're sick," I told him. But Sly says he knew by the lame way I said it his eyes had done their magic.

"Sick with love," was his answer, and let drop my arms. And maybe he did have some kind of magic because I just stood there. All around us the bump of the music and insane people screaming and crying and hugging the way they do on New Year's. I clutched my *Corona* bottle like it was some kind of staff holding me up, and Sly took my other hand and led me out of that place as if he was my own personal Moses. Outside, on the porch, he took my beer and tossed it into a bush.

"You don't need that," he said. "You're with me." Says now that at the time he had no idea what kind of a favor he was doing me *and* the baby. Then we stepped over a couple of bodies and down the front steps and into our new life. That's Sly's corny ending line. He always forgets the bit about how I had to go behind the bush to pee first.

"Things have changed around here," said Aunt Ruthie when I first showed up. I hadn't seen her in three years. I kept meaning to look her up, but you know how it is? For one she'd moved. Plus, life gets in the way. Meaning a group home, time in Canada, time in Montana, and so many people's couches and the backseats of cars I lost count. Sly's the one bugged me to find my aunt. Said she was family. We'd known one another about a week by then. "Where is she then?" I'd ask. "It's not my fault she moved." Then one day I'm up on Beacon Ave with my homegirl, Erica, when I spot my cousin Tina walking home from school. No matter what else I forget, I never forget faces. Took Tina a minute to come up with who I was though. I could see her playing connect the dots inside her head. That's okay. She was little the last time I saw her. Now she's almost as tall as I am.

"I'm your cousin Annie," I remind her.

"Oh yeah," smiles Tina. I tell Erica, "Later, girlfriend, I have to walk my little cousin home." Turned out the new house was only a couple of blocks from the old one.

"Look who I found, Mom," says Tina when we walked in the door.

Aunt Ruthie was in the kitchen, standing in front of an easel. She was fatter than I remembered. She made me think of a seal, the way seals have these real pretty heads, all sleek and smooth, and then their body fans out into a fat tube. Her kitchen table was covered with tubes of paint and jars with paintbrushes. Last time I saw her she had her nose stuck in books, studying to be a nurse. This time she's a nurse into painting. Mind you, nothing she paints really looks like what it's supposed to be, but the colors are nice. Just as well because she hangs them all over the living room. My other girl cousin, Rhonda, who's older, explained it to me. How my cousin Brad is serving time in Clallam Bay prison way out on the Peninsula for something he didn't do. The stress of running from jail to courthouse, and now all the way to the prison every other Saturday to see her son, had poor Aunt Ruthie breaking out in hives. She had to do something. According to Rhonda painting relaxes her. But she didn't look too relaxed when I showed up. If she was pleased to see me she didn't let on.

Soon as we're off the bus Sly starts walking like he's out to prove something. His rooster walk I call it. His mom's house isn't far from Aunt Ruthie's. It's different though. Out front there's a nice-looking hedge that has its leaves instead of a fence with its pickets snapped off. Aunt Ruthie hates her fence. Says it's like coming home to a mouth full of broken teeth every day. She's been on the landlord to fix it, tells him he needs to fix the toilet too. Right now you have to jiggle the handle every time you flush.

We stand on the sidewalk looking at Sly's mom's house.

Sly holds my hand. He knows I'm nervous, and he is too. I can tell, because he keeps sniffing. It's a nervous habit he has.

"Your mom that scary?" I ask. I imagine a lady with real big arms. And right then a short skinny lady pops out from behind the hedge, holding onto a pair of hedge clippers almost as big as she is.

"Hey, Mom!" says Sly. He sounds surprised. "What are you up to?"

"Massacring the hedge." She is a bit scary. She has lightning bolt eyes that flash back and forth from Sly to me and back again. The way I imagine God's eyes.

Sly's sniffing like crazy. "This is Annie I was telling you about, Mom." He tugs on my arm. What does he want me to do? Put it up and wave it around like I'm in school and got the right answer? I wonder what he's told her. His mom puts down the shears and stands with her hands on her hips, as if somehow that will make her look bigger. But without the shears she looks smaller. She's wearing blue jeans and a T-shirt, and work gloves. She's okay I guess.

"Well, well, well," she says. She's smiling now, except it's the kind of smile that makes me think she wants to laugh. I hope it isn't me she finds funny. "Hello, Annie," she says, and pulls off one of her gloves to shake my hand. "I'm Maria."

I don't care much for introductions, they make me feel as if everything that's wrong with me is what gets noticed. Right off I wish I were wearing different clothes. This lady probably recognizes Sly's shirt. But I'm cool. "Pleased to meet you," I say.

Sly clears his throat as if he's about to make a speech, and then does, right there on the sidewalk. Telling his mom how much he loves me and that I'm going to have a baby. Then tells her the due date. I have never been so embarrassed in my life.

"Oh?" she says, and her eyes get round and her eyebrows go up.

So I explain, real quick, that it's not Sly's baby. Just in case she thinks Sly got me pregnant and is mad with him about it on top of everything else she's already mad with him about.

"Oh?" she says again. And then Sly butts in again and tells her he really wants the baby anyway, no matter whose it is, and as far as he's concerned he *is* the father because he plans on taking care of it.

"Oh?"

This lady's eyebrows cannot possibly go any higher. I just wish she'd say something else. She still looks like she might laugh, except now I can tell it is Sly she finds funny. I can't say I blame her. Standing there trying to explain himself he looks puffed up and shriveled at the same time.

"So, Joshua, you bringing Annie in or what?"

Joshua! So that's his real name! I nod like crazy. "Please, Joshua, please." He knows I'm clowning him.

Inside the house there are photos in frames all over, mostly over the fireplace and on top of the TV. I wonder what it must be like to come home and see a picture of yourself in a frame. There's pictures of Sly when he was little, his sister and his dad too. His dad is dead I know, but I didn't know he was a black man. He looks nice holding his children on his knee. This place is a cross between a greenhouse, a gift shop, and the library. Everywhere I look plants hang down or spring up. And there's all kind of baskets and shells, and little statue things sitting on shelves and standing in corners and on top of the coffee table. But best of all is shelves and shelves of books. Aunt Ruthie has some books, nursing books mostly, but she keeps them in her room. I've always wanted to live in a house with books. I don't mean to be rude, but I can't stop looking at things, scanning the shelves, trying to see what's there.

"Annie's like you, Mom," Sly explains. "Reading every

chance she gets. She's been reading to me from library books. Trying to convert me." Sly hates books. Says he's street smart and book dumb. "I tell her she better come up with something better than fairy tales. Except even they don't sound so bad when she reads them."

He is too clever, which is why his name is Sly. Sly as in fox, he told me, the trickster who knows how to survive. He's laying it on thick for his mom, this business about me and books. And sure enough, she's beaming. I feel silly. It's not like I even go to school anymore.

"I used to have a library card," I say, for something to say. "Except I goofed up and lost a bunch of books by mistake. Now I owe so much I can't use it anymore."

"Well browse around," she says. "Maybe there's something of mine you want to borrow. As long as you bring it back. I don't charge late fees, but I do want it back."

Says for me to take my time, she'll be in the kitchen whenever I'm done, and do I like peach cobbler? She flashes me a pretty smile and drags Sly off to show him something. I can tell she's easing up on him a bit though by the way she calls him Josh instead of Joshua.

I can't believe she's left me alone. Every time I got to a new foster home the foster mom hawked me like I was there to rip her off. And no matter how long I was there they never wanted to let me out of their sight. Except for this one place where the mom let me out her sight *all* the time. With her son. That boy was way bigger than me. He'd push me down onto the floor when we're supposed to be watching TV, bend my arms back over my head and push his disgusting stinky thing in my mouth. But try and tell someone something about their own son and they slap you stupid and call you liar.

Now I'm alone with this lady's things and I only just met her.

I find a copy of *Wuthering Heights* and start flipping through. I saw the movie one time, one of those old black and white movies. I like those the best. Then I hear Sly getting into it with his mom, him telling her she doesn't understand, and her saying she's got his sister to think about, and she can't have the house torn apart. Plus he needs to be in school. I'm thinking Sly needs to chill, but it's not my business, so I keep looking at books. I leave out of there happy, with two books and a stomach full of cobbler and ice cream. Sly's pouting. Turns out he missed some court date. I tell him I agree with his mom on that one: he shouldn't have been tagging in the first place. Mostly I feel so good I can't care about him too much just now.

Aunt Ruthie had it in for Sly right from the get-go. At least take off your hairnet I warned him the first time I took him over there. That was right after I found out where she lived and she said I could stay. But Sly says if people can't relate to him for who he is that's their problem. The way things turn out it seems most of the time it's *his* problem. People like my aunt, she looks at his tattoos and baggy pants and hairnet, and no one can tell her it's just a style.

"*Life*-style," is her come back. "And rule number one, I don't want it—or him—in my house."

Aunt Ruthie has a bunch of rules. Curfew. Clean-up. School. Five-minute showers. Hello, Auntie. We live in Seattle. It's not like we're going to run out of water. Her main thing is she doesn't want me lazing around the house in front of the TV all day. To make her point she's put a sign over her couch that reads, *This Is Not A Flophouse.* But tell me how I'm supposed to register for school when I don't even have any transcripts? Auntie says she's taking a day off work to sort things out, but she hasn't got around to it yet. Meanwhile, Sly's not allowed in, and I'm not allowed out past ten p.m. Meanwhile we spend a lot of time on her couch while she's at work and my cousins are in school. Mostly we leave the TV off though.

To begin with, I didn't tell Sly I was having a baby. Better to let him think I'm fat, was how my mind figured. I knew if he knew he'd leave me. I tried not to eat. And because Sly didn't want me to, I didn't drink. He has this thing about girls and alcohol. So at first I was getting thinner. I hoped the baby had died. But then it got so there was a butterfly in my insides. Not the kind of butterflies you get from shoplifting. This one fluttered about like it was the first day of spring, and then nothing. Just folded its wings and sat on a flower. I knew it was the baby.

The day I told him we were butt naked under a blanket on Aunt Ruthie's couch, my stomach hard and round as half a basketball, the butterfly doing its thing. I figured he'd have to know sooner or later. So I just blurted out that I was pregnant, but it wasn't his, and waited for him to hit me. Instead, he cried. Big splashy tears and a noise that made me think of rusty pipes. He turned away and buried his face in Auntie's cushion. I didn't know what to do so I stroked his hair. Without gel it was silky and not quite black. When he asked me "whose then?" I told him I don't know. And because I was thinking about the man in the alley with the yellow hair, and hoping this baby doesn't have yellow hair, I also told him about the man in the alley and what he did to me. All of it made him cry more. Then he said he needed a cigarette. He pulled on his pants and sat on the edge of the couch for a minute with his head in his hands. Talk about thin: the knobs on Sly's spine stand out like a mountain range. Then he went outside to smoke. Just about the first thing Aunt Ruthie does when she walks in the door is sniff around for cigarette smoke. I thought, for sure that was the last I'd ever see of him. But five minutes later he was back. He told me a story.

"When I was a little kid I had a dog," he said. "I loved that dog more than anything. My mom let me take her to bed with me. Not just on the floor, or on top of the bed, but all the way under the covers, curled up in my arm, her head on the pillow."

"That's sick," I said. "What kind of a dog anyway?"

"A little brown mutt with a feathery tail. She hated baths. One day she'd just had a bath and was doing that crazy thing dogs do, shaking the water off, bucking and running circles she's so happy it's over with. Right then my sister comes in the house with a whole string of her friends. My dog wasn't named Lightning for nothing. She bolts out the open door and under the wheels of a car that just happened to be passing. All before I could even call her name.

"My mom's got this theory." He sniffed a couple of times. "She says all my love for my dad I poured into that dog, and when I lost the dog it was like I lost my dad all over again. My mom's full of bullshit theories." He got this look on his face like he might cry again. "I guess I really want this baby, Annie."

I still don't know why he told me all that. "You're twisted!" I told him, and gave him a smack. "You trying to say my baby's a dog?"

But Sly's full of surprises "What's your Aunt Ruthie got in her kitchen?"

He didn't wait for me to answer, and just headed in there. I heard him opening the fridge and cabinets. "Get some clothes on," he called out to me. "I'm fixing you eggs. You got to eat."

He made me eggs with cheese and onions, toast on the side, and then sat and watched while I ate. I've never had anyone love me before. But eating those eggs I figured I knew what it felt like. Then Aunt Ruthie came home unexpected, and found a half-naked Sly in her kitchen. She flipped. He wasn't allowed to explain anything, not allowed to wash the pan, not allowed to even put on his shirt and shoes. He was O.T.D. as in Out the Door.

"I was just trying to take care of Annie," he called back.

I didn't say a word. Turned out Auntie was home early because she was taking me to the dentist, and I forgot.

"Why do you hang with all Mexicans if you're not Mexican?" I ask Sly.

We've just finished making up, which with us is pretty much the same as making out. We're down here on the waterfront because it's Aunt Ruthie's day off, and Spookie's place is strictly off limits, seeing as he's the one dragged us into a fight in the first place. Sly's throwing his French fries for seagulls. I've already eaten mine. What I really want is a beer.

"Who should I hang with?" he wants to know. He's got this hang-up because he's so mixed. His dad was black and Jewish, his mom's Gypsy and Welsh. He calls himself a Four-Way. "There are no gangs for Four-Ways, you know. It's all about one way. What did you think I was anyway?"

"Mexican," I say. I don't really, but I know that's what he wants me to say.

"My point precisely."

"But you're not."

"I am now."

"You're with me now, so maybe you should grow your hair long and be Indian."

"Maybe I will."

But the tattoo on his neck still claims *United Latinos*. So does everything else about the way he looks. And soon as Sly gets with his homeboys he changes on me. For one he drinks. I can't drink, but it's okay for him. Last night at Spookie's he was drinking like he'd just come out of ten days in the desert. Or rehab. Plus I didn't care for the meeting that was going on. *Retribution* was their word of the hour. I wouldn't have been there, except I'd already missed Auntie's curfew again and figured I may as well stay gone. It was just my luck that something had to come down. I know Auntie's going to ask me about it too. It was all over the TV news this morning, and the newspaper. *More Gang Violence* the headline reads.

"This meeting is man's business, baby," Sly had the nerve to tell me. His eyes were glittering, partly from the beer and partly because he'd been pumped up from the moment Loco showed up with the news about Soldado getting stabbed.

"Man as in *Macho*," I told him. He acts like I'm not supposed to know what's going down or what the word retribution means. But it's okay for Dolores to speak up, put her two cents in. So she's Spookie's main squeeze. Which bothers me right there, because Sly doesn't need to be hanging with anyone who runs with different girls. The problem with Spookie is he thinks he is somebody. So what is Sly then? He's the one with the brain, and I'm his woman, so why can't I speak? You know I said what I had to say anyway. That Sly does not need to be going wherever they're going, and for sure he doesn't need no gun strapped to his ankle, because what do the Asian Bloods have to do with us?

Can you believe Spookie tried to get between me and Sly? Tells Sly, "Keep your woman in line, brother. She's got a big mouth." Sly needed to know better than to let anyone talk to me that way because *no one* keeps me in line. Plus that Dolores with her titties hiked all the way up to her ugly face, well she needed to keep her eyes to herself. Standing there with her beer and giving me the evil eye. What was I supposed to do? Yes, I went off. Then Sly leaving out of there with the rest of them, me stuck behind with Dolores and a whole bunch of empties.

"Don't tell me what happened," I told Sly I don't know how many hours later, when he tried to get under the blanket with me on Spook's couch. By then he's sorry. It's Annie, Annie baby, there's nothing to worry about because he's never going to put himself in harm's way, not with me and the little one to think about. I had to keep slapping his hand away, him trying to put it over my stomach to check on the baby to see if it was sleeping or what. Didn't the fool know *I* was sleeping? Oh come on, Annie, he says, he just needed to cover his homies' backs was all. I understood, didn't I? They look out for him, it's only right he look out for them.

I didn't all the way forgive him though till we came down here and he bought me this I.D. bracelet and paid to have *Sly loves Annie* engraved on it. But now he's showing off again. He's run out of fries so he's showing the gulls his knife. What are they supposed to do? Freak?

"Leave the birds alone, Sly!"

He tests the blade for sharpness on his fingertip. First a sudden line of red, and then drops of blood. I grab his finger and suck, making like it's something else I'm sucking.

I have been super-careful not to lose Sly's mom's books. I ring her doorbell and wait. His sister opens the door. Sofi. I know her face from the pictures in the living room and Sly told me her name. I don't like the way she looks at me though. I hold out the two books.

"I brought these back," I say.

You'd think she'd never seen a book before. I clarify.

"They belong to your mom."

Would you believe she closes the door almost all the way in my face?

"Mom!" I hear her yell. "Josh's girlfriend is here to see you!"

All of which is extremely rude. But seeing as she *is* Sly's sister, and seeing as her mother is cool, I leave the door the way it is and do not disrespect her back.

Things feel better when the door opens again and her mom stands there.

"Annie," she says. "Wonderful to see you. Come in."

This lady likes me. Right off she offers me tea and more books. I don't usually drink tea, but she's got tea with interesting names like *Mango Peach* and *Ginger Snap* and *Licorice Spice*. Whoever heard of tea made out of licorice? Myself I like Red Vines not licorice, but I'm up for trying something new. Her daughter's banging around the kitchen at first, on my account I guess, trying to check me out.

"So where's my brother?" she asks after a bit.

"Filling out job applications." I flash my best smile. This answer I know his mother will like. It also happens to be the truth, so I really don't appreciate it when his sister decides to get smart.

"Did you hear that, Mom? My brother working! *Where?*" I'm not the least bothered when she finally leaves.

Sly's mom wants to know about my new school. I sip my tea, wondering does Sly tell her everything. I explain that it's not a real school, just some catch-up place at the YMCA with half a dozen kids and some beat up desks. It's only for half a day.

"I hated school when I was your age," she says. "Now I'm glad I stuck with it. Goodness knows life's hard enough." She hops up to refill the kettle, and suddenly the name "Mama Shorty" comes to me. It fits her just right. For one, she's shorter than me, plus she's Sly's mom which means she's almost my mama too. She keeps telling me all the trouble she got into in school, but the important thing was she read books, and how wonderful that I'm a reader too. Watching her, there's something that makes me think of a big person stuffed into a little body. I like the way her hands move when she talks, and how the bracelets she wears jingle up and down her arms. She doesn't seem old, even though up close she's got all kinds of gray in her hair.

We drink more tea, Mango Peach this time, and I start telling her things about me, and don't even mind because she tells me about herself too. What I can't stand is when shrinks want to know me from A to Z, while they just sit clammed up in their chair. Mama Shorty—I'm not ready to call that to her face yet, but the name's still rolling around inside my head—gets the atlas off her shelf to show me London on the map, which is where she grew up. When I ask her how come she doesn't talk funny, she says it's because she's been here so long. Then she flips the pages and shows me some place called Hungary, which is where Sly's grandma came from. She was the Gypsy part of his Four-Way.

"Hungry!" I say. "Sounds like where I should be living. These days I'm hungry all the time!" Right away I realize I shouldn't have said that because now she'll think I'm scavenging for food.

"Hun-*gary*, Annie, not hun*gry*," she says, and laughs, but not in a way that makes me feel stupid. Just a friendly kind of laugh I can join in. By this time we're both of us on the floor in the living room with the atlas spread out between us. Then, naturally, she offers me lunch, and before I can say no, it's back to the kitchen, where she whips something out the fridge and heats it up. Pretty soon we're talking our way through chicken stir-fry with vegetables. I don't even pick out the broccoli.

"You must have been the one who showed Sly…I mean Josh…to cook, huh?"

"Josh cooks? Where?"

"All the time, over my Auntie's house. When she's at work. She doesn't mind." The last part isn't totally a lie. What Aunt Ruthie doesn't know she can't mind.

I don't know what makes me think about my buddy Charlie as in Charlie Horse. The best horse ever. He does this. Just pops up out of nowhere, when I'm thinking about something else. It's like there's a part of me always trying to get back to that moment when he jumped with me on his back, and suddenly it's him and me flying over the gate again. There's not much in my life I want to live over. Mostly I try and forget things.

"Would you believe I stole a horse one time?" I ask now, and Mama's eyes get round, and she says "oh?"—just like the first time I met her.

"For real. It says horse thief on my record. Says I stole someone's prize show jumper, though technically speaking I only *borrowed* it. I explained to the cops. How could I be stealing when I left it in the same field I found it in? Or the next-door field anyway. But you know how cops are."

Mama laughs then, and wants to know where was I? Where were all these fields and horses? I tell her the whole thing.

"Okay. I was living in some group home, right? I told my caseworker it was not a good placement for me, because he knows how much I hate restriction, but he tried to tell me there was no place else left to take me. To this day I still don't know where that place is. Somewhere way past Tacoma, miles from anywhere, nothing but flat fields and Mount Rainier rising up out of nothing in the background. I tell you, Charlie was my only way out of there."

"Charlie?"

"The horse. Because those little country roads take forever with hardly anything on them but tractors and milk trucks, so how else was I going to make it to the main highway? It was fun climbing out the window, you know, with sheets. How they tie them together in the movies? And it was easy getting over the wall and into the field where I knew the horse lived. The problem was, it was still real early, everyone sleeping, and way dark out. So I couldn't see the horse at first, just hear it. Munching grass. I stood in the corner of the field, calling "Here horsey, here horsey," kind of whisper calling because I didn't want to wake anyone up. Then my eyes started to adjust and I saw him, just a little ways away from me, a big ol' horse. Except at first he just kept right on ignoring me, munching and munching his grass. And wouldn't you know it? When I tried to go over to where he was, he just moves off. 'Ah, come on, horsey,' I say. I hadn't got around to calling him Charlie yet, that comes in a minute. But I was getting paranoid that any second lights would start flicking on in the house and someone would notice I was gone. Because let me tell you, in that group home they didn't wait for no damn roosters to start rising and shining, and already there was this little line of pink creeping into the sky. So I explained my situation. 'Please, please, Mr. Horse, I really need out of this place, please, pretty please.'

"Wouldn't you know it, that horse stopped eating and listened? Lifted his head and looked right at me. I could see good by then, and dang, he was big. Huge! And that's when I named him Charlie because it seemed more friendly than plain ol' Mr. Horse. It was a sort of a joke though. You know…Charlie as in Charlie horse when your leg cramps up. I probably should have called him Pumpkin or Marmalade or something because he was orange, but Charlie's the name that came to me. Anyway, I guess he liked it because as soon as I called him by it he trotted right over. Be funny, wouldn't it, if Charlie was his real name?

"Getting on his back wasn't so easy, mind you. It took running and jumping and grabbing his mane, all at the same time, and as soon as I was on, he took off. Dang he was fast! It was all I could do to stay on I was laughing so much. Plus he was slippery. It's not like I had a saddle or anything. But then I sort of got the hang of things, and lay down along his neck and held onto his mane. Lucky for me, he was headed in the right direction because I sure didn't know how to steer. Then, suddenly, there was a gate…right smack in front of us…and this is the good part. He flew! I didn't know horses could fly. But Charlie flew. I swear he flew! Maybe he sprouted wings or something, like one of those Pegasus horses. It felt like I was in the air forever, the gate way down under me, and all around a pink light filling the sky and the air cool and fresh on my face. It was the best time of my whole life. Then the cops came along and spoiled it. Said I *stole* the damn horse."

"So what happened?" Mama wants to know.

"Oh, the judge made me do a bunch of community service." Actually, I don't really remember what happened after. But it was probably something like that.

It's a week or two later when Aunt Ruthie corners me.

"So when were you planning on telling me?" she wants to know.

She doesn't say it right off, soon as I get in. She waits while I stick my head in the fridge and rummage around for something to eat. As usual, she's at her easel. All she wears these days is nursing scrubs. Her good ones she wears to work, and then soon as she gets home she changes into old ones to paint in. Mostly she hums when she paints, though every once in a while she cusses. So I know something is up when I walk in and she's completely quiet. No "Hi, Annie." No "What have you been up to?" No hums.

I feel her eyes hawking me while I make a peanut butter and jelly sandwich, and soon as I'm done she tells me to put the food back in the fridge. To Aunt Ruthie cleaning up means *before* you sit down to eat. She'd have you wash the plate before you use it if she could. But I know what's going on is more than that, especially when I make a beeline for the living room and she tells me no, get back here, and puts down her paintbrush and folds her arms. I sit at the table: the little bit of it not taken over by her paints and brushes and jars of stinky cleaner. Plus now there's some big box dumped down in the middle of everything. I chew on my sandwich with Auntie watching me and try to figure what I've done wrong. I'm thinking broken curfew, too many phone calls, dirty laundry on the bathroom floor. The box reads, *Pampers Disposable Diapers: Newborns: 96 count.* But the meaning of a box of *Pampers* is totally over my head. Maybe it isn't even me, I think. Maybe something's up with Brad. Maybe he got turned down for parole. Then Aunt Ruthie zaps me with her *when was I planning on telling her?* line.

Of course, right away I know what she means, but I play innocent. It's instinct. I do the same thing with the cops. "Tell you what?" I say, and lick peanut butter off my fingers. I should have known Ms. Eager Beaver Social Worker would catch up with me sooner or later. Suddenly, more than anything, I want to get smart-mouthed before Auntie can say another word. It's standard practice in situations like this. Whenever it feels like things are getting out of control, or might get out of control. Or if it seems like I'm about to find myself out the door of wherever is home at that particular time, or lose what little bit I have all over again. Or if I *know* someone's already made up their mind about me, and everything I've done wrong and what a mess-up I am, then I figure I may as well help the whole situation along. Blow the whole thing sky high and get it all over with. Smart mouth sentences just make themselves up, the words tumbling out before I even have time to even think. This time it's, *Oh, I thought you knew. It's obvious isn't it?* To be followed by a shrug and another bite of my sandwich. Except this time the words won't say themselves and instead I'm crying.

Aunt Ruthie sits beside me and puts an arm around me.

"I had Brad when I was your age," she says. "It's not the end of the world. It changes your life, but it's not the end of the world." She gets up and goes to the sink, tears me off a piece of paper towel and sits back down. I blow my nose.

"I never thought I'd have anything good to say about your no-good boyfriend, but at least he's thinking straight." I look at her. I haven't a clue what she's talking about.

"How do you think I found out?" she asks. "He came by. With those," nodding toward the *Pampers*. "He's worried about you, he said. Said he thought you hadn't told me yet and I should know—which I should—to make sure you eat right, and take care of yourself. Said he'd already taken you to the doctor's and the baby's due in June. He bought the *Pampers* because it seemed like it was never too soon to be prepared. Says a friend of his mom's has a bassinet you can use."

I can't read Auntie. She doesn't seem upset. I'm laughing and crying, and there's snot in my throat. Sly actually came by and talked to her?

"What is this? A conspiracy?"

Aunt Ruthie snorts. "Oh yeah, between me and your little gang-banger boyfriend? I don't think so. Though maybe it's going to take one to take care of you. Oh...and Annie. There is one other thing. He mentioned in passing that he's not the father."

"So? He says he wants to be."

Aunt Ruthie's hand feels good on the back of my neck. "Yes, I have to hand it to him. He did say that too." She shakes her head and sighs, like she can't quite believe any of this is happening. I try to imagine how Sly must have looked standing on her porch. Whether he was sunk down into himself doing his humble routine, or whether he looked her straight in the eye.

"Just tell me one thing, Auntie."

"What's that?"

"Was Sly wearing his hairnet?"

She screws up her face trying to remember.

"No, come to think of it, I don't think he was."

We're huddled on the top bleacher at the University of Washington spring pow-wow. My belly's so big it's all I can do to button Sly's shirt. The butterfly turned into an acrobat sometime back and right now it's doing flips. I wish it would quit. The M.C. finishes commending someone named Joe Running-Deer Williams for another year of sobriety, and I lick my lips thinking about the sips I took off Dolores' beer last night. My first taste in months, and oh so sweet. Down in the arena the jingle dancers are up, ages thirteen through seventeen, my category.

"I was a jingle dancer once," I tell Sly. "I placed second one time."

"The prettiest jingle dancer ever," he says, and cat rubs my cheek with his, then slides his hand onto my belly to feel "Junior" move. It bugs me the way he calls my baby Junior, like it's a boy, and his son at that.

I like the girl in blue, number 419. My jingle dress was blue. Who made it for me? I try to remember. Some foster mom, one of the nice ones, Indian for sure…The drumming starts up, and so do the dancers. I watch their moves closely. I still like the girl in blue, but the pink girl has the better moves. How old was I when I danced, the year I came in second? Nine maybe…I liked the sound the jingles make. Wearing them is your own music when you dance. Even up here, above the sound of the drums, I can hear their tinkling.

I'm half watching the dancers, half panning the crowd when I spot my homegirl. I jump up. "Hey, Erica!" I wave. And suddenly there's the horse again, Charlie, and a flutter of that feeling from when we flew over the gate. Like a kite pulling at its string. Right away Sly pulls me back down and wraps his arms around me. "Forget her, we're together, baby," he says, and the flutter stops, and the kite falls out of the sky. When I look again, Erica's disappeared.

The dancers are still dancing, though I can tell by the drums they're about to finish. I wiggle free from Sly's grip and stretch my arms over my head. I'm ready to eat, to move. The baby gives an enormous kick. It feels as if its got boots on. The way I see it, it's got me prisoner from the inside. I can't get Charlie out of my head.

"Did I ever tell you about the horse I stole?" I ask Sly.

"Huh?" he says. He's rubbing his face against me again, but not listening. The dance ends, and the M.C. calls for a break. Climbing down from the bleachers to get something to eat I look for Erica again, or someone else I know. Sly reaches for my hand, and I imagine myself giving him a tug, the two of us leaping to the bottom, our big shirts filling with air like parachutes. Except I know with my belly I'd crash like a stone. Soon as we reach the main floor we plunge into the crowd, hands laced together, heading toward the Indian tacos, toward the smell of the fry bread.

Tree

Crooked trunk
growing from a stump
twists around
on a crooked spine.
Its cracked brown skin
soaks sun and rain
and its branches
beg the sky.
Sometimes they shake
free in the wind.

Jenkins came early, before breakfast, to tell me I had a phone call. I knew right then the kids weren't coming. I still had rollers in my hair because I always try and fix myself a bit when they come. My eldest, Sandra, was on the phone. We're sorry, Mom, but the car broke down. Right then I started crying. I cried all the way through talking to the little ones. The way things have turned out Sandra is mommy to Margie and Danny more than I ever got to be. I'm thankful the judge didn't pack them off with strangers, thankful Sandra's old enough to care for them. But I never planned on being anything but a mom to every one of my kids. Besides, Sandra has her own life too, has her own two babies to take care of. This morning, Elisa wouldn't talk to me at all, and Luis and Jaime weren't even there. They'd been running the streets again, Sandra said, getting more than Uncle Ramon could handle or wanted to handle. I wasn't sure what to say. Not with her sounding so worn down and Jenkins right there, jangling her keys and looking at her watch to make sure I didn't go over my five minutes. In the end I just asked Sandra what was wrong with the car. She said the head gasket had blown and she didn't know where the money would come from to fix it. By then my five minutes were up, and Jenkins marched me back to the housing unit. I cried the whole way, knowing it's going to be at least a month till the next time they can visit. It's a long drive from Yakima.

I never smoked in my life till I came here. I took up smoking to sit out in the quad. It's a chance to get out. Smokers get to sit on the benches along the wall where there's an overhang, so even if it rains you don't get wet. I blow smoke and sit there with the rest, listening to them talk. I'm not one to talk much. If there's too many on a bench, or sitting too close, or talking too loud, the guards split us up. Sitting out there, I try not to see the fences or razor wire or guards. I just look around at the green things. The tops of pine and spruce all along the north side of the fence, the bushes round the edges of the quad. I pretend I'm in a park. In the middle of the quad there's a tree that's not supposed to be there. Someone tried to cut it down, but now it's growing again out of the stump. For five years I've watched that tree instead of my kids. It was a little thing at first, now it's getting to be a real tree. Reminds me of my Jaime. He was born with a crooked spine but kept right on growing anyway. He's got one shoulder higher than the other, and he can't run good. But he can do other things.

Sometimes I wonder how tall that tree will be when I get out. *If* I get out. Everybody says a life sentence don't mean life. My roommate TK says that. I tell her it depends on how old you are when you get here, and what kind of shape you're in. I'm not young anymore and I've got diabetes. My mother was diabetic. She was only fifty-two when she died.

Soon as she got me inside the door, Jenkins ordered a room search. She didn't like TK's attitude. All TK was doing was lying on the bed with her arms behind her head. But right away Jenkins called for back up.

"What the fuck," said TK. "You want me to jump to attention and salute you the moment you walk in here?"

TK's different from me. For one, this place doesn't faze her. For two, she's young. And skinny. She wears a nose ring and has pretty pale red hair, and is just about the palest person I ever saw. Poetry's her thing. Everytime I turn around she's writing poems in her notebook. She's also a Wiccan, which is some kind of religion having to do with witches and means she doesn't believe in God. That scares me. But at least she's kind, most of the time. Sometimes she says things about Christians, especially Catholics, and teases me about the picture of the Sacred Heart of Mary I keep on my nightstand. She says it looks like an advertisement for open-heart surgery. I call her my roommate and not my cellmate because it makes this place sound livable. Besides, we're in these buildings that are kind of like long cabins divided into different rooms. They're not cells. There's no bars and there's even little windows. But we're still locked up.

This is only the second place in my life I ever remember living. In Yakima, I was always in my mother's house. First it was her house, and then when she died it was my husband's house. My mother meant for it to be mine, but Ray wasn't comfortable with that, so I signed it over to him. I dream about that house sometimes. When I was a kid I'd sit on my front steps with other kids from up and down the block, all of us eating apples from the tree that grew next to the walk. Though mostly I remember these little girls from across the street, and they're the ones show up in my dreams, and I'm braiding their hair, and we're eating apples big as beach balls. Then one day it got to be my kids on the steps, and I was inside the house, in the kitchen. Now I'm in this place.

Sometimes I feel like I can't get through another day here. I felt that way this morning, sitting on my bed and bawling while Jenkins waited for backup. I cried all the way through her and some rookie girl rummaging through our stuff. Soon as they left, TK came and sat down next to me and put her arm around me. It's funny. She's only twenty-two, which is six years younger than Sandra, but sometimes it feels like she's as old as me. First she handed me a tissue, then she sighed.

"Guess your not gonna see your kids today after all, huh?"

I shook my head, and she gave me a squeeze. Usually no one wants to touch me because I'm ugly, and I know I looked a sight by then with my face swoll up and my nose running. But everyone needs comfort sometimes, and this morning TK's arm felt good across my shoulders. It's a funny thing in here. Touching. There's not supposed to be any, even though a lot of girls turn lesbian after they've been here a while. Most of them go back to being straight as soon as they're out. But in here it's lonely. TK was moved in with me to get her away from another girl. I know TK would rather be back with Patty than stuck here with me. She and Patty got real close. I see them sometimes, sitting together on the smoker's bench. If they think the guard's not looking they let their fingers touch. Just for a second. I think it's wicked to split them up, even if the Bible says what they were doing isn't right. They weren't hurting anyone.

After a bit TK says, "Your kids won't forget you, Hills. Kids don't forget." I knew she was thinking about her mom. TK doesn't know where her mom is. She hasn't seen her since she was twelve. "Your kids are lucky, Hills, having a mom like you."

That made me laugh, even though I wasn't all the way through with crying. "Oh?" I looked at her. "My kids are lucky to have a mom who's a murderer?"

She stuck her lips out and stared off at the opposite wall. Her pale red hair hung down around her face. "Your kids are lucky to have a mom who loves them so much she'd kill rather than let anyone hurt them."

I didn't say anything. I was thinking how he'd hurt them

plenty of times. Ray. Their father and my husband. He hurt all of us.

"I'm never getting married," said TK. Like she knew what I was thinking.

Suddenly she was on her feet in front of me, clapping her hands and jumping up and down like a little kid. Much younger than Sandra. Sandra never jumps. She's big and slow already. Like me. But TK's skinny and light. So skinny she's hungry looking.

"OK! So your kids aren't coming today. Come to the workshop instead."

"No way, TK," I say. "What am I gonna do in a workshop?"

"Write," she says.

"I don't know nothing about writing," I say. "You're the poet."

TK grabbed my hands and tugged, the way Elisa used to do when she really wanted something. "Come on Hills. It'll do you good."

My name's Hilda. Hilda Hernández. But everybody in here calls me Hills because of my shape. I'm big. Lumpy and *shapeless*, my husband used to tell me.

"Besides, you know plenty about sitting," TK went on. She's like Elisa in that way too. She knows how to talk somebody into something. "You can just come and sit. You don't *have* to do anything. But we talk some shit in there. It's fun." She was still tugging at me when I looked down and saw the pale scars along the insides of her wrists. I'd seen them before, but this morning they made me want to do something to please her.

"Okay," I said. "Long as I don't have to do nothing."

A face like mine was a sin, Ray used to say. He must have been drunk when he married me. According to Ray I was a plastic surgeon's dream. Funny thing is though, half my kids look like me. Except on them it looks cute. I studied myself in the mirror one time to see if I could see in my face what I see in theirs. They don't have lines and scars or front teeth missing. Sandra's twenty-eight and Margie, my baby, is eight. Maybe I was cute once but I'm forty-five now and I don't need anyone to tell me I look older. Jesus loves you for what's on the inside, was what I used to tell myself. That's before I killed Ray. Now there's times I'm not so sure Jesus loves anything about me.

The hardest thing to get used to here is the showers. The way those shower doors are, huge gaps top, bottom and both sides. You have to stand directly in front of the door, out of the reach of the water spray in order to be covered. Nobody ever saw me without my clothes before. Even with the doctor there was always a sheet. In here there's male officers, in our unit. Knock, knock, they say. Staff entering. Male staff. Then they walk right into the shower room, stooping to look all the way under them doors, laughing, making faces. All in the name of a leg count. Sometimes when they laugh, I swear I hear Ray laughing too.

The loudspeaker announced breakfast, and I could feel TK watching me while I cleaned myself up a bit. I didn't want everyone to see I'd been crying. I splashed cold water on my face, patted it dry, and took the rollers out my hair. I had the comb in my hand when she came up behind me and took it and combed my hair for me. She's never done anything like that before. When she was done she picked up my spray can and gave my hair a little spray.

"You'll do," she said, which nearly started me off again because my mother used to say that to me, and I used to say it to my kids. But then the rookie came by and unlocked the door.

"S'posing they don't let me in?" I asked TK on the way to the cafeteria.

"We'll work it out," she said. "They know your visit with

158

your kids is off. The workshop's open to whoever wants to go. Pending good behavior. And you're Miss Perfect."

"But you're supposed to sign up in advance."

"This is advance. We haven't even had breakfast yet."

TK knows how to get what she wants. Before she was moved into my room they told me that she was manipulative. That's the word they used. If it had been me asking about the workshop by myself I would have been put off. I've always been put off. Used to be I'd tell Ray I'd leave him. Was gonna take the kids and go. He always talked me out of it. One time I got as far as packing but he convinced me I'd end up homeless and the state would take the kids away. But he'd always take care of me, he said. His kids too. Why did I think he worked so hard? Mowing lawns, trimming hedges, fixing fences. I couldn't argue any of that. He had his own truck by then, with his name on the side.

Sandra didn't have the time of day for Ray. She was nine years old when I met him, ten when Luis was born. By the time things got really bad she was already a teenager. So she left. I didn't know where she was for a while. I used to worry. What if I did leave with the other kids and she came home and I wasn't there? As it turned out, she never went far. Never left Yakima. She started coming by when Ray wasn't around, started helping me with the little ones. She just wanted to stay out of Ray's reach.

Maybe if I'd learned to speak up more, stand up for myself, things would have turned out different. But then, TK does speak up and she's in this place too. It's all the same to her, she says. Life is shit wherever she is. She looked pleased when she got it sorted out for me to go to the workshop though.

"Told you," she said.

Guards were all over. Saturday morning everybody's coming and going to different classes and programs. Mostly Bible classes, parenting, or cooking. To make us into good

Christian mothers, TK says. Like you already are, Hills. The poetry workshop's different. Creative Expressions it's called. According to TK it's therapeutic, meaning it's supposed to calm people down. That's why they allow it. Half the people in this place are bipolar. TK is. Everybody here's on medication for something. If you're not an addict when you get here, you will be when you leave. That's what people say.

On the way to the workshop, TK walked with quick little steps and I had to ask her to slow down. My legs hurt. They do sometimes, from the diabetes. TK had her poetry notebook hugged to her chest, and I don't care what she says, or how she feels about life, this morning she looked happy. Pretty too, with her red hair blowing back from her face and glinting in the sun. Then half way across the quad we passed my tree, its branches moving back and forth in what little breeze there was, its bark a warm red with the sun on it. I wished I didn't have to go anywhere at all and could sit out all morning just looking at it and feeling the air. By the time we reached C building, where classes are held, I wished TK had never talked me into going. The only class I've taken since I've been here is a Bible class. TK says she'll check out anything *but* a Bible class. She took an Alternative to Violence class one time and came back disappointed. She thought it was just called Alternative Violence.

This morning she marched into that classroom ahead of me with her hair tossed back over her shoulders. Inside, long tables and chairs were set up in a sort of circle around the room. Six or so people were already sitting. One of them was Patty. Her eyes shone when she saw TK. But TK marched right past her and up to a short blonde woman who four or five other people were crowded round, all of them trying to talk to her at once.

"Uh oh," I heard someone say. "TK's on a mission."

"Hi, Bev," TK said to the blonde woman. "This is Hills. She rooms with me."

Then she ditched me and went to sit with Patty. Bev said

something about being glad I was there, but I only half heard her because I felt as if everyone was looking at me and more than anything I wanted to sit down and not be noticed. If there had been a back row I would have sat in it. Instead I sat across from TK and Patty, and TK winked at me. She and Patty held hands under the table. I thought that was a bit bold. No guards were in the room, but they were right outside the door.

Except for a woman named Maureen, who took the same Bible class as me, there was no one else I knew. Most of the people there were young. I didn't fit in. I saw TK lean over and whisper something to Patty, and then giggle and rip a page out of her notebook. She crossed the room and shook it in front of me like she was a bullfighter and that was her cape. By then I'd noticed that everyone but me had notebook and pencils. The palms of my hands started to sweat.

"Tra la! For you," she said. "I brought an extra pencil too. Just in case."

"All I'm doing is sitting," I said under my breath.

Bev, who runs the workshop, didn't seem like a college professor to me. She was small and slim and blonde and wore blue jeans. She had little hands that made me think of birds. They flew when she spoke. At first it was kind of rowdy, and Bev just joked along with everyone else.

"Come on, Bev," said someone. "Swap badges with me just this once."

Bev had a red badge instead of the green ones we have to wear. "Sorry, no can do," she said. "But I'll tell you a joke I heard in a bar last night."

"Happy horse shit! What would I give to go to a bar," groaned this one girl, Ruby, who just got out of the hole. And it went on like that. I expected one of the guards to stick their head in the room any minute. But after a bit things quieted down enough for TK and a couple of other people to read poems they wrote during the week. I'd already heard TK's. She always reads out loud as she writes. I still don't get it. It has something to with death. Just about everything she writes has to do with death. Suicide mostly. One of the other poems had to do with death too, but it was funny. It was called Road Kill, about the meat we get to eat in this place. Seagull instead of chicken, the poem said. The woman who wrote it works in the cafeteria. She's a black woman about my age, and everybody likes her and calls her Custard. I don't know why. There was a lot of laughing and pounding tabletops after she read. People laugh any chance they get in here. I laughed too. But even my laugh is quiet. TK asked me that one time: How come when you laugh no sound comes out?

Then Ruby made us laugh some more by doing an imitation of Jenkins strutting up and down with her chest stuck out. Some one yelled at Ruby to sit her butt down, before Jenkins stuck her head in to see what all the noise was about, or the next thing she knew she'd find herself back in the hole. Ruby had no sooner sat down than Jenkins did stick her head in. Finally Bev got everyone quieted down by having us close our eyes and get comfortable. Lay our head on our arms or whatever. She started to talk. Today was the day all the fences were coming down. Today we were out in a forest, lying under a tree in the sun, feeling it warm on our skin. Someone snickered and said they knew what they'd be doing if they was lying on the ground in the forest. But mostly it was quiet, people letting Bev's words flow over them. For me it was as close as I've got to being out since I've been in. I was under my tree in the quad, except it had moved itself to the forest. Then it was time for us to open our eyes and write whatever came to mind. Nothing came to my mind. Half of me was still under my tree. So I just sat. Then the bell rang for movement time. Ruby whooped.

"Cigarette break!" she said.

There was a scraping of chairs and everyone trooped out to the quad. I sat on a bench next to TK, and Patty sat on the edge of the next bench. Jenkins was out there watching them like a hawk. I watched my tree. We all three blew smoke.

Suddenly TK says, "Hills, why don't you write something about that old tree you love so much?" And half turned her back to me and talked to Patty.

Life is funny how things come in a flash.

The bell rang and I went back in that room and the words just wrote themselves. Bev came round and looked over my shoulder, and wanted me to read it out loud. I said no way, and she asked me would I mind if she read it. I got red-faced and started to sweat again, but said I guessed not. So she did. Some people clapped. TK looked like a proud mother.

"I know what tree that is," said Custard.

"Jesus, Hills," said Ruby. "I always thought that old tree was ugly. But you make it beautiful."

I couldn't stop smiling.

I didn't mean to kill Ray. If he'd come for me, probably nothing would have happened. But he went for Jaime. It was in the kitchen. Right after supper. Ray was chipping ice out of the ice tray with an ice pick to fix himself a drink. It was about the only time he opened the refrigerator. Jaime said something Ray thought was smart-mouthed and he went for him. He still had the ice pick in his hand and I had the iron skillet in mine because I'd just washed it. The ice pick flashed by Jaime's neck and Jaime cried out. I hit Ray with the skillet, and he crumpled.

What might have happened doesn't count for anything. Jaime didn't have so much as a scratch and Ray's skull was caved in. I left the kitchen in handcuffs. May 6, 1990. A Sunday night. The last time I cooked dinner for my kids, or bathed the little ones, or brushed Elisa's hair down her back and trimmed the split ends off the bottom.

When we got back to our room TK taped my poem to the wall next to the sink.

"It doesn't have a title," she said. "What's it called?"

I shrugged. "Tree, I guess." TK nodded, and read it out loud again. Suddenly I didn't feel so heavy. She finished and we both were quiet. TK had that pouty look to her face that she gets when she thinks. I sat ready for something more. I heard my own heart beat, felt stirrings, felt my own blood move.

The Birthday Party

Busting out of a Vegas motel with Lou's birthday books hugged to her chest, and everything else left behind. Nothing except the white halter dress she's wearing and the books. Not even the poems she wrote and hid from Mo. Not even shoes. Star outside, with the engine revving, hollering for her to get her butt in the car, and Annie laughing so hard she nearly peed on herself. Then Star burned rubber out the parking lot, her face beaded with sweat, her knuckles white on the steering wheel.

Annie laughed now just thinking about it. She stretched out between white sheets, hands laced behind her head. Safe. Mo thought he ruled her. But she was here, and he was there. She turned her head slightly and glanced over at the nightstand. Generic. She'd seen it in a hundred motel rooms. The same lamp too. Except this time, instead of some dude's watch or cufflinks—or Mo's gun—there were Lou's birthday books, in a neat stack under the brim of the lampshade, waiting to be wrapped.

"What's wrong with toys?" Mo had wanted to know when she asked him to drop her at a bookstore. "Your kid a nerd?" Mo was the kind liked to lean back while he drove, one hand loosely on the wheel, leaving the other free for whatever it was needed for. That day it twisted itself in Annie's hair, a sign of affection just brutal enough to pull at her scalp. Then he pinched her cheek and called her the library lady, told her she'd look sexy in glasses. Lucky for her he was in a good mood, and feeling flush. He dropped her in front of Barnes and Noble and tossed her a couple of fifties. Said he'd swing by in an hour.

So she forgot about time. He knew she was no good on

time. She sat cross-legged on the floor of the children's section, took off her shoes so as not to pierce the insides of her bare thighs on their dagger heels, and started flipping through books she'd pulled off the shelf. Trying to decide which ones a three-year-old boy would like best, while the tips of her long black hair swished over their pages. There were both the story and pictures to consider.

"Can I help you miss?"

Annie looked up. The woman was gray-haired, wore owl glasses and a neat

pleated skirt. Annie smiled.

"No thank you. I'm fine."

The woman lingered for a moment, and then went away.

So many choices, it took time to narrow them down. They had to be the kind of books Annie should have had when she was a kid, but never did. She laid a dozen possibilities on the floor and knelt over them, turning pages, running her fingers over their jewel-bright colors. It became necessary to see how the words sounded, because if you planned on being the kind of mother who reads out loud to her children, as Annie did, then the sound of a book really mattered.

"Are you sure I can't help you?"

The woman was back, with an uncomfortable little twist to her mouth. Did the woman mind her reading so loud, or was it her clothes? Annie wondered. Did bookstores have a dress code? Glitter and spandex not allowed. Or was it because she was Indian?

"I'm fine." She smiled again, a little too wide this time, and pulled out the two fifties from the waistband of her shorts and waved them. "And I have money." This seemed to embarrass the woman, who fluttered her hands, and said she didn't mean that. But at least she went away again.

After doing the math in her head to see how many books she could afford for a hundred dollars, Annie picked six, all hard backs. These she'd just finished paying for, still half-floating in a dream world of words and pictures, when Mo showed up and grabbed her from behind, whirled her around, and smacked her. What did she think? He was giving her the afternoon off?

"I told you one hour, bitch."

"Hey!" protested a woman in blue jeans.

Other customers in line, who up till then had paid no mind to the girl decked out in flamingo-pink satin—this was Vegas after all—now decided it was time to openly stare. But instead of throwing the books back on the counter, or grinding them under the heel of his custom made Italian shoes, Mo merely turned and walked out, leaving Annie to run behind him. This she did, like a child trying to catch up with its parent, her spiked heels clattering on Barnes and Nobles burnished floor.

"Do you need any help?" the woman in blue jeans called after her. But all that mattered to Annie was that she had Lou's books. Outside in the sunshine, she was almost relieved to see Sabrina sitting up front of the car next to Mo. Normally this would have been cause for a fight right there. As it was, the back seat afforded her the opportunity to slide Lou's books safely out of sight, to be retrieved later.

Annie sat up in bed, and hugged herself. She wasn't used to keeping promises. Least of all to herself. Or her kids. But she was back. Just like she said she would be. Too bad she didn't have any wrapping paper or bows so she could wrap Lou's present. Maybe Star would make a quick stop to get some on the way to the party. Where was Star anyway? The other bed was empty, its white sheets crumpled, a pillow on the floor. She called out Star's name a couple of times and stuck her head in the bathroom. No one. Just damp towels and make-up strewn over the counter. She padded across the room to the window and pulled back the drapes to see what kind of day it was. Behind the Motel Six sign the freeway, behind the freeway a flat gray sky. Yuck. But at least she was back in Seattle.

What time was it? she wondered, and picked up the phone to dial the front desk. Two thirty already! Where was Star anyway? Star said she'd arrange a ride. She called the front desk again. "Hey, this is Carmen in room 307. Is my roommate down there by any chance? Well have you seen her today? She left? When? I mean, did you see when she left? Well, did you see who she was with? Okay, okay. I know you're busy. Hey, do you guys have any bus schedules down there?"

She sprang into action. So Star had ditched her. She'd deal with that later. She pulled her T-shirt over her head, flung it on the bed and ran into the bathroom. Adjusting the shower took a minute, cold then burning hot, but then the warm water kicked in and Annie showered quickly. How was she supposed to get from here, out by the airport, to wherever it was she was supposed to go, she wondered. She knew the park, could even picture it in her mind, but couldn't quite think of the name or where exactly it was. Picnic area number one, her Aunt Ruthie had said when she'd talked to her on the phone last night.

Out of the shower, she wrapped herself in a towel, and brushed and blow-dried her hair. So many times she'd thought about cutting it, but the tricks liked it long, black and silky, all the way down past her butt. To tricks she was Carmen, the pretty senorita from Acapulco. Well, the least she could do now was curl the front a bit with the curling iron, the way she did for them. Do something pretty for Lou.

When she was done with her hair she outlined her almond shaped eyes in black-eyeliner, and her lips in deep plum which she then filled in a brilliant red. There wasn't much she could do about the bruise on her cheek. She tried covering it up with a thick layer of foundation, but individual teeth marks still showed through. Mo was a cannibal. Only a cannibal would bite someone like that. She wondered would it scar, and looked herself over carefully under the light. In truth she looked fine, way too fine for one measly scar to wreck. She blew herself a kiss in the mirror.

"Go ahead, girl!" she said, and dropped her towel. She was so nice and skinny now, maybe no one would recognize her. Or had she been this skinny when she left? She couldn't remember. Now, what to wear? Humming to herself, she hurried back into the room and rummaged through the suitcase. Didn't Star have anything but shorts? It wasn't exactly shorts weather in Seattle yet. She pulled back the corner of the drapes to double-check the sky, and spotted a patch of blue.

"Alrighty then!"

In the end she dressed quickly in denim shorts, a white tank top and a pair of Star's sandals, which were a little big, but at least didn't have ridiculous heels. The shorts were okay, and the tank top only slightly wrinkled. Except, maybe the shorts were too short. Annie ran to the bathroom to check her butt in the mirror and make sure it was all the way covered. She didn't need to go to Lou's party looking like a ho even if she was one. What she needed was to be out the door. Grabbing a sweatshirt, and some change from Star's nightstand for bus-fare, she saw two ten-dollar bills lying there and stuck those in her pocket as well.

There was a girl with a stroller at the bus stop. Blonde, with hair that made Annie think of Princess Di. She wore a blue raincoat over lavender leggings, and sneakers. Seattle had no style. Mostly she looked tired, circles under her eyes the same color as her leggings. Her baby was sleeping. One peek and Annie could tell that baby's daddy wasn't white. She smiled.

"Cute baby. How old is he?"

The girl looked Annie over, and for a moment Annie thought she might turn her back. Instead she smiled.

"Nine months," she said.

"Cute," said Annie again. She leaned over the stroller, her long hair hanging down in curtains. "What's his name?"

"Jason."

Annie leaned closer. "Hi Jason." Jason chortled and grabbed a fistful of Annie's hair and tried to stuff it in his mouth. His front teeth were in but mostly he was gums. Annie laughed, and his mother said, "Let go of the lady's hair, Jason," and "sorry 'bout that, his manners are awful," as Annie, still laughing, tugged her hair free.

Jason reminded her of Lou when he was a baby. His gummy grin whenever she put her face near. How he always grabbed her hair or her nose or her cheeks and used whatever it was to pull himself closer. One time he managed to get his mouth all the way over her nose. She laughed again, remembering.

"I have a kid," she told the girl. "Two kids, actually." Sometimes she nearly forgot about Frankie. He'd been so young the last time she saw him. But she loved Frankie too. He was her baby too. "Boys," she said. "Two boys. Today's my eldest' birthday."

Why did this girl look so surprised? What did she think? She had a monopoly on babies? "For real?" she said. "Where are they?"

Maybe she thinks I'm too young, thought Annie. Everyone thought that. Though Princess Di here didn't look to be more than eighteen or nineteen herself. Besides which, Annie was eighteen now. Had the I.D. to prove it, even if it was fake.

"They're with their grandma," she said. Which was basically true, although last night they had been at her Aunt Ruthie's house, and not with Sly's mom. Still, according to Auntie she was a grandmother too, said that was their tribe's tradition. But this princess didn't need to know any of that. "I just came from work," she added, as if that would explain everything. As if she owed anyone an explanation.

"Oh," said the girl, looking Annie over again. She started pushing the stroller back and forth, as if Annie had somehow disturbed her precious baby and she now needed to soothe him. She was definitely a princess.

"How old are they?" she wanted to know next.

Sometimes Annie found herself unable to stop talking, even when she wanted to.

"Lou is three," she said. "Today. I'm on my way to his party. My big boy! Three years old, I can't believe it! And Frankie's fourteen months. They're both named for my brothers."

"That's nice…"

"My brother Lou died. And my brother Frankie I haven't seen since I was little. We used to be in a foster home together, and the mom kept him, but she didn't want me."

"That's sad."

Yes it was sad. It had just about ruined her whole life. There were all kinds of people, social workers and cops, who asked questions about her family and she wouldn't say a word. But a stranger she could talk to. A stranger she could tell anything. *Anything.*

And all this girl had to say was "that's sad."

"If you really want to know, my brother Frankie was kidnapped." Which was also basically true. The way Annie saw things now, foster parents were kidnappers. "By the cavalry and the Catholic Church," she added, because what did this princess know about tribal history? Although none of it quite fit Frankie's situation. But then, who cared? Annie saw the bus coming. So did Princess. She gave Annie one last look over.

"Are you Indian?"

She just had to ask didn't she? Sometimes Annie thought life would be easier if she wasn't Indian. Because as soon as they knew, people always expected her to have problems, expected her to be an alcoholic. Like her mother. As if that were the fate of being born Indian. Well, if she wanted to, if she cut and curled her hair, and bleached it a bit, she could pass as a white girl. Her skin wasn't *so* dark. Except, who in their right mind would want to be white?

"Yep. I'm an Indian."

"I thought so. You have the most beautiful hair," said the girl, and added, "I bet your kids are gorgeous." Which was *so* true Annie forgave her for being a princess— after all no one could help what they were born as—and helped her up the bus steps with the stroller.

"Bye baby Jason," she said, before heading to the backseat, where she always sat, where she could keep an eye on things.

The bus hummed along the freeway toward downtown. Annie stared out of the window, and daydreamed about Lou and how it was going to be to hold him again. Then adjusted the picture to let Frankie in too. She had a kid tucked up under each arm, the three of them snuggled up on the new leather couch she was going to get just as soon as she had a job and somewhere to live. She was reading to them from one of Lou's birthday books, even if Frankie was still too young to understand the story. Just thinking about them this way made her feel warm and fuzzy inside. Fizzy too, like the bubbles in soda-pop, rising and rising. Then suddenly she realized she'd left Lou's books on the nightstand, and her fizzy went flat.

"*Shit!*"

She swung her way to the front of the bus and stood beside the driver. Please pretty please, would he stop the bus? She'd left something back at her motel and she absolutely had to get it. The driver was an old guy with large pink ears and a gut jutting out over his thighs. He stared straight ahead.

"This bus is an express," he said. "No stops."

Annie could feel peoples' eyes on her back. The princess's too. She hated that.

"It's my son's birthday," she pleaded. "And I've left his birthday present back at my motel."

"It don't make no difference what day this is, young lady, this is still an express."

"Well…couldn't you just pull over?"

"Lady, please! We're on the freeway. Now I need to ask you to take a seat."

Annie was about to tell him she didn't mind, she'd walked along freeways before, when a quick glance outside showed her they were almost all the way to downtown now. It was too late to go back. She sank down into the seat directly behind the driver and across from Princess, not caring what she or the old lady sitting next to her thought. Baby Jason stared up from his stroller and Annie stared back. This was one of *those* times, she thought. Starting out for one place and ending up someplace else without knowing how she got there. Unreliable, the judge had said, citing times she'd missed the kids' doctor appointments and taken them to McDonalds instead. Incapable, said her court appointed attorney. Whose side was he on anyway?

Except, this was nothing like any of that. Star had run out on her was all. If Star had lined up a ride like she'd promised, Annie wouldn't have been so rushed and forgetting things. Well, she'd just have to give Lou his books next time. By then she'd have them gift-wrapped. It's not as if she was going anyplace anytime soon. She was back for good now. What mattered was making it to Lou's party. She couldn't remember even one time when her mother had showed up for her birthday. Come to think of it, she couldn't remember ever having a party. The way she figured, Lou was one lucky fella.

Turning to look out the bus window again, Annie saw the domed roof of the Kingdome. Suddenly she was excited. This was home. If anywhere was home, downtown Seattle was it. The bus stopped at Fourth and Jackson and everyone piled off, someone else helping the princess with her stroller, Annie already scanning the faces of the people waiting at the bus stop, looking for the friendliest one.

"Excuse me," she asked the black woman with two small children. "I'm looking for a park...I forgot the name, but it's down by Lake Washington, and sticks out into the water...there's a trail goes all the way around..."

"Seward Park," said the woman. "That's Seward Park. The twenty-nine takes you there. You can catch it down on First."

First Avenue. That's where Annie had ended up the night she left the shelter. That had been the last time she'd seen her kids. For a whole year she had lived in that shelter, from the time she'd split up with her boyfriend, Sly, and fallen out with Aunt Ruthie. First off, Auntie couldn't stand the sight of Sly, and then threw a fit when Annie dumped him. Couldn't Annie see Sly was trying to turn himself around? That he was trying to be responsible? Which meant what, Auntie? Annie didn't need to spend the rest of her life with him. She'd liked Sly better in his old gang-banging days, anyway. Now he was boring. Besides which she needed her independence. None of which changed when she found out she was pregnant again. So she moved out of Auntie's, and into a shelter for battered women where they had a few beds put aside for teen mothers. For a whole year she put up with their rules and their curfew, and getting written up for every little thing. No better than Auntie's really. Forever hawking her, and snooping to see if she was drinking beer or smoking weed in her room. Finally they told her she had to go.

She woke that last morning to find Lou sitting on the floor in his Micky Mouse pajamas with a box of Cheerios between his legs, cramming cereal into his mouth like he hadn't eaten for a year. Frankie was awake too, sucking on his fists, and stinking of piss. Annie fixed him a bottle, snatched the cereal away from Lou, and turned up the heat. Lou started to whimper. "Don't even go there," she warned, but made him a bottle too. Anything to keep him quiet. "Get your butt over here little boy." She patted a spot in the bed with her and Frankie. Diaper changes beyond her right then. She needed to figure out where she was going to live. Child Protective Services was on her back too. Aunt Ruthie's was better than nothing. She telephoned, but Auntie was at work, and the only one home was her cousin Rhonda. Please, please Rhonda, could she stay there until she had something else figured out. Well, couldn't Rhonda talk Auntie into it? She'd do whatever Auntie needed, she promised, and stick to her rules for real, even curfew. Hey, she'd managed curfew in this place for a year. She was good on curfews. Tell Auntie that. Oh, oh...and would Rhonda watch the kids for a few hours while she got herself packed up?

Later Bridget, from staff, had come up the four flights of stairs and banged on the door to tell Annie her cousin was in the parking lot, waiting on the kids. And had Annie remembered she needed to be out of that room no later than ten p.m.?

"We're sorry to see you go Annie. You know that."

Yeah, right.

Lou and Frankie were in their pajamas still, both smelling of piss now. Annie threw a couple of extra diapers in the diaper bag, slung it over her shoulder, and carried the two of them down the four flights of stairs, one on each hip, Frankie still clutching his empty bottle. But Annie hadn't minded the stairs, or even carrying Lou who was old enough to manage them himself. Even bounced the two of them on the way down, and made them laugh. That day was the very last time she'd have to put up with all the rules and regulations of that place. Hello, she was not a battered woman. Annie had reminded Bridget of this countless times. So why did all these security rules have to apply to her? No one she knew was even allowed in the building.

Outside she handed the kids and the diaper bag over to Rhonda.

"They didn't eat any real breakfast yet."

"Breakfast?" said Rhonda. "It's nearly three o'clock."

"So?" said Annie, and kissed the kids good bye quickly. "See ya later, babies."

As it turned out that had been the last she'd seen of them. Of course, she had meant to go Auntie's that night, meant to work things out with her. But for the first time for more than a year she had no curfew. No kids, no strollers and no diaper bags. She had packed everything into garbage bags and stashed them in the lobby. To be picked up within the next two days, Bridget said. Annie had walked through those doors with nothing to weigh her down, and nobody to tell her what to do. Outside a frost twinkled under the floodlight in the parking lot. She turned up her coat collar and shoved her hands in her pockets and walked the few blocks to First Avenue, where, neon lights lit up the frost on the sidewalk, music floating up basement steps and out the doorways of clubs. Annie had no money, and no place to go. Hadn't even brushed her hair that day. She really hadn't meant to do anything but take a little walk down First to Pioneer Square and then back up to Third to catch the bus to Auntie's.

All of which she explained to the man in the camel-hair coat, who whisked her past security and bouncers and into a club. Really, she said, she could only stay a little while. But he had a way about him, warming her frozen hands between his manicured ones, a diamond nugget in his pinky ring, and a voice that made Annie think of crushed velvet. He ordered her a tequila sunrise and introduced himself as Mo.

Well, she was through with Mo now. All that behind her. She was making a fresh start, and going to do it right this time. "Yes, I'm getting myself into rehab," she had told Aunt Ruthie on the phone last night. "Don't sweat it Auntie, I told you. I'll do whatever I need to do to be with my kids."

An old man in a tattered coat shuffled toward the bus stop, and toward Annie in particular it seemed, his hand outstretched for change. Annie reached into her pocket, feeling for coins and pulled out the two ten-dollar bills. Unsure of where they came from, she gave them to the old man anyway. "Have a nice day, Grandpa," she said.

The clock on the railway station tower said ten minutes to four. Aunt Ruthie had told her to be there around four or four thirty, so she was right on schedule. Plus the sun had decided to shine, a pale beam of it pushing through cloud. In a little while she'd have Lou back in her arms. She pictured how it would be. Balloons flying from the corners of the picnic shelter, Aunt Ruthie heating up the coals, chicken on the grill, Rhonda setting out paper plates and drinks, Sly's mom jiggling Frankie on one hip. Except he was walking now, so maybe he'd be toddling around under the tables. Lou was playing on the grass. In her mind, Annie watched him play for a few minutes. He was so big now, his hair grown long. Then he turned around and saw her, and his face lit up. *Mommy!* Hurtling himself down the grassy slope and into her open arms.

"Yo! Annie!"

The voice called from behind her.

"Yo! Girl! Annie!"

She turned around. A young man with long dark hair stood on the sidewalk a few yards behind her, arms dangling at his sides. At first she wasn't sure who it was. His face was hidden by the shadow cast from his baseball cap, and he wore shades. But she knew Pollo, standing beside him, dancing uneasily from foot to foot, shaking his head. Annie's face lit up.

"Hey, Pollo, little man. Whatssup?" she said, walking back toward him. Pollo was one of the few people she actually wanted to see.

"Told you it was her." She could see now that the first guy, the one who had called her name, was Johnny Special. She didn't know what his last name really was. Everyone just called him Johnny Special, even the cops.

"Let it be," said Pollo. "I aint got no hard feelings."

"No hard feelings about what?" asked Annie hugging

him. Man, he seemed smaller and more beat down than ever. "Whatssup Johnny?"

"What's up is Pollo's mouth," said Johnny. "Open your mouth Pollo. Show her." Pollo shook his head. "Show her man! She needs to see." Reluctantly Pollo opened his mouth. His front teeth were missing.

"Man, what happened to you?" said Annie.

"Tell her."

"Naw, man. I told you, forget it."

"Forget what?" asked Annie.

"What cousin Pollo doesn't want to tell you is he got the crap beat out of him on account of you. Pull up your pant leg man, pull it up. Show her. Show her what they did to you." Johnny heaved Pollo's pant leg up. Annie saw a deep purple groove across the shinbone and another line, criss-crossed with stitch scars, like a zipper running up his leg.

"What's that got to do with me?" She was confused. Why did Pollo keep looking around like that, and shaking his head, his skinny braids swinging about over his narrow shoulders?

"You go stab someone," Johnny said, "and leave town in a hurry. So who you think that guy's friends come looking for? Anyone who looks Indian is who. Anyone they know knows you." Johnny's voice rose. "They fucked with a lot of people 'cause of you, and just about killed Pollo. You just breeze out of town with your pimp boyfriend and leave a fucking mess behind you."

Annie's head felt as if it were about to burst. She closed her eyes and saw shapes moving behind her eyelids. An intersection...it was raining hard, a bunch of people piling out of a car...her too. Then shouting, and someone writhing on the ground, the rain washing blood into the gutter. Mo pushing her into the car...sweat pouring down his face. Or was it rain? Or blood? The two of them sped away.

Her eyes flashed open. "What was I supposed to do? Stay here and get myself killed? I never stabbed that guy, I swear I didn't! I didn't even know him!" She pressed her temples, as if she could push the memory back inside to wherever she'd dislodged it from. "And I didn't mean for that to happen to Pollo. I'm sorry Pollo. I'm sorry. I didn't mean for you to get hurt. I know you're my friend." She was in tears now. "Anyway, I'm not even supposed to be here right now. I've got a bus to catch. I'm supposed to be at my son's birthday party. I haven't seen him for a year on account of this shit."

She never should of come back, she knew it. She should have stayed gone. With Mo. In Vegas where she was safe.

"It's okay, Annie. I wasn't gonna say anything..." Pollo stared down at the sidewalk, still shaking his head from side to side.

"Man, why you shake your head all the time?"

"Because he's fucked up on account of you, bitch!!" roared Johnny.

"Fuck you! Don't be getting in my face. And don't nobody call me out of my name!" Annie's fist was up and flying before she even thought about it. Just as quickly Johnnie blocked her and punched her in the eye. She fell backwards on the sidewalk and landed on her butt. Her eye was stinging and she couldn't see straight. Blood dripped out of her nose and onto her tank top. Pollo stood between her and Johnny, shaking all over now. He reached a trembling hand out toward Johnny.

"Stop, man! Okay?" he said. "What happened, happened. I told you. It's over."

"For you maybe," said Johnny, and turned and walked away. After a few steps he turned back. "I wouldn't stay around too long girl, if I was you," he said. "Word might get around that you're back." A couple of tourists passed by, the woman twisting her head to look.

"Pay them no mind," hissed the man.

Annie was up on her feet now, one hand under her nose and the other over her eye.

"Fuck you Johnny Special!" she yelled. "There aint nothing special about you."

Pollo put his hand on her arm.

"What's he done to my face, Pollo?" she asked, lifting her hands.

"Hmm. Look like you need some ice. You getting a shiner."

"Shit! How am I supposed to go to Lou's birthday party with a black eye? And blood on my shirt. Man, what's he going to think?"

"He'll probably be pleased to see you Annie, no matter how you look. You can borrow my shirt if you want. There, look. Your nose already stopped bleeding."

"But my eye's gonna turn purple. Damn! I can't go there looking like this. I wanted to make a good impression you know. I'm trying to get my kids back. My Aunt and my babies' grandma's not going to think shit of me coming there looking like I just had a fight."

"You did just have a fight..."

Annie shivered. The sun seemed to have given up trying to shine, and she'd left her sweatshirt on the bus. She rubbed her arms and walked briskly along First Avenue, past the old man she'd given the money to, away from the twenty-nine bus stop and toward Pioneer Square. Pollo limped beside her. A bus came along, headed toward Pike Place Market. They were right by a stop, so Annie hopped on. It was the free fare zone and the driver waved her transfer aside. Pollo followed her, swinging himself into the seat next to her.

"Where's the party at?" Pollo asked. "I'll come with you if you like."

Annie didn't answer. She stared out of the bus window and imagined the party again. Aunt Ruthie at the BBQ grill, turning chicken and hot dogs, Sly's mom lighting the candles on Lou's cake, her cousins crowding around, everybody talking, eating, laughing. Who else was going to be there? Not Sly, she knew that. Sly was gone someplace. But some of Lou's little friends from childcare for sure, along with their parents in jeans and jumpsuits. She saw herself through these parents' eyes. A beat-up teenage hooker coming across the grass toward their children. "What happened to you this time, Annie?" Aunt Ruthie would ask. When Lou turned around he didn't even know who she was. She'd look him up some other time, when she had the books. For now better to just ride the bus a while and chill with Pollo.

Trains

Found her on the floor I did, this morning. In her bra and panties. Managed to get herself out of her nightie and get that far with dressing herself when she took a tumble.

"What were you going to do then, love," I says to her, "if I hadn't been coming in about now? Planning on staying on the floor all day were you? That's what you've got the buzzer for. No good if you don't use it though, is it love?"

I could hear my voice getting loud. There's absolutely nothing wrong with her hearing, but so many of them are a bit deaf you get in the way of turning the volume up.

She was excited this morning, bless her heart. Today was the day she expected her granddaughter, all the way from America. Another morning a tumble like that first thing would have put her in a right dither. Out of sorts for the rest of the day. But she was happy as a lark soon as I had her up. Just about running to her wardrobe she was. She wanted to pick out something nice. I can understand that.

"Dress you up like the Queen today shall we, love?"

"Yes," she says. Even her voice was brighter. And maybe her idea of a queen wouldn't sit right with Buckingham Palace, purple velvet pants can you believe? But she looked right smart, a nice purple broach on her blouse. What mattered is she liked what she saw when she looked in the mirror.

"Smashing," she says. "If I do say so myself." I took that as a good sign too, her talking, even if it took her forever to say it. Some mornings she won't talk at all.

"So who are we this morning?" I asked her when I had her seated at the table. "Who am I serving breakfast to this morning? Susie or Zsuzsa?" She's got two selves she says, her English one, and the one she left behind in Hungary.

"Both," she says. "I'm starving."

You got to hand it to her. She's got a sense of humor. I'm not sure I would if I was in her shoes.

* * * * *

Zsuzsa wants to see the photograph of Sofi again. It's been so long since she's seen her granddaughter she worries she'll get her mixed up with someone else. So many people coming and going. Time to go potty, time to take pills, time to eat lunch, time to lie down, time to sit up, time to take a walk. Right bossy, some of the girls are. She never knows who is going to walk through the door next, though if it was a man that would make her sit up. The only men ever show their faces around here are her sons. Mostly her dead son, Rollie, who drifts in and out as only the dead can do. Oscar when he sees fit. As for the other two they may as well be in America with their sister for all she sees of them. But a total stranger can walk in here one minute, and out the next with whatever they want, long as they wear a sky-blue nurse's dress with a royal-blue elastic belt. Lucky it's Sheila here this morning.

"You're stuck with me all day today, love."

Well good, Sheila is her favorite. At least she remembers who Sheila is. The only colored one out of the lot. That makes it easier. Sheila takes an interest too. Not that some of the others don't, only that Zsuzsa is never sure who it is taking an interest, and by the time she's worked it out they're gone again.

"What is it love? What are you looking for?"

"My granddaughter."

"Well, she's not here yet is she? Doesn't come till this afternoon you said."

"Not *her*! Her picture!"

Oh dear, there she goes, sounding cross again. It's just that it takes so much effort to get the words out. Nothing left of her voice but a husky whisper—who'd of thought she used to recite whole poems?—and then to have to say two things instead of one. But Sheila understands that she needs to save her energy for Sofi.

"There it is lovey, right on the mantelpiece where you left it."

Zsuzsa shuffles over to where a picture is propped up above the fireplace. All the others in frames, and then this one. She rests both hands on the mantelpiece and peers at it. She still can't see very well. Carefully, carefully she lifts it between thumb and forefinger to bring it close. She peers again. So, that's Sofi. A nice looking young woman. Dark eyes, dark curly hair, brown skin. Well, she could be anybody for all Zsuzsa knew. Could be Sheila's daughter. Who would have thought she'd end up with colored grandchildren. Not that she minds, it's just that who would have thought? Slowly she turns the picture over to check for writing on the back. There is some, but she can't read it because she doesn't have her other glasses. Most likely they're on the bookshelf on the other side of the room. Perilous this, holding onto the mantelpiece with one hand, twisting her torso to try and get turned around, while down on the carpet her feet dance their lunatic dance, treading water where there is no water. All for a pair of glasses. If her daughter were here she'd have something funny to say about it. *Hold on, Mum. No need to get your knickers in a twist!* Mary said things like that. But my goodness, look at Sheila! Look at the way she moves. Lovely. Two strides and she's across the room.

"What's this then?"

"Your glasses."

"Oh yes."

Then the business of getting them out of the case, the other ones off her face and the right ones on. Such a palaver, legs jelly the whole time. At least Sheila lets her do it herself. Some of them just lose patience and take over. There! Now she can read what's written on the back of the picture. *To*

Grandma from your loving granddaughter Sofi. Blimey. Is
that all? After all that effort?

* * * * *

Spent most of the rest of the morning looking at her pictures,
we did. She's got them all over, everyone in her family. We've
looked at them all before, lots of times. But I didn't mind
doing it again. She calls it her tour.

"I'll give you a tour of my life," she says.

So round we went, arm in arm, like we were on an outing,
in a museum or something. Mind you, the picture that catches
your eye when you first walk in is her son Rollie. That's her
son that died. He wasn't quite right in the head, and went and
drowned himself in the river. She's got him done up in oils, a
proper portrait. Her tours always start with Rollie. She calls
him her guardian angel, and always blows him a kiss. Then
we do the rounds. She blows more kisses at her dead
husband's pictures, and once she got a bit weepy in front of
her wedding photograph. But mostly she tells me stories
about her children and grandchildren. She's got great
grandchildren as well now, little boys, in America. But she
says she can't tell me a thing about them because she's never
met them.

"Who's this handsome fellow?" I asked when we stopped
in front of one of her old photographs. You know the kind.
So old they're brown and white instead of black and white.
I've wondered about that picture. She turns it to the wall
sometimes, for days on end. That's enough to make a body
curious. Today it was turned back the right way. A photo of a
man, with black eyes and a handsome mustache: very snazzy
looking, wearing a brimmed hat and a waistcoat with shiny
buttons. Next to him is a little girl with a handkerchief on
her head and tied under her chin. One time when I asked
Susie who they were she told me to ssh and mind my own
business, there's things a Gypsy won't talk about. Another

time she told me he was a prince from the Arabian Nights. Her mind had already begun wandering that day, her left foot twitching, and that wispy look she gets when she's tired. This morning her mind was clear as a bell though. She knew who everybody was.

"That's my father," she said. "With my sister Rosa."

"Are they Gypsies then?" I asked her.

"Oh yes," she says. "They're both Gypsies. *Roma*, we used to say."

I checked about this Gypsy business with her son Oscar one time. "What's this about your mum being a Gypsy?" He looked at me like I'd said she was an orangutan. "Hungarian," he said. "Mother's Hungarian."

* * * * *

A child with wild hair is how Zsuzsa remembers Sofi. Undisciplined hair, her husband used to tease. Ssh Colin! Zsuzsa would chide him She's just a little girl. You'll give her a complex. She meant about being colored. Sofi's hair was naturally wild and woolly. What it had needed was to be put into some nice plaits. Like the West Indian's did their children's hair. She had asked Sheila once: Do you plait your children's hair? Sheila had two girls. But no, no, her girls didn't want anything to do with plaits anymore. They'd had their hair straightened and wore it smooth, with headbands. *Like English girls?!* Zsuzsa exclaimed. She thought that was silly and told Sheila so. And Sheila, who wore her own black hair in a neat French twist, had thrown her head back and laughed. Said they were English girls.

"Time for a wipe, Susie love."

Zsuzsa opens her eyes to find herself hung all to one side in her chair, a long string of spittle dangling from her mouth. What is Sofi going to think, seeing her grandma drool like this? As far as Zsuzsa is concerned, drooling has to be one of the worst things about this wretched Parkinson's business. She takes the tissue Sheila offers and dabs at the corners of her mouth.

"Thank you." She closes her eyes again. Inside her head a waltz plays, and a man in a white suit steps forward to ask her to dance. It is Colin, the way he looked when they first met, although she can't remember his ever having a white suit. He's quite handsome. Round and round she swirls, enjoying the smell of his after-shave, Old Spice, quite distinct. But when she pulls back a little to smile at him, it is her son Rollie's face she sees, and then Papa winking at her. Everyone is dropping in for a visit today. Wanting to get a look at Sofi most likely.

* * * * *

I'd just come back in with her dinner tray when the phone rang. Usually I pick it up when it rings because Susie never answers. She can't get to it fast enough. Used to get in a right bother, all tangled up in the wire. Her son, Oscar, got her a cordless, but she doesn't like it. Says she doesn't know how it works. Most times she lets it ring off the hook when there's no one around, even if I put it on the little table next to her chair. I know because I've talked to Oscar a number of times and he said he'd been trying to get through to his mum all morning and no answer. Best to phone on mornings he knows one of us is here, I tell him. It's not like there's someone here round the clock, though if you ask me it's getting so there should be.

"Is that you, Mum?" said the voice on the telephone.

I was so surprised you could have knocked me down with a feather. Neither of my girls ever called me in someone's home before. Only on the staff phone, up at the main house, and hardly ever then, but never in one of the bungalows. Well, they wouldn't put them through, on switchboard, would they? They'd take a message. That's one of the things they drill into you here. Respecting privacy. It's a bit different up at the big house, but the bungalows are people's homes. That's what they stress. I put my hand over the mouthpiece. Susie was looking at me bright eyed as a squirrel, hoping it was Sofi no doubt.

"It's my eldest, Debbie," I said. "Heaven knows what she wants." My heart was pounding. No news is good news, they say. Turned out Debbie got herself in a right pickle. Caught smoking in the school toilets she was, then turned around and called the prefect that caught her a cow, then got lippy with the teacher the prefect called in to help. To top it off she told the Headmaster he was an old fart to his face. She was telephoning from his office. I could tell he was standing right behind her, breathing down her neck. Hear his wheezing all the way down on my end I could. He is a bit of an old fart, but I'm not about to tell Debbie that. Soon as she was done he gets on the phone. I understood, didn't I, that it was *imperative* I come in for a conference? Of course I bloody did. All his fancy words and la-de-da tone did was rub me up the wrong way. Like I was the one the one he really wanted to haul up on his carpet. Well, it's always the mum's fault isn't it? If the kids don't turn out right, blame their mum. I could have smacked Debbie a good one though. Lucky for her she told me over the phone.

"Debbie's in trouble again," I explained to Susie soon as I hung up. "The way she's going she'll get herself expelled from school. Her dad's going to go off the deep end when he hears about this latest."

* * * * *

Papa is inside Zsuzsa's head making speeches again. He reminds her, in a firm tone, that her name is no longer Zsuzsa. In England she is Susan. What about her secret name, the one that she must never even whisper to a *gadjo*? Ah, that is the name she must forget most of all. What language does Papa speak? English, Hungarian or Romany? Identities change as quickly as a change of clothes these days. One way or the other, everybody's doing it, everyone copying the Gypsies, ethnic all the rage. Her own headstrong daughter wanting to be known as Maria instead of Mary. There she goes now, her lovely legs inside purple stockings. Mary darling, you're not going to go to school dressed like that are you? Oh yes she is. Flouncing out of the house, yelling back over her shoulder: *Maria,* Mum! My name is *Maria!*

"Dinner time, Susie."

Zsuzsa's eyes blink open. Who is it, bothering her? One of those school dinner ladies? Well, today she's not going to eat that muck. She bats the air with one hand and nearly keels over in her chair. Where is she? Whose house is this? Is this the war? London kids tagged like parcels and sent off on trains. Except no one wants her. Take one look at a little brown-skinned girl and send her back.

She closes her eyes again. Just as she suspected. Butter beans. Well, Mary's right about that. School dinners are muck. Say grace and here they come. The dinner ladies with their gray dishrags, mopping up the tables before you've even had a chance to eat, pointing accusing fingers at the food left on your plate. Hitler can drop a bomb on her butter beans for all she cares. She never wanted to come to England in the first place.

"Wakey, wakey Susie love. Your dinner's getting cold."

"If it's butter beans just bomb them."

Impertinence. One of the dinner ladies laughing right in her ear. What's so funny she'd like to know, hurrying along into the kitchen now, little shuffling steps. But it isn't butter beans after all. Instead there's roast beef and a dried out Yorkshire pud on the tray, and gravy made from a mix. Real gravy isn't that color. Silly, if you ask her. There's nothing difficult about making gravy. Mix a tablespoon of flour in the meat drippings, brown the flour, add the water from the greens a little at a time. Greens water is loaded with vitamins. She's explained it all to Mary. That's where the vitamins go when you cook the greens, darling. No sense in pouring good vitamins down the drain. You use them in the gravy, but don't stop stirring or it will go lumpy. Mary was getting to be quite a handy little cook.

"Mary made the gravy."

"What's that love?"

"My daughter Mary made the gravy."

"Did she? She did a good job didn't she? Time to take your pill love…"

Who is this woman in the room? Somebody she didn't invite to the party. Someone in a blue dress, right there, next to the table. Whoever it is brings their face closer. A nice brown face, with a friendly smile.

"Who are you?"

"It's only me love. Sheila. Wandering a bit are we? You'll be fine soon as you've had your pill."

"Who let you in?"

"I came in the back door same as usual."

"Well that's alright then. If the dog jumps on you, just tell him 'down.' He probably wants a biscuit."

* * * * *

It got so she wouldn't budge from her chair, not even to go to the loo.

"No," she said. "Sofi might come, and I'll miss her."

Mind you, her place is small enough she can see both doors from her chair, front and back. Then there's the big picture window next to her chair that anyone coming up the path has to pass by. Most of the time the only person you ever see is Mr. Griffin. He's a nice old fellow out of one of the other bungalows. I don't go in his place much, but I see him out and about taking a bit of exercise with his hat and his cane. It takes him forever to go a few yards. There he was today, creeping along, nearly falling over when he stopped to tip his hat to us.

"Quite the dandy isn't he?" I said to Susie. "Shall I invite him in for tea then?"

I was just pulling her leg, trying to get her mind off worrying about Sofi.

"No," she snapped. "He's too much of a race horse for me."

She says the funniest things sometimes. But in the end I gave up trying to humor her. Gave up on the loo too. Just put on the radio for her, and ran up to the big house to get myself a bite of lunch.

"Be back in a jiffy, love."

While I was out and about, I decided to make a quick nip round to get a pound of Sainsbury's sausages for supper. I wanted to soften Brian up a bit before he found out about Debbie, and he's a man loves his bangers and mash. When I got back I found Susie pulled forward in her chair, about to take a nosedive onto the floor.

"You won't find Sofi down there love," I said.

"I got stuck." Then, as if I'd caught her doing something naughty. "I need to use the pot."

There's never anything quick about getting Susie on and off the loo, and once I had her in there, sitting like the Queen on her throne with her trousers round her ankles, she decided she had some business she needed to do. I gave her too many prunes for dessert, she said, and sent me out again with strict instructions to watch for Sofi. I settled myself in her chair, waiting for her to finish, and started up thinking about Debbie and her dad again. It was on my mind to give him a quick call. *Everything alright, love?* I'd say, just to sound him out. *Don't forget I'm doing a twelve-hour today. I'll be home in time to fix you some grub, okay Pet?* But I didn't want to bother Susie asking to use the phone.

He's old fashioned, my Brian is. Leave it to him and he'd smack Debbie right into the middle of next week. I tell him he should have gone into something other than brick-laying. All he can do is think in a straight line. Everything's either on the level or its not. Sometimes it's hard to tell the difference between him and my dad, the way their minds work. According to Daddy, if Debbie had been born in Jamaica she'd be a whole different kind of a girl, yes indeed, and get a thrashing whenever she needed. Not like these English kids running wild and talking smart aleck to whoever they pleased, even their own parents. My Brian, like a fool, sits there and agrees with all that. Where on earth does he think I grew up? I'm from here mate, I tell him, same as you. He can agree with Daddy all he likes. He's still England through and through, and pale as a London sky in winter.

* * * * *

Zsuzsa closes her eyes. Just for a minute, she thinks to herself. The radio is on, a nice violin concerto playing, Mozart it sounds like, the violins quite lively. Ah, here's Papa again, with his violin. Hello Papa. He rubs rosin on his bow. We are not from Esztergom, she hears him say. Who is he talking to? He pulls himself straight, lifts his felt hat and makes a little bow. Where is Esztergom, Papa? But already his violin is tucked under his chin, the notes flying out like small fast birds.

She lifts one hand from her lap as if to conduct, and then lets it drop. Behind her closed lids the faces in the restaurant are plump and pleased. Yes, their glances over linen tabletops are clearly pleased. Their glasses clink. Up there, on that small stage, Papa is fine. Up there, nobody minds his black eyes and the copper glow of his skin. His unruly black hair and bristling mustache—fine. The roll in his walk and the way he holds himself so straight—fine. His velvet waistcoat with the pearled buttons and his dead man's shoes with new leather soles he stitched himself—all of it fine. Sándor Kovács, the Gypsy Violinist is applauded. Over by the door, Sheila applauds too. Fancy seeing her here. She is waving her hand and saying something. Easiest just to wave back and smile. No, Papa is not from a squalid place called Esztergom. He does not live amidst stench. He is not despised. His children do not wear rags and ooze sores. He is from Budapest, before that from Szengai, before that who knows where? Wherever the roads took him.

The music changes. Something heavy and orchestral begins to play. Too heavy for Zsuzsa's taste, too somber, too many oboes. A melancholy instrument, the oboe, whereas today is the day her granddaughter Sofi arrives from America, a happy event, in need of happy music. She lifts her head from where it has sunk—these days she spends more time than she cares to think staring at her knees—and looks around for Sheila. She was here a minute ago. *Turn this thing off, please Sheila,* she will say. *Change the channel. Play something you like. Top of the Pops.* But no signs of anyone in a sky-blue dress. Only a little girl running through leaves. Red and yellow leaves, so it must be autumn. The little girl waves her arms as she runs, and Zsuzsa sees she wears mittens, so maybe it is already winter. The puzzle is, who is she? Perhaps it is Mary, when she was little. But then it becomes obvious from the wild tendrils of her hair that the girl is none other than Mary's daughter, Sofi, eight years old still and unchanged from her last visit. All of which makes perfect sense seeing as Sofi is the person she's been expecting all day.

"Hello Sofi, darling."

She is not surprised when Sofi does not respond, knowing as she does that this is another one of those dream things, or whatever they are, one time framed rather nicely inside another. Something she once tried to explain to Oscar—a hopeless task—but that made instant sense to Rollie. The problem is the music. The wrong music is playing. With Sheila not around there is nothing for Zsuzsa to do but heave herself out of her chair and turn the radio off. Or maybe she'll fiddle with it and find another channel. She succeeds in pulling herself onto her feet, but no luck at all getting the silly things to walk her across the room. Interesting though, even rooted to one spot like this she finds herself continuing to run. Was she really this active, on Sofi's last visit, before she became ill? It's lovely to run. The running, it seems, has been going on for some time when suddenly Sofi stops in her tracks and turns, panting and out of breath, which allows Zsuzsa to recognize the little girl, who is not Sofi at all, but none other than herself. Mittenless, cheeks red with cold, blowing on cold fingers, a worn blue wool jacket over long cotton dress. She recognizes the dress right off, the bands of yellow and red ribbon around its skirt, remembers watching Mama sew the ribbon on. Seeing herself this way is a surprising enough turn of events to cause Zsuzsa to sit down, which in itself is confusing because who is it that sits? Herself as she is now, or then?

Either way, gradually there comes the realization that she is on a train. Good, she thinks at first, an adventure. She can do with one of those after all these years of being a housewife and mum. A response which suggests to her that she is indeed still in the present, whatever year this is now, a time in which outside her window the ridiculous Mr. Griffin once again tips his hat. But then, almost immediately, she becomes unquestionably a little girl, and for a moment feels disappointed. For while there is no doubt about it being a train, this is not the adventure she hoped for, because there is also no doubt about *which* train.

Peering through its smoke smeared window, all she sees are flat brown fields and tight little snowflakes clawing their way out of a closed sky. She knows if she turns around, she'll find Mama crying on the seat beside her, biting into the back of her hand to keep from making noise. And there's Papa on the seat opposite, looking stern, sitting next to a *gadjo* lady with blue eyes and fur on her collar and her mouth in a twist. Nothing for little Zsuzsa to do but lean her head against the window and listen to the clickity clack, clickity clack of wheels on tracks, while out there in the room the music keeps trying to catch itself up to the sound of the train. Which with an oboe is a hopeless thing to try.

What Zsuzsa wants to do is turn to Mama, pull her hand away from her mouth and wrap her arms around her, snuggle against her and drink in the sweet sour smell of her clothes and her skin. Then, when she is close like that, to whisper into her ear, hand cupped around her own mouth so there is no chance of Papa hearing, and ask about Rozsa. Where is my sister, Mama? All Papa ever says is Rozsa will catch them up. He says it in Hungarian, because that is what they are now, Hungarians, who do not understand or speak Romany. When they get to London, they will become Londoners, like papa's brother already is, and learn English. Forget this place, little one, Papa says. But Zsuzsa does not want to forget. So sad and brown the fields outside, better to close her eyes and remember it the way it will be, next summer, when she is gone. Better to conjure up whole fields of yellow sunflowers, (how many sunflowers in a single field, Papa?) each flower its own bright sun.

* * * * *

I never expected to marry Brian, did I? It was a joke at first, him and me. Met him right down here, in Guildford. *Far From the Madding Crowd*, I used to say. I read that book in my last year of school, wasn't hardly through with school at the time, that job in Guildford hospital the first real one I ever had. I was seventeen. Lord knows how I ended up down there when I was still living in Brixton with Mum and Dad. I used to ride the train down, liked it too, just to get away from the traffic and grime and non-stop push and shove of London. Couldn't believe it when I got here, no rubbish in the gutters.

My job was wheeling the food trolley around the maternity ward and doing the washing up after. But there was this bloke, see. Everyday he came by, delivering oxygen tanks and picking up the empties. Had a nice pair of shoulders on him, and this lock of straight brown hair flopping down over one eye. Who knows what I found so charming about that combination? I look at him now, sprawled out on our settee with his belly gone soft as rice pudding, hardly any hair left on his head, and I ask myself that question. But back then I'd have my eye open for his lorry. Watch out the kitchen window while he parked it. Wait for him to open the driver's door and spring out, start lifting those big canisters on his shoulders, like they were nothing.

All this while I was drying the cups and saucers, mind you. I'd have a saucer in one hand and dishtowel in the other, the hand with the towel moving slower and slower until it stopped altogether. Probably had my mouth hanging open too. If you listen to the way my best mate told it back then, I had dribble running down my chin. Judy, her name was, straight out of Barbados, and working in that kitchen longer than any of us. *Check our Sheila everybody*! she called out one day. *She got de hots for the white boy.*

After that it was a matter of a few bets and a dare, and before you know it I was going steady. Got love bites on my neck. Taking the last train back to Waterloo every night, barely making that last tube connection to Brixton. Made up all kinds of stories I did, for Mum and Dad, about working late. I'd telephone them from outside the pub, Brian hanging all over me. Me trying not to giggle, telling them I'd just missed the nine-thirty and the next train wasn't for more than an hour.

I loved those rides home, especially that last stretch on the tube. There'd be nobody but me and a handful of people on the whole train, all of us black by then, which was how I knew I was getting close to home. Sometimes I'd be the only one still awake. Lit up I was, a glow in me insides like hot coals in a furnace, the train all lit up on its inside too. Streaking through those pitch-black tunnels its windows were mirrors. I'd turn toward the window and study my face. Touch all the places Brian had planted kisses, examine the shape of my mouth, my nose, eyes, all of it reflected in the train window clear as if it were my bathroom mirror.

* * * * *

Such a young woman Zsuzsa's grown to be, standing beside the mound of her mother's grave. Her double-breasted coat of navy wool is worn to a shine over several winters, sleeves too short now. These she tugs over bare wrists, while a fine rain falls and beads itself upon her dark hair. Or perhaps she wears her good scarf over her head. The one made of softest wool and covered with a design of wine-colored roses that was a gift from Rick, her blue-eyed admirer in the American airforce, now flown away to Italy.

Mama died of sadness is what Papa says. Her grave is brown and cold. A Gypsy is hard pressed to find a place to bury their dead in this bleak corner of London. Though, of course, they are no longer Gypsies, have not been since before the war and it is now one year after. *What happened to Rozsa, Papa?* This is the question Zsuzsa longs to ask but dare not. There are things she reads and hears on the radio now. Terrible things, talked about in shops and pubs and in front of bus stops. So terrible, people cover their mouths and parts of their faces as they speak, as if to create a shield from the smell, or the sight, or the knowledge of the unspeakable. Of this Zsuzsa reads and hears as much as the next person. The Jews, the newspapers always say. Yet Zsuzsa wonders, rubbing her arms in this damp chill, at the secret that caused Mama to shriek and wail behind closed doors, to repeatedly cry out her Rozsa's name the day Auntie Maria arrived head bowed and thin with news from Europe.

Papa breaks a bottle over the mound that is Mama under it. He had problems finding even a small bottle of Gin. He would have preferred Schnapps. We make do, he says. He says it in the old language, the rims of his eyes red from weeping. We adapt. That is how we Roma have always survived. They huddle in the rain. Papa, with his arms around Zsuzsa, his brother János, and his sister, Maria. They the only ones left. Amidst the bombed out shells of buildings Papa breaks the bottle over Mama's grave, and sings and weeps. He sings in the old language as London people hurry past, hidden under umbrellas and turned up collars. Papa sings while the sparrows in sodden trees do not. And doesn't Papa notice Mama has not survived?

Papa is still singing when the rain turns to snow, huge snowflakes whirling out of the sky, everything instantly blanketed white. The light, never strong, becomes very dim, then dimmer still and becomes night. Still Papa sings. And because it is dark, and because Papa sings, and perhaps also because of the snow which muffles sound, Zsuzsa neither sees nor hears the train at first. Then with a roar it comes thundering along this last stretch of track, and into a place of hard sudden light amidst darkness, where nothing or no one can hide. Is it the train that creaks and moans so, its boxcars shuddering, as men in high boots thunder along the platform? There is a moaning, unmistakable now, and a smell, the wheels of the braking train creaking over the tracks, a hiss of steam. Papa has gone, her uncle and aunt too. Zsuzsa is alone on the platform with the men in boots who do not seem to see her but whom she fears. Although not as much as she fears their dogs, their leashed Alsatians that sniff hungrily at the frozen air, and strain toward the boxcars, dogs that fret and bark on the end of their short chains.

* * * * *

She woke up weeping, didn't she? I was writing up how her morning went in the logbook we keep in the kitchen when I heard her. Peeked in the room and found her crying, biting the back of her hand to keep from making noise. She was so quiet at first I thought I must be hearing something on the radio, part of the music. I'd left it playing for her because she likes that. Outside was nearly dark, a horrible greenish gloom in the room. It gets dark ever so early this time of year. I switched on the table lamp and kneeled in front of her.

"What is it then, love?" I said, and rubbed her knees and her arms, the teeth marks on the back of her hand, mopped up her face with a tissue. "Is it Sofi? Are you worried because she's not here yet? Is that it?"

She slept for a bit longer than usual today. Usually she only dozes for ten or fifteen minutes in her chair and then she's awake again ready for a cup of tea. I always tease her. *Ready for another innings, are we?* But this afternoon she slept for a good half an hour, and later in the day too than most days. I reckon she woke up groggy from sleeping heavy.

Maybe I shouldn't have mentioned Sofi so soon. The name was barely out of my mouth and she started to cry harder, rocking herself and wringing her hands. I'd never seen her so upset before. Then she clutched at me, she's got quite a grip on her at times, and I could tell by her eyes, she was scared out of her wits.

"What is it? What is it love?" I said.

There are times she's hard enough to understand without her crying, days when her voice gets stuck down in her throat. Though up till then she'd had a good day talking. But all that crying made her voice weak. Her words came out slurred, and bunched up on top of each other. I leaned in to try and catch what she was saying, but even then I wasn't sure I heard right. Something about her sister Rosa, and something about a train. I caught the last part right though, I'm sure of that.

"Sofi's on the wrong train," she said.

"What train, love? What train's she supposed to be on?" I was still stroking her arms, her shoulders, rubbing her legs, she felt so cold, anything to try and soothe her.

"Not *that* train," she insisted, and rocked some more. Up to then I hadn't really stopped to think about how Sofi was getting from the airport to her grandma's place. I guess I thought one of her uncles would pick her up direct from

Heathrow, though a train makes as much sense as anything. Driving to Heathrow is madness these days, and there's a train connection in the terminal brings a person right here. Still, she'd need someone to pick her up from the station. She'd have luggage, wouldn't she? I'd assumed it was all arranged.

"Which train, love? Which train is it?"

All she would do was rock and cry. Finally I picked her up like she was one of my girls when they were little—she's no bigger than a twig—and I sat her on my lap, this little white haired lady, me doing the rocking, just trying to get her calmed down.

"Shall I give Oscar a jingle love? Ask him what's going on."

"Yes," she said after a long pause. "I suppose so."

Oscar wasn't home, but his wife was. Lucky she knew what was going on. Sofi wasn't due till tomorrow she said. Mum had the days mixed up. Yes, she was quite sure of it. Oscar was picking Sofi up from the train station tomorrow at three and bringing her right there. Would I like her to speak to Mum herself?

"It's Joyce, lovey," I said. "She wants to talk to you." I held the receiver for her. Usually she does it herself, but with her upset like that I didn't want her to drop it and get more upset.

"Yes," I heard her whisper. "Yes. Alright then." She looked very sheepish when she was done. "I got mixed up," she said. "Sofi comes tomorrow."

"That's alright, love. Everyone gets mixed up sometimes. Now, how about a nice cup of tea?"

Later, in the kitchen, dipping a biscuit in her tea, she seemed more her self, and I thought, well maybe she's forgotten it, whatever it was. She does forget things very quickly you know. Not things that happened a long time ago—she's got them all sorted out. But her short-term memory is for the birds.

ANNA BALINT is the author of *Out of the Box*, poems, Poetry Around Press, 1991 and *spread them crimson sleeves like wings*, stories & poems, Poetry Around Press, 1993. She co-edited *Poets Against the War*, an anthology of poems protesting the Gulf War; 1991. Her stories and poems have appeared in numerous journals including *Calyx, Briar Cliff Review, Raven Chronicles, Caprice, Stringtown, Radiance, Emeralds in the Ash.*

Balint received the 2001 "Leading Voices Award" for outstanding work with urban youth in the Puget Sound Region in the field of creative writing. In 2002, she received a Seattle Arts Commission literary grant for development of new work.

She lives in Seattle, where she teaches creative writing.

CURBSTONE PRESS, INC.

is a nonprofit publishing house dedicated to literature that reflects a
commitment to social change, with an emphasis on contemporary writing
from Latino, Latin American and Vietnamese cultures. Curbstone presents
writers who give voice to the unheard in a language that goes beyond
denunciation to celebrate, honor and teach. Curbstone builds bridges
between its writers and the public – from inner-city to rural areas, colleges
to community centers, children to adults. Curbstone seeks out the highest
aesthetic expression of the dedication to human rights and intercultural
understanding: poetry, testimonies, novels, stories,
and children's books.

This mission requires more than just producing books. It requires ensuring
that as many people as possible learn about these books and read them. To
achieve this, a large portion of Curbstone's schedule is dedicated to
arranging tours and programs for its authors, working with public school
and university teachers to enrich curricula, reaching out to underserved
audiences by donating books and conducting readings and community
programs, and promoting discussion in the media. It is only through these
combined efforts that literature can truly make a difference.

Curbstone Press, like all nonprofit presses, depends on the support of
individuals, foundations, and government agencies to bring you, the reader,
works of literary merit and social significance which might not find a place
in profit-driven publishing channels, and to bring the authors and their
books into communities across the country. Our sincere thanks to the many
individuals, foundations, and government agencies who have supported this
endeavor: Connecticut Commission on the Arts, Connecticut Humanities
Council, Eastern CT Community Foundation, Fisher Foundation, Greater
Hartford Arts Council, Hartford Courant Foundation, J. M. Kaplan Fund,
Lamb Family Foundation, Lannan Foundation, John D. and Catherine T.
MacArthur Foundation, National Endowment for the Arts, Open
Society Institute, Puffin Foundation, United Way, and the
Woodrow Wilson National Fellowship Foundation.

Please help to support Curbstone's efforts to present the diverse voices and
views that make our culture richer. Tax-deductible donations can be made by
check or credit card to:
Curbstone Press, 321 Jackson Street, Willimantic, CT 06226
phone: (860) 423-5110 fax: (860) 423-9242
www.curbstone.org

IF YOU WOULD LIKE TO BE A MAJOR SPONSOR OF A
CURBSTONE BOOK, PLEASE CONTACT US.